MY HUSBAND'S MISTRESS IS DEAD

Other Books by Saundra

Long Live the Queen
A Hustler's Queen
A Hustler's Queen: Reloaded
Hustle Hard
It Ain't About the Money
Her Sweetest Revenge
The Treacherous Wife

MY HUSBAND'S MISTRESS IS DEAD

SAUNDRA

kensingtonbooks.com

Content warnings: miscarriage, traumatic birth, kidnapping, child abduction, murder

DAFINA BOOKS are published by

Kensington Publishing Corp.
900 Third Avenue
New York, NY 10022

Copyright © 2025 by Saundra

To the extent that the image or images on the cover of this book depict a person or persons, such person or persons are merely models, and are not intended to portray any character or characters featured in the book.

This book is a work of fiction. Names, characters, businesses, organizations, places, events, and incidents either are the product of the author's imagination or are used fictitiously. Any resemblance to actual persons, living or dead, events, or locales is entirely coincidental.

Without limiting the author's and publisher's exclusive rights, any unauthorized use of this publication to train generative artificial intelligence (AI) technologies is expressly prohibited.

All rights reserved. No part of this book may be reproduced in any form or by any means without the prior written consent of the Publisher, excepting brief quotes used in reviews.

All Kensington titles, imprints, and distributed lines are available at special quantity discounts for bulk purchases for sales promotion, premiums, fund-raising, and educational or institutional use. Special book excerpts or customized printings can also be created to fit specific needs. For details, write or phone the office of the Kensington Sales Manager: Kensington Publishing Corp., 900 Third Avenue, New York, NY 10022. Attn. Sales Department. Phone: 1-800-221-2647.

Dafina and the Dafina logo Reg US Pat. & TM Off.

ISBN: 978-1-4967-5228-4
First Trade Paperback Printing: September 2025

ISBN: 978-1-4967-5229-1 (e-book)

10 9 8 7 6 5 4 3 2 1

Printed in the United States of America

The authorized representative in the EU for product safety and compliance
is eucomply OU, Parnu mnt 139b-14, Apt 123
Tallinn, Berlin 11317, hello@eucompliancepartner.com

Prologue

The city lights twinkled below me as I sat in my office, the bustling sounds of Los Angeles muted by the thick glass windows. It had been more than a day at Walter and Hanks Accounting firm, my mind still reeling from the unexpected visitor a week prior—Erika Jones. Her impromptu visit had shaken the very foundation of my seemingly perfect life.

Growing up in the foster care system of Los Angeles, I had learned to rely solely on myself. Education and career became the pillars of my stability, shielding me from the scars of abandonment and loneliness. Despite the success I had achieved as a senior account analyst, life had its own gut-wrenching plans for me.

Meeting Andre Perry, a charismatic, successful, and highly intelligent gentleman, had been a turning point in my life. Tall, handsome, and irresistibly charming, Andre swept me off my feet quickly. I fell in love, unaware of the shadows lurking behind his charming facade. Six years into our marriage, life seemed blissful on the surface. Successful careers, social status, and dreams of a family filled our days. There was nothing we both craved more. Yet, the echoes of two miscarriages still haunted me, leaving a void I tried to fill with career achievements.

Then came Erika Jones, a woman with a past intertwined with my husband's secrets, or at least that was her story. Her accusations shattered the illusions I had crafted, revealing cracks in our marriage I had been blind to. What started as a confrontation in my office spiraled into a web of lies, deceit, and ultimately, betrayal.

As I grappled with the truth and the weight of Erika's revelations, I realized that my life was not what I thought it was. Secrets, infidelity, and hidden agendas threatened to unravel everything I had built. With each revelation, I delved deeper into a world of darkness, where trust was a luxury and betrayal lurked at every corner.

I thought surely there was no way things could get worse, that is until my husband's mistress entered my world . . . *and now she had been murdered*!

Chapter 1

I aggressively snatched the free pillow that lay beside me and positioned it over my head. I wanted nothing more than to silence the persistent, annoying ringing of my cell phone that was breaking through the beautiful silence of my peaceful bedroom. It was Saturday and I'd promised my body the luxury of a full eight hours of uninterrupted, blissful sleep, but that was now null and void. "Ugh," I whined out loud, reluctantly rolling over onto my side, and reaching for the phone. My tired eyes squinted at the brightness of the phone screen.

"What, Reese?" I said, my tone laced with grogginess.

"Why are you still in bed at ten thirty?" Reese chuckled through the phone. Reese was my best friend; we were more like sisters. We met in college on registration day. I was standing in line minding my own business when this unknown tumbled straight into me out of nowhere, and nearly knocked me over. I soon discovered she was trying to escape the unwanted attention of this nerdy guy who was badgering her for her phone number. As soon as we both regained our balance, she apologized. A week later we ran into each other at the campus library and started talking. She ended up inviting me as her plus-one to a party she'd been asked to attend, and we've been inseparable since then. Even in our freshman year Reese was popular. Everyone on campus liked her, and we had so much fun.

"Ain't you supposed to be on a ten-mile run or on that laptop of yours, going over numbers for a client?" she teased.

I playfully rolled my eyes. "You are not a comedian, so stop. I'm a little tired, so I made an executive decision to indulge my brain in some extra sleep. Isn't that what normal people do on Saturday?" I let out a yawn and shifted my body up in bed. I could feel the exhaustion as it radiated throughout my body.

Christened by someone other than my biological parents at birth as Brooke Hall, I was handed over to and raised in the Los Angeles foster care system. I never had the privilege of knowing who my real parents were, why they gave me up, or if they even loved me. One of the things I learned early on in foster care was that I had other things I could use my time being concerned about. Needless to say, I had known my share of hard times. But determination was rooted deep in my bones, and beating the hand of adversity that had been handed to me at birth was my goal. I graduated from UCLA with a 4.0 GPA. Straight out of college, I landed my dream job at Walter & Hanks accounting firm as a senior account analyst, and within two short years I had been promoted to financial manager. I was just getting started though. Despite this accomplishment, I still hungered for the number one spot, and I was known to work sixty hours a week.

"Well, how about that sleep you dreamed of today, you get tomorrow? It's beautiful outside, and I have the bursting urge to go out and do some shopping today. Would you please join me? We could grab lunch and catch up," Reese suggested.

"Oh, Reese, as tempting as that sounds, I can't. I brought some files home that I must review and a few reports to skim through as well." I glanced over and could see the sun trying to burst through my Calvin Klein curtains, where a visible gap was the result of me not having pulled them closed tightly enough. Oh, how I longed to be out in the sun, free, laughing, and doing some retail therapy. But that was not on my short-term goals list.

Reese released a sigh, and I knew what was coming next. "Brooke, haven't you worked enough this week? That is the reason you are so tired. One plus one equals two," she lectured, fussing over me with her usual concern.

"I know, I know," I replied, nodding. "But these two clients are important. Their company is fairly new, and they are already in trouble. However, I think I can help them before it gets out of control."

"If you say so."

"How about we do lunch this week?" I negotiated. I really did want to hang out and do some shopping.

"Nope, I'm not falling for that. I'll be getting a call with that 'I'm sorry, Reese, but I need a rain check. I have this or that, I absolutely must tackle.' She mimicked me. Her voice sounded like mine; she was hilarious. "Yep, that bullshit, not drinking from that cup."

"Hee, hee," I chuckled out loud, my cell phone still pressed to my ear. She had cut me to the quick with her truth.

"But I do have an idea. You remember Anthony?"

I didn't like the sound of her having an idea. It could be the undoing of my willingness to be great. Reese's ideas had dragged us both to downright near compromising situations. But we always stood by one another, through thick and thin, so thankfully we had survived them all.

The air-conditioning was sneaking in on me, sending a chill through my body. I pulled the covers up to my shoulders for warmth. "Yeah, I remember him, the new guy you are playing around with," I remarked on her dating habits. Reese was never serious with anyone she entertained. She saw those guys as a moment in time. The irony was most of them actually liked her and never saw it coming when she called it quits.

"Oh, here you go . . . yes, him." She giggled. "How about we go on a double date? See, Anthony has this friend . . ."

I cut her off immediately. "No, no, no, and NOPE!" I shook my head from left to right as if she was standing in front of me. Although I'm pretty sure my reaction didn't surprise her at all. Nevertheless, I'd remind her anyway. "I already told you; I will not be going on any more double dates that you orchestrate. Have you forgotten about that last loser you set me up with? He was married!" And that was one of the near-compromising situations I was speaking of. Here I was out on a date with this handsome guy who resembled Common. We were out dining at a nice five-star restaurant when none other than his wife walks in, sits down at our table, starts clapping out loud so that she has everyone's undivided attention. She then proceeds to enlighten me that the man I am on date with is her husband of five years. Talk about being beyond embarrassed, I thought I would have to wear that shame around for the rest of my life. Since that debacle of a night, I swore off double dates and being set up. But, as usual, Reese was unfazed about that incident and apparently isn't giving up.

"Listen, I apologized for that, it was like a small hiccup, I had no idea he was attached."

"Nah, I'm good. Besides, as we both know I'm too busy

to date. No man deserves to be robbed of not having my time," was always my go-to excuse.

"What do you have time for? Please enlighten me. Because from what I understand, all you do is work, work, work. Here I am studying to become a doctor and thought we were supposed to be the busiest people on the planet. But I have more free time than you. Come on, go out with us?" Reese begged me. "You will have so much fun."

I twisted the corners of my mouth and released an irritated sigh; Reese refused to have a relationship with the word *no*. If she googled it, she would never find it. So, it would be a waste of my time to say it, especially if I expected her to drop it, so instead I said, "I'll think about it. But I'm not promising anything," I added just to be clear. Because if I didn't, the last thing she would remember me saying is, "I'll think about it," which she would put in terms of me saying "I'll do it."

"Okay, sounds good, as long as you'll think about it." Her tone perked up. "Listen, I got to go, Calvin is beeping in on the other end." Calvin was another one of her friends. As I said, Reese was never serious when it came to dating.

"What about Anthony and that double date?" I asked for the sake of teasing her.

"You are not a comedian. Now bye." She ended the call.

I chuckled, then chanted out loud, as I threw the covers off of me, "Give me the single life." I was content with being alone. Maybe too content. I was focused on my big picture. Companionship was not a priority. Growing up in all those different foster homes, I was used to being alone, feeling unwanted and unloved. So, love was nothing I craved. What I truly wanted was success, and I would work hard until I had every drop of it.

Chapter 2

The atmosphere inside Edge Gym was as invigorating to me as always. It filled me with immediate excitement and tranquility whenever I stepped inside. I even enjoyed the scent in the air, which I described as a fragrance of comfort. Reese said I was crazy. She in turn described the air in the gym as a musty sweat. She hated working out but that didn't stop me from dragging her there whenever I could, which was often. Because no matter how busy I was, pursuing my career on the ladder to success, I was just as tenacious when it came to my body and health goals.

I made it a priority to work out at least three days a week at the gym. In addition to that, I went on a five- to ten-mile run two days a week. I also did my best to eat as healthily as I could. However, like most people, I indulged in foods that were not the best for me but tasted too good to completely give up. I called them my guilty pleasures. That gave me even more ammunition to make sure I didn't miss my workouts or runs. Today was no different, I was at the gym ready to burn some calories and gain some energy. I always felt like a million bucks when I completed a workout. But at this point, I was starting to believe I would never be able to get my weightlifting started, due to the malfunctioning exercise equipment.

"Come on, machine," I fussed about the stubborn lift machine. It was refusing to cooperate and allow me to load it with my desired weight. I had been at this for almost five minutes with zero success. I could feel the frustration that was surely etched on my face as I struggled. Determined to conquer it so that I could get my lifting on, I continued.

I turned slightly to my left and watching me was a tall, no less than six-feet-four-inches tall, chocolate-colored, well-built, undeniably handsome guy. His presence gave me a slight tingle in the pit of my stomach. His juicy lips formed a smile and I nearly swooned.

He offered his assistance. "Can I help with that?"

I wasn't a fan of a man thinking he could do all the things that a woman could not. In most circumstances I would've turned him down flat, but I was ready to work out, and after all he was such a delicious-looking piece of eye candy.

Before I knew it, "Yes, please," rolled from my lips like sugar and spice. I watched him as he flexed his toned body around the lift machine he had been using and was soon standing next to me. I took a step back to clear the way so he could get to the lift machine. I watched with pleasure as he tackled the problem. I surveyed his shoulder muscles as they stretched with each movement he made.

He turned so suddenly I couldn't remove my eyes before he caught me. "There, it's fixed," he announced, his white teeth on display.

"Thank you so much!" I said.

"I'm Andre Perry," he said, extending his hand out to me. I figured this was a cue for me to offer up my name even though I really didn't want to. But he had just helped me out of the bind I was in. I figured the least I could do was be polite.

Slowly, I raised my right hand to meet his. "Brooke." I purposely left out my last name, for all I knew he was a serial killer. We stood there, our hands gripped together like they were mated and engaged in their own conversation. I pulled mine away first. Then silence. "Well, I need to get this workout started. Thanks again."

"It was my pleasure," he replied with a slight smile and amusement that twinkled in his eyes.

I nearly blushed. I had to get moving before I said or did anything to embarrass myself. "Excuse me." I stepped around him and gave the machine my undivided attention. After a few minutes of lifting, I moved on to the next machine. The workout was getting good, my muscles were responding to the pressure, and perspiration was glistening on my skin like a good rubdown with Vaseline.

Two machines later I was on the elliptical and for some odd reason my mind drifted back to the stranger, Andre Perry. I stalled in my thoughts for a minute because that surprised me. I honestly never gave a guy a second thought, no matter how fine he was. I wasn't the kind to ponder a handsome face for too long. I loved men, their masculinity gave me chills, but they were just not in my short-term goals. But Andre's glistening skin, white teeth, and nice body were now crowded spaces in my mind that I'd had no idea were vacant. I turned up "Surrender" by Kut Klose on my Beats. I needed to surrender my thoughts to something other than a stranger.

Doing Pilates was last on my list for the day. My heart rate was up and steady, which I could appreciate. I was tired and it felt wonderful. "Whew," I grunted, wiping the perspiration from my forehead with wobbly legs. My mission workout for the day was complete.

I walked into the locker room feeling accomplished, the

adrenaline from my workout still flowing through my veins. The locker room was empty except for a few women getting ready to leave. I quickly located my locker, entered the combination, and retrieved my keys and workout bag. As I turned to leave, I caught a glimpse of myself in the mirror. Sweat-drenched and with a rosy glow on my cheeks, I couldn't help but smile. There was something empowering about pushing my body to its limits and seeing the results firsthand.

Exiting the locker room, I made my way toward the gym's exit. The atmosphere inside Edge Gym had done its magic once again, leaving me feeling energized and revitalized. I glanced at the time on my phone and realized it was getting late. As I stepped outside, the cool evening air hit me, a stark contrast to the warmth of the gym. I took a deep breath, relishing the feeling of clarity that often followed a good workout. Now, home was my destination.

Pulling into my driveway, I pushed the button to allow one of the doors on my three-car garage to open. Shutting off the engine I reached for my gym bag and exited the car. Unlocking the door, I stepped inside and kicked off my sneakers. The familiar scent of home welcomed me as I walked into the living room. I set my workout bag down and headed to the kitchen to hydrate myself with a glass of water. As I drank, my thoughts drifted back to Andre Perry.

I wondered what it was about him that had caught my attention. Was it his charm, his willingness to help, or simply his striking appearance? I shook my head, trying to dismiss the thoughts. It was time for a much-needed hot shower, followed by some relaxation. Later I had plans to hang out with Reese at one of the hottest clubs in LA, and I was excited. It had been a long time since we'd taken the club scene by storm. It was sure to be epic.

* * *

The line at Plush had been excessively long but as usual we had no trouble getting in. Reese was somehow acquainted with the owner, Pierre. So, our names had been placed on a VIP list that basically said we were platinum, which meant no line, no waiting. Plush, with its neon lights, ambiance of sophistication and allure, was one of the few "IT" clubs in LA. Crystal chandeliers hung from the ceiling, and the bar area was the focal point where cocktail waitresses oozed in between and around customers with backlit bottles that shimmered like jewels. Celebrities from all over the world partied here. I had been to Plush on several occasions with Reese, and each time I had enjoyed myself. I was sure tonight would be no different. I was dressed in a cute pair of Dior red bottoms with a Nili Lotan black crisscross bare-shoulder top, and white paper-bag shorts. With a smooth mocha-colored skin tone, a slight dimple on my left cheek, I stood no less than five feet, eight inches tall, with a thin waistline and just the right amount of roundness in my hips that screamed *great genes*. My soft, straight, naturally colored chestnut hair hung loosely in the bob style it had been cut in. I looked as though I had been plucked right out of the pages of *Ebony* magazine.

Standing close to me checking a text on her cell phone was my equally beautiful friend Reese. She had a sun-kissed skin tone and was only an inch or so shorter than me. Reese was around the same size as me but just a bit rounder in the behind, which she totally loved. Dressed in a maxi dress that was so tight it would simply be impossible to pinch an inch, Reese would have to not make any sudden movements tonight if she didn't want to have a major wardrobe malfunction.

"Brooke, I swear we are about to have a good time tonight. It has been way too long." She gazed out into the crowd of people. The DJ was on fire, playing Rihanna's song "Pour It Up." I bobbed my head to the music because I was feeling as good as I looked. I worked so much I had forgotten this part of life existed, but the bright lights and shimmering bottles woke up the fun-loving monster inside of me. Reese eventually led us to the bar.

"What can I get for you ladies?" the muscularly built, medium height bartender asked us.

I had no idea what I had a taste for, but a drink was a must. Getting tipsy was definitely on my list of short-term goals tonight.

"Reese, what are you going to have?" I asked.

"I have no idea, something strong for sure," she answered back.

"I can handle that for you," the bartender said with a mischievous smile

"I bet you can," Reese encouraged him with a playful smirk. "Give us a shot of Patrón."

The bartender poured up the shots with a practiced hand and handed us the glasses. He winked at Reese, and she couldn't help but grin. She turned to me, and we lifted our glasses and clicked them in a toast then downed them fast. The warm liquid spread through me like a wildfire, adding a touch of boldness to the evening.

I leaned into Reese. "That bartender sure is cute," I pointed out.

"Fine as hell is what he is. But he's a kid for sure."

I agreed with a nod of my head just as Future's "Turn On the Lights" came on. "I am so glad we came out tonight!" I shouted with joy.

"Me too. It was way overdue, and I'm going to be sure I enjoy myself. Hell, because you might go into hibernation after this," Reese teased.

"Shut up." I playfully rolled my eyes at her. We started laughing.

"'Turn on the lights,'" Reese sang. I joined in, threw

my hands in the air and vibed to the beat with a little hip movement. We were still standing in front of the bar, so I didn't want to give away too much, just keep it cute and classy.

The effects of our first shot had kicked in, leaving us feeling carefree. While enjoying the buzz, Calvin, one of Reese friends, approached us. After a quick exchange, he asked Reese to dance. Before I could protest being left alone, she was off to the dance floor. I threw caution to the wind as I turned back toward the bar. I figured now was as good a time as any to grab that second drink.

"Let me guess—another shot of Patrón?" the bartender asked. But I had other plans. It was early and the last thing I wanted to do was end up drunk before the night had even started. I was what you would call a lightweight when it came to drinking. It didn't take much for me to start feeling light and breezy, but I knew how to coast it. At least I used to, back when I was in college. Tonight, I decided that I would put it to the test to see if I still remembered how to handle my liquor.

"Nah." I grinned. "Maybe later. For now, let's do a Long Island iced tea but go light on the tequila."

"Small world," a voice to my left remarked. Even before I looked over, I had a feeling it was directed toward me. I was surprised at the face staring back at me and the familiarity in the voice, now matched up. I recognized him right away.

"Brooke, right?" The music was loud, but his tone steady enough not to scream over the noise. I heard him well.

"In the flesh," I said, my voice a bit louder than his. I was surprised by my own reaction, which had to be influenced by that shot of Patrón. My response wasn't one I would typically use with a stranger. Yet, for the second time in one day, Andre Perry from the gym was getting strange reactions out of me. And just like this morning, the man was looking exceptionally good, and he smelled incredibly yummy.

"Is this your first time here?" he inquired.

The bartender delivered my drink. I cradled the glass in my hand. "Actually, no. I've been here a few times. How about you?" I asked, then sipped from my straw. The bartender may have been young, but damn he was a mixologist for sure. The drink had the right amount of everything in it.

"Yeah, I've been in here a few times," he confirmed.

"Oh my God, Brooke. I haven't danced like this in so long." Reese stood in front of me, out of breath and giggly. She threw her right hand to her chest and took a deep breath. "Calvin just wore me out." When she noticed Andre was standing next to me, she stopped talking. "Wait, I'm sorry . . . excuse me, I didn't realize you two were talking. I didn't mean to interrupt." She apologized, looking at Andre first then at me.

Andre smiled and reassured her, "No need to apologize, it's okay."

I introduced them to each other. "Andre, this is my best friend, Reese. Reese, this is Andre."

Reese stepped in closer to me, then leaned in and whispered in my ear, "Girl, he is fine as hell." She put so much emphasis on the word *hell* I was sure I felt the vibration bouncing off of it. I tried not to smile, but I simply couldn't fight the urge to agree with her and I couldn't hold it in. Andre also smiled, clearly aware he was the topic of conversation.

Calvin appeared again next to Reese's side and was soon dragging her back to the dance floor. "Hey, don't kidnap my friend," she jokingly threw over her shoulder, as she disappeared into the crowd. Their playful banter made me chuckle.

I turned my attention back to Andre, who was still

standing next to me at the bar. "Yep, that's my best friend." I said, and we both laughed.

"So, I take it the rest of your workout went okay? I mean, I didn't see you struggle to fix another machine."

"No, actually, you saved the day. The rest of my workout went smoothly after that, thankfully." I took another sip from my drink, which was still in my hand. The one thing I never did in college, and was still a habit of mine, I never set my drink down anywhere.

"That's all good news. I'm just glad I could help out. My mother would have been very disappointed if I had not. She always used to tell me, 'Andre, always assists a woman whenever she is in need.'" We shared another laugh.

I couldn't believe I was talking to a man who was cool enough to bring up his mother when speaking to a female that he'd just met. That had me thinking I had just hit the jackpot. It told me one thing for sure, he was raised by a strong woman who instilled in him how to properly value and respect women. Perhaps he was one of the good ones.

"I don't know what I would have done if I couldn't lift. All the other machines were taken, and lifting is a major part of my workout."

"That it is. Judging by how you look, I think you have lifted yourself to perfection. You are not in need of it."

Was he openly flirting with me? I could only grin in return. "You don't look too bad yourself. That six-pack is one to be proud of." Again, a bold move by me, and I wasn't feeling the least bit shy.

As the music shifted, we migrated to a quieter corner, away from the pulsating beats. We continued to talk. I couldn't help but admire Andre's intelligence and his perspective on various topics that were brought up. We laughed upon discovering we shared common ground in food, music, and different meaningful conversations. Time seemed to slip away unnoticed. Before I knew it, we had talked for hours, and it was time for the club to close. The only thing I regretted was I had not danced once. Reese, on the other hand, had shut the club down on the dance floor. Andre Perry had somehow done something no other man had ever done before successfully in one night. He had fully captured my attention, and that was no easy task. There were other men who had asked me for much less and not succeeded.

Chapter 3

After hanging out with Andre at the club, he asked me to go out on a date with him, but I was a bit hesitant. Dating meant making a time commitment, and with my work ethic I didn't have a lot of that. While I had enjoyed his conversation it wasn't enough for me to switch up my schedule. But I had given him my phone number, which for me was a huge, positive step.

Over the next few months with Andre's consistent encouragement, we went on some dates, and we grew closer than I would've ever imagined. Never did I think I could be as attached to someone as I had become with Andre. The entire experience was something I couldn't describe. It wasn't something I wanted to give up.

When Andre first invited me to meet his mom, I said yes with hesitation. Tonight, he'd made plans for us to meet for dinner. He suggested a trendy restaurant downtown that had a reputation for serving exquisite dishes and offering a sophisticated dining experience. I wasn't surprised at his choice. Since we started dating, that was the only type of place he seemed to frequent. I dressed in a chic black dress paired with elegant heels, wanting to make a good impression for our evening out.

As we arrived at the restaurant, I couldn't help but feel a bit nervous. Meeting Andre's mother was a significant step, and I wanted everything to go smoothly. Andre, however, seemed calm and collected, as I squeezed his arm extra tight while he led me inside with a reassuring smile.

The restaurant was bustling with activity, the ambiance elegant and inviting. We were escorted to our table, and as we settled in, I noticed Andre glancing around, perhaps looking for his mother's arrival. Just as we were about to order drinks, a pleasant voice interrupted us.

"Andre, darling! There you are," a sophisticated-looking woman exclaimed as she approached our table. She was impeccably dressed in designer attire, her demeanor exuding confidence and elegance. This was surely Mrs. Perry, Andre's mother. He swiftly rushed to his feet to greet her with a kiss on the cheek and then pulled out a chair for her.

"Mother, this is Brooke." Andre introduced me with a warm smile. "Brooke, meet my mother, Vivian Perry."

"It's a pleasure to meet you, Mrs. Perry," I greeted her politely, offering a smile, with my hand extended out to her.

Vivian's response was polite but distant, and not once did she even attempt to touch my extended hand. "Likewise," she replied, her tone cool and composed.

I instantly regretted offering her my hand. Maybe she was a germophobe; if so, I hoped I hadn't offended her.

Throughout dinner, she made subtle yet pointed comments that left me feeling slightly uneasy. She inquired about my background, slightly probing into my upbringing and career. Her remarks about the restaurant's ambiance being "quite charming for a casual night out" and how she preferred establishments with a more exclusive atmosphere hinted at her preference for a certain level of sophistication. And clearly, Andre had missed the mark.

Andre apologized to her repeatedly for every issue she innocently raised; but clearly she was making a point to make me feel uncomfortable. I tried my best to engage in polite conversation and maintain a pleasant demeanor, but I couldn't shake off the feeling of being scrutinized and judged. Andre, sensing my discomfort, interjected with light-hearted topics and anecdotes, trying to steer the conversation away from any potential tension. He wanted to assure me that all was well, and things were going great.

As the evening progressed, Vivian's comments became more veiled, hinting at her expectations for Andre's future and the type of company he should keep. She made subtle comparisons between me and other women Andre had dated in the past, highlighting their backgrounds and social circles.

Despite her disapproval demeanor, I couldn't bring myself to dislike Vivian. I wasn't even sure if she was intentionally trying to put me down. I didn't think it was personal, I was just a different species she'd probably never encountered before up so close. There was an air of refinement about her, and I sensed that her comments stemmed more from her protective nature and desire for Andre's happiness rather than malice. Any mother would be concerned. However, her words did leave me feeling somewhat inadequate, as if I didn't quite measure up to her standards. I had known the words *foster kid* to be considered taboo for a lot of people. But I had worked hard to become the woman I was. Surely, anyone, even Vivian, once they got to know me would not be able to deny I was a good person.

As dessert was served, Andre excused himself briefly, leaving me alone with Vivian. Seeing an opportunity to connect, I tried to steer the conversation toward more neutral topics, asking about her interests and experiences.

Surprisingly, Vivian opened up a bit, sharing stories from her travels and her love for art and culture. By the end of the evening, despite the initial tension, I found myself developing a respect for Vivian. She was a woman who knew what she wanted for her son and was unapologetic about her expectations. I couldn't fault her for that. I mean, who would? While her comments may have stung at times, I realized that her intentions were rooted in love and a desire to see Andre happy and fulfilled. All she wanted for Andre were things I was more than capable of offering him. Since we'd started dating, I had given love that I didn't even know I possessed.

As we said our goodbyes outside the restaurant, Andre thanked me for handling the evening with grace and understanding. He assured me that his mother's comments were not a reflection of how he felt about me, and that he appreciated my patience and kindness. And that he knew in his heart she would grow to love me.

Driving home, I reflected on the evening's events. Meeting Andre's mother had been a challenging experience, but it had also given me insight into the dynamics of his family and the importance they placed on certain values. Despite the early anxiety, I felt a sense of reassurance knowing that Andre stood by me and valued our connection, regardless of any external judgments.

The next day, as I recounted the dinner experience to Reese, she listened intently, offering words of encouragement and support. She reminded me that sometimes navigating relationships with family members could be tricky, but what mattered most was how Andre and I felt about each other.

As I settled into bed that night, I couldn't help but feel grateful for the experiences that had brought me closer to Andre and helped me understand the complexities of relationships and family dynamics. Drifting off to sleep, I felt a sense of contentment knowing that despite the challenges, love and understanding could bridge even the most difficult of situations. But there was something that Vivian had said that weighed heavily on my mind. It wasn't exactly what she said, it was more the fact that it was she who revealed it and not Andre.

Andre Perry had been married before.

Chapter 4

One year later

The Morning View estate in Malibu, California, was simply breathtaking. Nestled right in the middle of six acres surrounded by swaying palm trees and panoramic ocean views, it was paradise on earth. The property was equipped with six luxurious bedrooms on the mansion's upper floors, perfect for accommodating a select group of close family members and friends overnight. As I arrived at the estate I was greeted by a gust of activities. Florists and caterers were moving about the place in preparation for the pre and main events to make sure everything was absolutely perfect. I was eager to be alone with my own thoughts, to think about my life, all that I had endured from when I was a child up until now. I spent most of the day exploring the property, until it was time for the rehearsal and then dinner. During rehearsal I couldn't help but feel a sense of gratitude and disbelief.

The countdown was inevitable, and I was about to take a step in my life that I would have never thought possible a short year ago. As I had reflected earlier during my walk, the journey that had led me here had been full of ups and downs, challenges, and victories. In retrospect, every waking moment was worth it.

"I can't believe you're about to get married, Brooke. I just can't believe it. I'm trying to let it sink in." Reese shook her head slowly, then crisscrossed her legs into her chest as she sat on a chaise lounge across from me. We were relaxing comfortably in our huge room that doubled as a suite at the wedding venue. Being my maid of honor, she had vowed not to leave my side until the deed was done. Lucky for me, she had a kung fu grip on that vow.

"Trust me, I can't believe it either. I'm still pinching myself to be sure it's real," I admitted with a soft giggle.

Reese watched me with a curious gaze then let out a chuckle. "I mean, for eight years I practically had to drag you out on dates, while you kicked and screamed every step of the way. Then Andre comes along with skillful wits and smooth charm. And twelve months later you are about to walk down the aisle. I mean, whatever voodoo magic the guy was practicing on you, girl, you fell for it hook, line, and sinker." A hint of suspicion laced her tone.

I could only laugh and smile at her summation and dramatic assumption as I thought of one of the most famous blind dates she set me up on. "Well, I think it helped that he didn't already have a wife and kids at home," I teased.

"OMG! Really, Brooke, are you ever going to forget that shit?"

"Ummm, nope." We both giggled. But too soon I was able to detect the seriousness on Reese's face. Something was bothering her, and I knew my friend would eventually say it.

Reese sat up and stretched her legs back out to touch the floor; a thoughtful look covered her face. "Brooke, I know you don't like me asking this or bringing it up. But you know me, and I have to . . ." Her eyes fluttered as she shut them for a brief moment while intertwining her fingers. I could literally hear the bones as they popped. She sighed. I waited but was losing patience quickly. I wanted to know what was on her mind.

"Are you absolutely sure about this? I mean really, really . . . sure?" She said the words slowly and deliberately. Then her right brow went up in an arched position. "You know what, fuck it." She slid to the edge of the couch, her demeanor seeming to shift to something urgent. "Look, I just don't think you should marry him. Andre may have swept you off your feet, showing you the lifestyle of the wealthy. But the guy is a rich, arrogant asshole." Her words were blunt and filled with emotion.

I blinked at the weight of her truth as she saw it. But I wasn't surprised at the brazen outburst. Since the engagement and even before that, she had expressed her concern about Andre. Reese was my best friend, and I never wanted her to think that I didn't trust her opinion. It mattered to me deeply. But I had learned to accept that she and Andre would not see eye to eye. It was something about his demeanor that just didn't sit well with her. Nevertheless, my stance was always the same, and I thought I had been clear, but here we were again.

"Reese, I thought we were done with this weeks ago." I stood up, my tone filled with concern and frustration. "I love Andre . . . he's not perfect, I admit that. But he is a good guy, a gentleman." I started to pace back and forth, rubbing my forehead. Then I looked at Reese, my eyes begging her to understand. "And he's not arrogant. Andre is just used to a certain lifestyle and has a certain expectation." I tried to reason with her. I wished she could see him in the same light as I did.

Reese rolled her eyes. "Exactly, the dude is arrogant. And his mother . . . well, I just don't see how you're going to put up with her. She treats her son like he's twelve years old and he allows it by answering her every beck and call. She looks down her nose at everyone who's not on her so-called social scale, and that includes you, Brooke. In the beginning, I too thought she would get over herself and see what a wonderful person you were for letting all that class and status shit she brews all the time fly out the window. But the woman can't be moved. Surely by now you see that."

The mention of Andre's mother raised my brow. Vivian Perry had not been the most welcoming of me from day one, but she did it with such bougie and class I couldn't be upset. After a while, I finally put my finger on it and was able to get to the right perspective. Sure, she didn't think I was good enough for her son. That being said, I had come to know how to deal with her. I wasn't worried about Vivian at all. I could handle her. Besides, I didn't have to live with her. I wished I could get Reese to understand, but I was tired of the whole conversation.

"Reese, you are my best friend, and I know you are concerned about me. But I'm happy. Truly I am." I had to assure her of this. "I love Andre, and he loves me. He shows me in every way. Please just be happy for me."

Reese exhaled. "I love you, Brooke, blood couldn't make you dearer to me, so I will try. But he better know I'll run him over with my car if he hurts my friend," she threatened. Her lips finally curved into a soft smile, and I was thankful.

"That much I think he knows already. He might even be a little frightened of you."

Andre knew that Reese was not his biggest fan. But he just said, *She'll come around.*

At this point I wasn't so sure about that. He would have to literally jump through a hoop, and I mean a round one. But I didn't want to think about it at the moment. I wanted to have fun, and have girl talk with my bestie, before I became Mrs. Perry. I reached for the bottle of champagne we had on chill. "Now let's finish this bottle of champagne, it's my wedding day."

"Well, since it's your wedding day and not mine, I'll pour you a glass." Reese stood up and retrieved the bottle and popped the cork. The bubbly oozed out, ready to help us celebrate.

"Join me in introducing Mr. and Mrs. Andre Perry." The crowd erupted with thunderous applause and the thrill of excitement pierced my whole body. The moment felt completely surreal and almost magical. I blinked my eyes about a thousand times to fight back the tears that were trying to escape my eyelids. I would not mess up my makeup.

Andre guided me to him. He leaned into my ear and softly whispered, "You look so radiant, I adore you, Mrs. Perry." His words filled me with warmth, my heart was complete, and I could only grin as my lips met his.

"*WHEEWWW!*" A female high-pitched voice in the crowd screamed, catching our attention. Andre and I eyed each other and couldn't help but burst into laughter. The atmosphere was filled with laughter and joyous sounds from the guests until the celebration was soon taken over by the live band as they started playing. The energy of the music drew more guests around us, and soon everyone wanted to share their words of good wishes and happiness.

"Congratulations, Brooke." Three of my coworkers sang, their voices in harmony as if they had practiced for hours. Their genuine happiness and excitement were evident, as smiles spread across their faces. I felt a rush of gratitude and warmth, appreciating the friendship, and support.

"Thank you ladies for coming." I didn't have many people in attendance from my side. There were a hundred guests in attendance and over eighty percent of them were Andre's family and friends. I had invited a few coworkers and, of course, Reese, who was considered my family. So, while Andre had five groomsmen and a best man to boast about him during the toasting, my toast was quick and to the point because I only had Reese and three of Andre's cousins, who I barely knew, standing in for bridesmaids. While I was more than appreciative that his cousins had said a kind word about me, I couldn't wait for that part to be done. By the time everyone was raising and clinking their glasses in toasts, I was more than ready for my favorite part of the ceremony. The cutting of the cake.

I enjoyed stuffing Andre's double-chocolate slice into his mouth. He looked so handsome trying to lick it off. I couldn't resist kissing him until most of it was off. So many people had been rushing toward me the entire night that Reese had to take a back seat. Finally, she was able to break through to the cake table and reach me.

"You look so beautiful in your dress, Brooke, and are the most gorgeous bride ever." Reese hugged me tightly. I could see Vivian approaching as my face peeked over Reese's shoulder.

Vivian wore a look of pure skepticism about something, but of course I couldn't be sure what it was. "The wedding dress turned out okay, I suppose. Nevertheless, a custom-made dress flown in from France would have been more fitting for Andre's standing. But I do understand it's hard sometimes for people to arrive at their new station." Her voice carried disapproval.

Here I was, standing in front of her wearing a Valentino haute couture dress that cost $20,000. And my new mother-in-law was disgusted with me and calling me out as an upstart. About five feet, nine inches tall, with a super thin frame of maybe hundred and twenty pounds, light-skinned and superior attitude Vivian looked animated. With her head held high and nose in the air, she squinted her eyes at Reese as she sized her up.

Reese stared her back down and a slight smirk appeared across her lips. "Well, when you have a figure like Brooke's you don't need a hundred-thousand-dollar dress flown in from France to create a conversation." Her snide remark was on purpose, and she wanted Vivian to swallow it whole.

Vivian's eyes seemed to tighten into even smaller slits, and the corners of her mouth did as well. "And who are you again?" she asked Reese, knowing very well who she was, to counteract the shade she'd just been given.

Reese's nostrils flared and her body seemed to float from its space into Vivian's. I grabbed her hands and blocked her body entirely, just in time. "Reese, thanks so much for making sure I got through this day. I couldn't have done any of it without you, my dearest friend, and sister."

Reese cut her eyes at Vivian with a vicious look and rested them there. "No worries, my friend. I wouldn't have missed this bougie affair of uppity Black folk, even if one of my legs had been freshly amputated yesterday." She smirked and sucked her teeth for good measure.

"I—" Vivian started.

Andre interrupted her and followed up with a warm smile. "How is my beautiful bride?" He approached and embraced me into a hug. Once again, his lips were on mine, and I was in bliss. Vivian's antics disappeared, but only for a moment.

"Why? Oh why, son, did you have to jump that godawful broom?" Vivian's words felt like a stab in the back. "My reputation in all social circles is ruined," she complained. Her tone was full of emotion that only she could understand. Her remarks were meant to offend me and put me in my place.

Andre slowly turned to her, his expression calm. "Mother, as I explained to you before, it was Brooke's wish, and I'm confident your reputation will remain intact." He turned to me, winked, and silently mouthed *I love you*. I gave a half smile as he turned back to Vivian and took her hands into his. "Now let's have a son-mother dance." Vivian put up a fake fuss, then relented.

"Aggh," I sighed under my breath as they strolled off to the dance floor. I could not believe the audacity of Vivian, especially on my wedding day. I could feel the heat rising from Reese as she stood close to me, tapping her foot impatiently, her eyes glued to Vivian's back.

"Disrespectful," Reese mouthed, shaking her head with contempt, biting down on her bottom lip, and trudging away in irritation.

Was Reese right? How would I put up with Vivian? I considered myself to be a patient person; growing up as a foster child and never living with the Brady Bunch of families, I knew the funky side of people. But Vivian was a challenge. Nonetheless, I wanted to remain positive, be optimistic, and give her time, give her a chance. Maybe she just had to warm up to me, be absolutely sure of my love for her one and only son and that I would be dedicated to their family. Or perhaps she would never change toward me. Had I simply underestimated her and hoped for what could never be true? Maybe I had bitten off more than I could chew.

Chapter 5

Six years later

The married life had been good to me, our time together as husband and wife had been adventurous. In between taking long vacations, cherishing our time together, and conquering the demands of our careers, six years had flown by. Both of our careers were successful and thriving. However, there was a notable difference between us in our professions. Andre was the owner of his business, or more accurately, his own boss. When I first met him, he was already a millionaire, having inherited his late father's brokerage firm. The business was already prosperous when Andre inherited it, but over the years he had grown it into an even bigger empire. Now Elk Perry's Brokerage, which was named after his father's grandfather, was one of the top ten brokerage companies in LA. I couldn't help but feel proud of his accomplishments.

As for my career path, I was steadily climbing the corporate ladder and now I was up for partner at Walter & Hanks. And I couldn't have been more nervous and excited at the same time. But I had been resolute in pursuing my goals and would not rest until my name was on the marquee, as they say. Andre and I were truly happy with each other and our achievements. But with all the money, success, love, and happiness there was one thing we both yearned for deeply that we couldn't seem to have—a child of our own.

Two miscarriages had deprived us of that happiness. Even though we both felt content with our lives, the second and most recent miscarriage had been even more devastating for me than the first one. Because the reality of it spoke a harsh truth that was difficult for me to accept. Despite the challenge, I was determined to get back to being myself with the support of my husband and, of course, Reese.

Dressed in a sleek Nike crop-top sports bra and a pair of compression leggings that hugged all of my curves, I felt confident with my body, it was still top notch. However, working on my mental well-being was equally important, and working out was a good outlet for that. I had my hair pulled back into a smooth, practical ponytail so that sweat could flow freely down my face with no strings attached.

Now all I needed was a nice pair of Nike workout shoes to match. I exited our master bedroom and headed to my shoe zone. To go anywhere in this house was like going on a journey, the house was that huge. We lived in Bel Air in a seventeen-million-dollar mansion, the house was 17,415 square feet with eight bedrooms, thirteen bathrooms, and an eight-car garage. I had protested when Andre chose this enormous house for just two people. But he had been adamant this would be our home, and I would love it. His previous property had been a penthouse downtown. He said he was now ready for a house in a gated community.

While I greatly appreciated the heated floors, two-story ceilings, and stone counters, I couldn't wrap my head around the fact this house had a freaking elevator in it. For my lifestyle I didn't even know if that was realistic. Vivian had rolled her eyes when she heard me questioning our new quarters.

"What do you propose you do, dear, only have the option to climb stairs?" she had said to me with so much sarcasm in her voice, it was clear she was embarrassed to be associated with me. After that remark I felt like a panhandler standing at the side of the road begging for change. Vivian had that effect on people.

But Andre had been right, I loved, loved, loved the house, especially my closet, which was the size of a bedroom. This space was hands down every woman's dream. The closet exuded luxury and organization. There were glass-paneled cabinets that stretched from floor to ceiling, an island in the middle of the room with sleek marble countertop. The closet was even decorated with furniture, so sometimes I came in with a glass of wine, tried on clothes that I had never worn, with the tags still on, and ended up falling asleep. Today would be a quick visit, though, because I only needed a pair of gym shoes.

The warm feel of Andre's strong arms as they wrapped around me from behind caught my attention. "Hey, sexy, are you single?" he whispered playfully in my ear. I giggled and blushed at the same time. Andre had that effect on me, I was like a schoolgirl meeting a guy and crushing over him for the first time.

"No, actually I have a husband, and he's the jealous type. He wouldn't like these strong arms wrapped around me." I grinned, totally enjoying our role-playing. I placed both my hands on either side of his arms and caressed them softly.

"Umm," I moaned as his mouth found the crease of my neck.

"Would this jealous husband of yours mind me feasting

on this delectable neckline?" he whispered in my ear, then playfully nibbled on it.

This time I giggled out loud. I was so ticklish. "Babe, please stop." I begged for mercy. We both laughed. He knew he was driving me crazy. I tried to pry myself from his grasp, but he pulled me back to face him.

"How are you feeling this morning?" he asked.

"Fine, thought I'd go to the gym. The doctor said it would be good for me to get back into my workout routine. You know it's good for the body and the mind."

Andre nodded his head in agreement, his arms still wrapped around my waist. "I'm glad you are feeling up to it. Plus, I know how much you love working out. But, Brooke, I will never understand why you prefer the gym when we have a top-notch one right here on the estate."

I freed myself from his embrace and grabbed my shoes so I could get going. This could start a whole new conversation about the in-house gym, and I didn't have the time. "I know, but it's something about being at the gym with all the other activity going on around me that motivates me. And I especially need that motivational feeling now."

"Alright," he relented, and I was thankful for that. "Well, I'm heading to the office. I have a board meeting in an hour. If I'm late Clinton will be tripping; my guy is like a clock with a mouth." We both chuckled. Clinton was a longtime friend of Andre's who sat on the board and held a prestigious position at the company.

"Alright, after the gym I'm going to return to shower then go into the office."

I turned around to find a displeased look on Andre's face. "Brooke, I want you to take it easy . . . there is no need to rush things. Take care of you."

Once again, I was annoyed. I understood his concern, but I was growing weary of hearing it. I'd grown tired of the *Brooke be helpless* messaging. "Andre, please STOP!" My voice boomed. I was unable to control my frustration. "I had a miscarriage, not a full heart transplant. Hell, this is the second miscarriage," I reminded him. Andre stood frozen, clearly shocked at my reaction and tone. His concern appeared deeper now.

He held up his hand in a truce. "I'm sorry . . . I'm sorry, okay. I don't mean to nag. I just—"

"No . . ." I cut him off. Perhaps I was overreacting. This wasn't me. "I apologize . . . babe, I know that you worry about me. But really, I'm fine," I reassured him. I inwardly sniffed back the tears that were trying to come out. I had promised myself that I was done with the crying. I had cried too long and hard over spilt milk. Was I being selfish and greedy? I had been given so much already. My life was perfect, I had a husband who adored me, and a career that I loved.

"Work is good for me, and you know how much I enjoy it. Besides, I'm up for partner, remember? Six months and a decision will be made. So, it's a must I show up and show out." I turned to leave, giving my booty a little bounce. Andre chuckled. He loved it when I did that. I gave him a wink over my shoulder.

"Well, I guess you got to keep that thang tight while you climb that ladder to success," Andre commented. Then he smacked me on the booty, and I giggled again like a schoolgirl. Andre laughed out loud at my reaction. I skipped out of the closet down the massive stairway, which led to the second floor. I hardly ever used the elevator. The stairs were invigorating and gave me energy.

"Good morning, Brooke." Melva spoke as soon as I hit the last step on the stairway. I didn't see her, but I knew she was close by.

"Morning, Melva," I answered back. Melva was one of our two maids. The house was so huge we had to have more than one. Sue was our other maid; they both had been with us since we moved in. Melva held more than a maid position, she was also in charge of the upkeep of the grounds, which meant she dealt with the contractors for all outside work. So, her title was senior housekeeper, and she did a great job.

"Morning, Brooke." Sue suddenly appeared.

"Morning, Sue," I sang out. Then Melva stepped into view. "Well, ladies, I'm off to the gym. Sorry I'm in such a rush, but I'm already late." I hurried out the door. My black Porsche was parked out front. I jumped inside, pulled around the circle driveway and waited for the gate to open.

My heart smiled as I thought about Andre, and the expression he had on his face whenever he looked at me. I was so fortunate to have him. That man loved and supported me always. I was blessed. I may not have been able to conceive a baby, but I had no real reason to complain, because my husband cherished me.

The sound of my Bluetooth chimed in, interrupting my thoughts. "Hey, bug a boo," I greeted Reese and continued to navigate through traffic.

"Brooke, where's your late butt at?" She rushed, talking fast. "I know you don't have me sitting here of all places at the gym, waiting for you."

I couldn't help but laugh out loud. "Well, ain't you the pot calling the kettle black, ma'am." I was more than happy to tease her, she had it coming. Reese was the queen of being late. For once she had arrived on time, and now she was ready to murder me. "I'm on my wayyy, Reesseee," I sang to tease her.

"You had better be because . . ." She continued, threatening me within an inch of my life. I laughed all the way

MY HUSBAND'S MISTRESS IS DEAD / 37

there. I was enjoying giving Reese a taste of her own medicine. This was a very good start to my day; the best part was that my best friend had shown up to get this much-needed workout in with me. I was amped up.

I arrived at the gym with a smile on my face, the banter with Reese having lightened my mood considerably. As I parked my car and stepped out, I couldn't help but feel a surge of determination. Today was going to be a good day, I could sense it.

Reese was inside, tapping her foot impatiently as I approached. "Took you long enough," she teased, though there was a playful glint in her eyes.

"I like to keep you on your toes," I replied with a grin, giving her a playful nudge. "Ready to crush this workout?"

"You know it!" Reese exclaimed; her enthusiasm contagious. We made our way into the gym, greeted by the familiar sights and sounds of clanging weights, rhythmic music, and the buzz of energy from fellow gym-goers.

As we started our warm-up routine, I couldn't help but feel grateful for moments like these—time spent with a dear friend, focusing on our health and well-being. The rhythmic movement of the exercise, the burn of muscles, and the overall flurry of physical activity that contributed to a sense of empowerment.

Reese and I pushed each other through various sets and exercises, cheering each other on as we both declared to have more body muscle than the other. It wasn't just about physical fitness; it was about fun, laughter, and pushing ourselves to be the best versions of ourselves.

"I needed this," I admitted to Reese, feeling a sense of lightness and positivity as our workout was winding down.

"Me too," she agreed, and flashed me a bright smile. "We should make this a regular thing again, Brooke. I'll show up, I promise."

"You pinky swear?" I teased.

"You are not a comedian. Stop." That was our favorite thing to say.

After an intense workout session that left us both sweaty and exhilarated, we headed to the smoothie bar for a post-workout treat. As we sipped on our protein shakes, we chatted about everything from work to personal goals to plans for the upcoming weekend. It felt good to be talking about something other than the miscarriage. I wanted to be treated as if I was normal, not a grieving female who couldn't do one of the most common and natural things— have a baby.

Chapter 6

"Now that Mr. Rodriguez's inheritance has been deposited into his account, we can begin to look at the full portfolio of his assets."

I gazed over the file in front of me. I was having a short meeting with my assistant, Janae. She had been working with me for the past three years and she was at the top of her game. I was confident that one day she would be sitting where I was. "However, I need you to set up a call with him to go over those potential adjustments that we discussed because of his wife's settlement."

"Yes, I already prepared the summary of questions that you suggested. I will email them to you in an hour, for final approval." This was the type of dedication Janae had for her position. She was detailed and very organized, all habits I appreciated in work ethics.

"Please do so. By tomorrow afternoon we will be able to view the market trends and see if we need to make any last-minute adjustments before the final projection. Make sure you are available."

Janae nodded as her fingers moved fast, typing notes

into her laptop. "I will block off the time on my calendar." Her organizational skills were above reproach. She was never late to a meeting, nor had she ever missed one.

"And—" I began to say, but my train of thought was interrupted by the ringing of my office phone. I knew it demanded my attention. It was Leah, my junior assistant, on the line.

"Mrs. Perry, you have Mr. Hastings on line one," she informed me.

"He wasn't scheduled for a call, was he?" I asked but was almost certain he wasn't.

"No, he was not," she confirmed.

I bit back my annoyance and instructed Leah, "Put him through. I'll be with him shortly."

I hung up and finished up my meeting with Janae. As I picked up the phone, I couldn't help but roll my eyes, "Mr. Hastings, hi." I was used to him, so I put on my professional hat, and reassured my client that everything was moving along as expected. Despite having to repeat that in three different ways, three different times, I eventually was able to get him off the phone.

I glanced at the time displayed at the bottom of my computer screen. I realized that it was 4:00 PM, and I hadn't even had a lunch break, or stopped to take a breath. After having met with Janae earlier in the day, then taking Mr. Hastings's unscheduled call, I had sat in on two different meetings, not to mention the reports I had examined in between. Somewhere along the line, as usual, the day had gotten away from me.

"Ahh." I leaned back in my chair for a pause and gazed out of my large office window. The bright sun was shining through, and it energized me. But there was a tug at my gut that suddenly pulled me back to the miscarriage.

Pain, a recognizable agonizing pain, ripped through

me. Asleep, my eyes popped open. I expected to see Andre's body to my right, beside me, but his space was surprisingly empty. I wanted to reach for my cell phone. I could see that it was close, within arm's reach. I moved my body to attempt to retrieve it. But as another sharp pain tore through my abdomen, I tried to scream. But the room blurred as the pain intensified. And a burst of hot liquid spilled forth. "Agghh!" I finally was able to scream. I moved my hand down to feel the puddle and came up with a glob of blood. And I knew. Andre burst from the bathroom where he had been. The pain was all over his face . . .

Buzz, buzz! The constant buzzing of my office phone yanked me back to reality. That horrible part of my life was over. Today I was not in pain, at least not from my abdomen. I could, however, feel the wetness from the tears on my cheeks. I had been crying. I reached into my drawer and retrieved some Kleenex with one hand, hit the answer button with the other. "Yes, Leah?" I spoke into the speaker and tried to keep a steady, upbeat tone.

"There is an Erika Jones here to see you."

"I thought my schedule was clear today?" I dabbed at my cheeks to dry the wetness that still lay there.

"That is correct. There are no scheduled appointments on the calendar today."

Perplexed, I tossed around the unfamiliar name in my head, and it didn't ring bell. I didn't know Erika Jones. Maybe she was a referral, but even still, people didn't normally just show up. And it was late.

"She says it's about Mr. Andre Perry," Leah said, just as I was about to instruct her to schedule an appointment.

The mention of Andre's name had me curious. "Bring her in." I gazed over my shoulder out the window at the view of the city, taking a moment to collect my thoughts. I turned back around just as Leah pushed the door open.

I quickly refocused as Leah moved to the side and an

unknown woman stepped inside the door. With smooth, mahogany-colored skin, a thin waist and about five feet, eight inches tall, there stood America's Next Top Model. I was mystified, but anxious to know who this stranger was who wanted to see me about Andre.

Anxious to hear what she had to say, I offered politely, "Please, have a seat. Thanks, Leah." I excused my junior assistant, who was still standing in the doorway. She gave me a curious look as she backed out, allowing the door to shut.

The lady took a seat and glared at me. Something in my stomach flared up again. *Uneasy* is how I would describe the feeling. "Brooke Perry." She announced my name as if she knew me from high school. But I was sure I didn't know her from Adam. She was a stranger with Andre's name on her tongue.

"Yes, I'm Brooke," I confirmed, still feeling confused why she had asked to see me, then marched into my office confirming my identity. Of course, I was Brooke. "How can I help you, Erika Jones?" I said her name this time. My tone conveyed a sense of expectancy.

"I'm here about Andre, your husband. Well . . . I've been seeing him and conceived a baby with him." She said this to me in a matter-of-fact tone, as if it was the most normal thing in the world. Her facial expression revealed the same neutral expression.

I was sure the lights in my office went out because for a moment, I saw pitch-black. All background noises faded, and I could only hear silence. It was even possible that I had temporarily lost my hearing. Her words had caught me off guard and cut me deeply. For some reason I gazed at my abdomen area, expecting to see blood spilling forth. But there was none. I felt nauseous, and there was a heaviness on me as if I was being weighed down.

"Lady, you're crazy. I do not know who you are, or

who sent you, but you are lying," I accused. My tone of voice was full of disbelief. "Now get out of my office, NOW!" My voice suddenly boomed with unexpected force. I wasn't sure if the words were coming out of my mouth or if I was thinking them. But this was real, she was real, so the words had to be coming out of my mouth.

"What do you mean, someone sent me?" Clearly, she was offended by my accusation. Nor was she deterred by my demand that she leave. "No one sent me . . . and I'm not crazy nor am I lying. But I do need your help . . . it concerns the child," she continued to explain.

I was appalled by her boldness and unwillingness to leave my office as she had been asked to do. Who was this person? Here this woman was, in my face, telling me that my husband had been unfaithful to me. Admitted that it was with her, yet she was offended by my words. I was dumbfounded. My unsteady hands reached for the phone, and I dialed security. I refused to hear any more from this deranged female. "Please, leave my office." I was now on my feet demanding she leave.

Security burst through the door and I directed them to remove her from the office and this building. Stan, one of the guards, asked her in a polite manner to please stand up. But she flat out refused. He gently reached for her elbow with the intention to assist her.

"Do not touch me, asshole." She jerked her head in his direction, then jumped to her feet. "I am capable of standing and walking without your assistance. She twisted back around to face me, then opened her hand. A piece of paper had been lying there, and she placed it onto my desk. "Please, I know this is a lot to take in. But meet with me and I will explain further." There was a plea in her eyes that was unmistakable.

"Ma'am, please, it's time to go." Again, Stan gently reached for her arm and this time he was able to grab ahold of it. He escorted her out and to my surprise she went quietly. I stared at the closed office door for at least two minutes, unable to look away. But when I did, and for the first time, I could see through the glass office window that a small crowd of employees had gathered. Leah opened the door to inquire if I was okay, and if I needed anything. Carl, a newly promoted financial advisor also entered with concern. I assured them that I was okay. Our offices were all but soundproof, so I knew they were not sure what exactly had happened. But the fact that security had burst into my office was a dead giveaway that something was amiss.

Chapter 7

My feet moved at a steady pace. Nonetheless, on the inside, I was running at top speed. "Ahhh." My head fell loosely from my shoulders as a breath of fresh air shot through my lungs, as I escaped Walter & Hanks. The sun embraced me, and I felt alive. Had I remained inside, I would surely have passed out. The air in there had become increasingly stifling. After replaying the whole Erika Jones ordeal over and over in my head at my desk, anxiety took over me, and I had to flee.

I was in a zone; I just couldn't process what had just transpired. An unknown woman just waltzed into my office, sat down face-to-face with me, and accused my husband of having an affair and conceiving a baby with her. How? When? Why? Andre Perry, my husband? Was she sure? This was implausible, there could be no truth to this fable. He would never do a thing like this to me. Andre was a proud, happily married man. Things were on track for us. Tonight was going to be another big celebration for us. Andre's company had reached another milestone on its road to success, landing in the top ten of LA-based brokerage firms. The party was being held at our estate; so much planning had gone into pulling off the perfect event. And here I was sitting in my car battling over some stranger's frivolous accusation about my husband, her claim that she was his mistress. Suddenly I could see it clearly; it happened all the time to celebrities. This had to be about money, right?

"Shit." The sudden ringing of my cell phone startled me. It was Andre. "Hey, babe," I answered, my tone upbeat as usual.

"Babe, are you okay? I just called the office, and Leah said you already left for the day." I could hear the concern in his voice.

Whenever I was at the office, Andre would call Leah and have her track me down because he couldn't get me on my cell. At work, I was usually all business, and everything else was put on the back burner. So, the cell phone was the first to go.

"Yeah, I'm fine. I had to get out of there a little early today. I have an errand or two to run before the party tonight."

"Oh, sweetheart, I thought between Shelly and the caters, everything was handled. I didn't want to put an additional stress on you."

"No, babe, it's nothing like that. Everything for the party is good. You know, Shelly makes sure everything is taken care of. She's the best. I just have a few things that I need for the party," I lied.

I felt so guilty for lying to him, but I didn't know what else to say on such short notice. How could I say, *Honey, some crazy lady just marched into my office and accused you, of all people, of having an affair and making a baby.* Nope, there's no way I could say that. No, I wanted to forget that foolishness ever happened, at least for now.

MY HUSBAND'S MISTRESS IS DEAD / 47

* * *

"Shelly, everything looks so beautiful?"

Shelly, our event planner, was amazing. She always delivered the vision. I admired the scene that was laid before me. Circular tables decorated with exquisite floral centerpieces offered a balance of intimacy and sophistication. The sun started to dip below the horizon. But lanterns adorned with soft candlelight dotted the pathways and would guide the guests to our front door. A live band played music in the background. The scene that was set was a testament to the power of collaboration and the enduring spirit of partnerships. The guests had started to arrive, and it was going to be a successful evening. But Andre and I expected nothing more.

"I'm glad you like it. Everything should be spot-on to your vision," Shelly said with a sweet smile on her face.

"It is." I beamed as Reese approached.

"Hey, friend." She gave me hug. "Shelly, I see you did your thing, as always," she complimented.

"Thanks, Reese," Shelly said. "I'm going to mingle a little before leaving," she announced and scampered off. I always invited her to attend the events. Sometimes she stuck around, and others she was on the run.

"So, I see you are here early. To what do I owe your promptness?" I teased Reese.

A waiter came by with a tray of champagne and she reached out and grabbed one. "Hmm." She pretended to think over my question. She observed some of the guests, the men in particular. "Well, I knew I was going to be flying solo, and I was hoping some fine men would be here tonight. Thought I'd get here early because most of your women guests are often thirsty, if you know what I mean."

"Reese." I playfully slapped her shoulder and laughed. "Girl, you are crazy."

"Yeah, maybe I am a little bit. But I need a date, a real one if you catch my drift. It's been a minute." She sipped her wine.

"Brooke, how are you?" Watson, one of Andre's rival business associates approached. They had known each other for a long time. While Watson was a rival, they got along pretty good, attended each other's events, and even hung out together.

"Hi, Watson, glad you made it tonight," I replied.

"You know I wouldn't miss Andre's celebration. Besides, he throws the best parties." I noticed Watson cut his eyes at Reese. "Reese, it's been a minute, but it's certainly good to lay eyes on you." He secured her right hand and kissed it.

"Nice seeing you too, Watson." Reese's tone was casual. Poor Watson, she never gave him any spark.

He still held on to her hand. "What's been keeping you occupied?"

"Residency takes up a lot of my time." Reese removed her hand from his.

"You should let me take you out sometime so you can tell me about your residency. I really would like to hear more about it."

"Umm, I'm just so busy. I barely have time to work out." My neck snapped in her direction. Why had she said that, of all things? Reese hated working out.

Watson ate her up with his eyes. There was no doubt he saw a dish he wanted to taste. "Well, I don't think you have anything to worry about if you miss a few sessions, you look great. Here, take my card, let me know when you have some free time." He reached into his pocket.

"Watson, what's up, my man?" Andre approached.

Watson pulled his hand from his pocket, where he had been trying to fish out that card, to shake Andre's hand.

"What's up, man of the hour. Congratulations on the success."

"Thank you, and thanks for coming out tonight. I know you've been busy starting up your brokerage firm."

"Yeah, man . . . we need to sit down soon for a meeting."

"No doubt, I got you. Have my secretary set it up. You know what to do," Andre said. He turned to me. "You look beautiful, sweetheart." He kissed me full on the lips. "Hey, Reese." He spoke with no enthusiasm or kindness.

"Andre." Reese gave the same energy in return. "By the way, congrats."

"Ahh, thanks, Reese." Andre smiled. He wasn't expecting her well wishes. The only thing Reese ever gave him was a *hi* and *bye* and that was their conversation. That's all, that's it.

"Watson, in the spirit of networking, come. I have a few people that you need to meet." He led Watson away before he could protest. Watson gave Reese a quick glance over his shoulder.

I shook my head at her and smirked. "You are something else. You barely have time to work out," I repeated her words. "You ought to be ashamed."

Reese shrugged her shoulders nonchalantly. "What, I couldn't think of anything else to say. Listen, I am not going to lie. Watson is cute, but he just ain't my type." She gave a slight frown; her lips were twisted sideways.

"Girl what do you mean not your type? Watson is a catch on the dating scene. Let me see . . . he is cute, smart, and wealthy." I counted with my fingers for good measure.

"Yeah, so is Andre Perry. And umm . . . yeah." Her tone was full of sarcasm.

"There you are, Brooke; I have been looking all over for you." Vivian slid in beside me before I could tackle Reese's shade.

"Vivian, hi," I exclaimed with all the cheer I could pull from within. For some reason the sight of Vivian revived the Erika Jones incident. Suddenly, I was all too aware of the unpleasant incident that had happened less than six hours ago. And here I was entertaining guests, kissing my husband and playing the dutiful wife. "I'm glad you made it. Andre will be happy to see you." I forced a gentle smile.

"Why happy? I'm sure he knows I am here, that is no surprise. I'm his mother—where else would I be on a night like tonight?" Vivian's head was spinning trying to catch the eye of all of the guests. I was surprised she hadn't called me up and asked for the guest list beforehand. That would have been a classic Vivian move.

"Brooke, I'm going to mingle." Reese eyeballed Vivian hard and strutted away. I knew she was not in the mood to be bothered with her. Vivian used her eyes to wave Reese away, the feeling between the two was always mutual.

"Brooke, you really must find another party planner. This Shelly person, is that her name? Where did you say she attended school?"

"I didn't," I replied, my tone steady and calm. But my forehead burned as if it was on fire as it pounded with a throbbing headache. "Vivian, please come. I must take you to Andre straightaway, he will be on his heels to see you." I had to get away from her, and quickly. The plan was to deliver her to her son and make a break for it.

I managed to temporarily distance myself from Vivian for the time being, but throughout the night she would sniff me out to complain and be her usual rude, stuck-up self. She tossed around every snide remark she could think of concerning the party. As usual I ignored her, which wasn't hard to do. Erika Jones had crept into my mind and had a grip on my thoughts. But it was becoming increasingly hard to hide my agitation.

"Brooke, are you okay?" Reese had asked me three times in the same hour.

My cheeks stretched back into a forced smile, the biggest I could manage. "Oh, I'm fine," I lied with a straight face. "Just getting a little tired. I had a busy day at the office," I added, hoping it made my lie more believable. But Reese knew me better than anyone else and could detect when my mood was off. The slight crease in her forehead told me she wasn't completely buying what I was saying. But to her dismay Watson approached her again. He wasn't giving up.

Andre slid his arm around my waist and uttered, "Thanks" to me for putting the event together. "You okay, you seem a bit disconnected," he whispered into the crease of my neck.

"Who, me? Oh, I'm fine. Just enjoying the camaraderie."

"Are you sure?" His tone held concern. "You would tell me if something was bothering you, right? No secrets between us."

His statement jolted an uneasy internal conflict into the pit of my stomach. I swallowed my emotion. "Of course. No secrets, right?" I threw his question back at his feet.

"Never from you, babe. I love you." He faced me and gently kissed me on the lips.

"I love you too," I returned. "Now go get back to your guests. They came here to celebrate this pivotal moment with you. I'm fine, so do not worry," I assured him.

"Alright, beautiful." He started to walk away, but then turned around. "Is it Mother?" He paused.

"What were you going to say?"

"Is it Mother, is she being too much tonight?"

"Oh, no, never." I lied straight through my teeth; a loving smile covered my face. If I'd smiled any harder my face would have cracked like glass. Vivian was always too much, but how could I say that to him, about his own mother? Andre worshipped the ground she growled on. He would defend his dear mother, and blame all her faults on the disloyalty of others. Trying to convince him otherwise would be like walking on hot rocks with no clear end in sight. It was not worth it. So, I gave him another loving smile and waved him off. Besides, Vivian was kibble and bits on my interest list right now. I had bigger concerns. Erika Jones . . . who was she?

Chapter 8

After the celebration of the night before, I was physically exhausted from mingling, making sure everyone felt welcomed and appreciated. I was also feeling worn out mentally because Erika Jones had erupted in my mind like a hot volcano, and I couldn't shake it. After tossing and turning most of the night and listening to Andre as he purred and slept like a baby, I decided to get out of bed and start my day. I brushed my teeth, grabbed my cell phone, and raced downstairs out into the California sun, which was shining beautifully. I sat at the edge of our massive-sized swimming pool and allowed my feet to greet its crystal-clear waters. Scrolling through my contacts, I searched Reese's name and selected it. She answered on the first ring. I told her I wanted to grab lunch and chat, and she didn't protest. I allowed my feet to soak for another five minutes, then raced back inside to take a hot shower and get dressed.

Since we both loved Mexican food, I had chosen one of our favorite spots that was not far from Bel Air, Mamá Por Dios. At home I was restless, so I arrived ten minutes before we were supposed to meet. I sat down and to my surprise Reese was right behind me.

"Whewww! It's too early for it to be this hot." She sat across from me.

"You know me, I love the heat, so I'm not complaining." I slid off my Burberry sunglasses and placed them on the table.

The waitress approached us. I took the liberty and ordered us both margaritas because I knew that would be Reese's choice as well.

"Oh, Brooke, I don't know how you handle it. That mother-in-law of yours . . . I wanted to scream at the sight of her last night. I've never met someone so blatantly rude and downright disrespectful." She vented, her face bunched up into a scowl.

I chuckled lightly. "Who, Vivian? She's not that bad." I used sarcasm for my own entertainment.

"I see why you were so preoccupied last night. That woman could throw a devout Christian off their game." She was still riled up from the encounter. The waitress brought our drinks over, then took our food order. We decided on queso dip with sausage; neither of us was that hungry. We asked the waitress to check on us in case we wanted to order more drinks. I was certain we would be ordering more.

"Actually, the issues I was preoccupied with last night had nothing to do with Vivian. Far from it." I stirred my margarita straw around in my drink, then took a thoughtful sip. I would need it to share this story with Reese in as much detail as I could. Intrigued, she raised her eyebrows one by one.

"Brooke, are you going to tell me, or do I have to sit here and age first." Reese sighed with frustration. I didn't realize between the stir of my drink and the sip, I was keeping her in suspense.

"Oh, sorry . . ." I snapped out of it. I could hear the clicking of glasses and murmurs of others in the background. "So yesterday, as usual, I had a long day at the office. It was getting close to the end of my day. I still hadn't had my lunch, so I was taking a quick breather at my desk. The next thing I know Leah is telling me a woman by the name of Erika Jones was asking to speak with me. I didn't have any appointments scheduled so my interest was piqued but I was about to send her away. That is until Leah said that she wanted to speak to me about Andre—

"Andre?" Reese repeated, cutting me off, her tone full of curiosity. I had expected this reaction from her.

"Yes, Andre," I confirmed. "So, I tell Leah to go ahead and bring her to my office. Leah opens the door and in walks this striking, tall *America's Next Top Model* type of chick. She takes a seat and proceeds to drop this bombshell. According to her, she's been having an affair with Andre."

Reese's eyes bulged and her response was a loud, "SHE SAID WHAT?" Her voice boomed and echoed throughout the restaurant.

"Reese." My eyes scanned the restaurant. Thankfully they were not too busy but there were a few people staring, as I had expected they might. "Calm down," I uttered.

The atmosphere in the room shifted from casual conversation to one charged with intrigue and disbelief. "I'm sorry, that shit just blew me away. I mean, what the hell?"

I hung my head low for a second, raised it again and sighed. "That's not all . . . she also claims there is a baby involved . . . a baby," I repeated. The words seemed heavy on my tongue as I said them aloud.

Reese seemed to go pale in the face. But I could see she was fighting hard to hold her composure in a public place. I could tell the turmoil inside her was brewing deep under the surface. It appeared as though she was holding her breath. Her jaw was clenched tight, and she pulled in her bottom lip as she shook her head with disappointment. "You know what, I'm not shocked. Brooke, I told you not to marry that fucking asshole," she said, clenching her teeth tightly. She scooted up in her chair, closer to the table. "I told you, I never cared for him or his weird-ass momma." She spat the words out as if they disgusted her.

I was so confused I fought back my emotions. I didn't know what to feel or what to believe. I knew Reese would initially be upset and would blame Andre. I had really struggled overnight with whether I should tell her or not. Reese already disliked him, and this was only going to make her hate him. But if it turned out to be a lie, how could I reverse what I had created? I was feeling so conflicted, but what other alternative did I have? Keeping the bombshell news to myself was equally daunting. Confiding in my best friend would lead to some clarity amidst the chaos roaming through my mind.

"Reese, I don't know what to do at this point," I confessed with a shrug; a sense of feeling lost and overwhelmed washed over me.

"Well, what does his ass have to say to this mess?" Reese asked bluntly.

"Who? Andre?"

"Who else? What does he have to say? What did he do, lie? Lie through his teeth that it's not true? I'm sure he did," she ranted and accused all in one breath.

I paused and contemplated how to answer as I sipped my drink. I was nervous to share with her that I had not confronted him about it. "Actually, he has no idea. I haven't mentioned it to him just yet."

"Wait, you mean he doesn't know? Why wouldn't you mention this to him right away, Brooke? Why wait?"

I nodded my head and shrugged my shoulders. There was no excuse I could give her that would make sense.

"Wow, Brooke! You are one strong-ass chick, because there is no way I could have stayed quiet this long. You smiled and gave him full support last night in front of his business partners, family, and friends. There is just absolutely no way I would've been able to pull that off. With the amount of anger that would have been seething through my veins, his whoring ass would have been dead yesterday, soon as I laid eyes on him."

"Trust and believe I was struggling inside to keep it together. But I have to think rationally . . . I can't be going off all half-cocked. Rushing to judgment . . . No, I must know the facts first," I reasoned.

"The facts?" Reese twisted up the edges of her mouth. If she had sucked on a lemon her face couldn't have been more scrunched up.

"Yes, the facts. We need to hear Andre's side. What if . . . what if this Erika Jones is lying? What if someone paid her to ruin us, ruin Andre? Things like that do happen."

"Brooke, really? Why would someone want to do that? Ruin Andre for what? What would be their motive? I mean, to what end? No, maybe . . . just maybe . . . Andre is just a whore who couldn't keep it in his pants." Reese shrugged as if that were a fact.

"Or maybe he's a loving husband dedicated to me and is being set up. I know it can be a lot to consider when such accusations are made. But this brokerage firm mess sometimes brings enemies and sometimes much worse. All these big money deals and such fail more times than not, and that leaves people with vindictive emotions. What's more, I'm his wife. I should give him the benefit of the doubt. If I won't, who will? I shouldn't just believe some woman . . . some complete stranger, who came in off the streets and accused him of having an affair and fathering a child. Besides, she brought no proof whatsoever. She didn't present me with anything that was based on the facts." I defended Andre and begged Reese to try to understand.

Reese sighed. I could hear the skepticism in her tone as she spoke. "Brooke, you are right, Andre is your husband, and you owe him something; I'm not sure what. But what I don't believe is that some random woman is setting him up. I just don't believe that. What would she have to gain?" Her question lingered in the air.

"Money . . . it's all about money, of course. Andre is rich, no one can deny that," I said with certainty. "But nevertheless, she asked me to meet with her, and she claims that then she will explain further. But I just don't know about that. Andre wouldn't like that, me meeting with a stranger."

"Well, this isn't Andre's decision to make. Of course, he wouldn't want you meeting with someone who might shed some light on his sneaky ways. But as you said, you want facts, and while I can't say you can trust this Erika Jones, she might be able to point you in the direction you need to go. And if it's facts you require, you need to go get them." Reese's words resonated with me, cutting through the fog of my uncertainty.

The house was eerily quiet when I returned home after meeting with Reese. I had gone into the office for a couple of hours. Although it was not planned, I wanted to busy my mind, and I knew checking a few emails and going over some reports would do the trick. And I was right. I was able to shake Erika Jones out of my mind for a couple of hours. But now I was home, and I was tired. A glass of wine and a hot shower would be the saving grace of my day. Andre wouldn't be home for a while. I was sure he was still at the office. Sliding out of my Chanel heels, I picked them up with the plan of heading toward the den. But at my feet lay a trail of rose petals, scattered as far as my eye could see. I stalled. I nearly jumped out of my skin as Andre appeared from nowhere.

I grabbed my chest. "Babe, are you trying to give me a heart attack?" I gave him wide grin. "What's going on?" I asked.

Andre continued toward me. "You do so much to support me, and tonight I want to give you my sincere thanks. I appreciate the party that you went out of your way to throw for me and my colleagues. You made it happen even though you've been working so hard at work. Waiting to hear about your partnership and still making me a priority. So, to start with, I have a hot bath waiting for you, then I prepared dinner."

I snapped my neck to the side in shock. "You cooked? Like cooked in the kitchen?" I pointed to the kitchen with my right hand, which held one of my Chanel shoes. "Wait, can you cook?" I teased him. We both laughed.

"Yes, I can cook." He licked his lips. "Come on, six years of marriage and you ask that?" His wide grin was so handsome. He played at being offended.

"Yes." I grinned, and nodded my head up and down. He pulled me into him and hugged me as we both still laughed.

He reached for my Chanel heels and held them both with his right hand while gently taking my right hand into his free left hand. "Now, follow me."

I followed slightly to his left as he led me toward the staircase, where rose petals were scattered along every step we took. At the edge of the stairs, he stopped and turned to look at me. "Listen carefully, Mrs. Perry. I want you to take your sexy self up those stairs, undress, climb into that warm bath, relax, and not a minute before you are ready, I want you to meet me down these stairs, for dinner. I promise to keep it hot and ready for you."

"Aww, thank you, babe." I treaded the staircase where rose petals adorned the whole area and continued to lead into the bedroom. I was impressed. This good husband that I had was one of a kind. Inside, just as he promised, I found a tub full of bubbles, surrounded by candles, and rose petals so thick on the floor it was like walking on thick grass. And not to disappoint, there was a bottle of champagne chilling, already corked, waiting to make my acquaintance. My heart did somersaults. Andre was so good to me, the man was loving and attentive, always.

It was time I followed his orders. Slowly I undressed, climbed into the water and it sucked me in, causing me to moan out loud. He had made sure that the champagne was positioned within a more-than-comfortable arm's reach. With a glass of champagne in my hand, I held the glass to my mouth and sipped.

"I see you are relaxed." I glanced up and there was Andre standing in the doorway.

"Yes, it's perfect. You did good." I lifted a leg from the water to tease him and he smiled. "Why don't you join me? There are still plenty of bubbles."

He feasted his eyes on me, and his look was seductive as he came closer. "While nothing sounds better, I just got a call from the office and need to run out for a minute. I'm so sorry," he apologized.

I sat up with my champagne glass in my hand. I was instantly disappointed. "No, babe, what about dinner? All of this you put together." I pouted.

"I know, I hate it too. But I have everything ready and waiting for you. And I just want you to enjoy it. I don't know exactly how long I'll be, so just go ahead and eat without me. I'll make it up to you, I promise." He leaned down and kissed me softly on the lips. Then he dipped his hand in the water and slid it between my thighs.

I moaned out loud as I gripped on to his arm, almost pulling him in with me. We both laughed. "Go on, get out of here before I pin you down," I said.

He stood and turned to leave but stopped and faced me again. "Oh, and I know you've had a long day. So, don't wait up for me." With that he was gone, and I was all alone to enjoy the appreciation dinner and bath he had prepared for me.

With each sip of champagne, I felt a sense of detachment. A bubble appeared midair, agitated. I raised my right hand and gave the bubble a light volleyball slap. The bubble burst into a million air bubbles and landed back with the countless bubbles that had me surrounded. I no longer had an appetite, and finishing off this bottle of champagne became my goal for the night, since I no longer had a husband to entertain me. Was Andre really going to the office?

The image of Erika Jones and her startling revelation resurfaced, casting a shadow over the romantic evening Andre had orchestrated. Why would he go to such lengths for this surprise, only to return to the office? Was there something else going on that caused his sudden departure? My mind now raced with questions as unwanted doubts crept into my mind.

"Ugh," I muttered, and shook my head and tried to shake the negativity out of it. I put the glass to my lips and swallowed all of its contents, determined to get rid of all the negativity that was threatening to cloud my evening. I quickly reached for the bottle and gave the glass a refill.

Chapter 9

I had followed the GPS, first to the interstate, then to a modest middle-class neighborhood. With each corner I turned, block for block, and the closer I got, I contemplated my decision to come here. But all too soon the GPS informed me, *You have arrived.* I was in denial, but now I found myself at the door, my right hand balled into a fist. I followed through with a light knock, then out of sheer nervousness followed it up with a second, only it was stronger. There was a doorbell in plain view, but for some reason I didn't use it. I gazed around quickly, wondering if someone had seen from their window, but except for the breeze and subtle smell of flowers, it was quiet. My fist threatened a third knock, but before I could do that, the door swung open.

"Sorry, I didn't hear you knock at first. It sounded more like a tap."

Once again, I was staring into the face of Erika Jones. I realized after talking to Reese that I should take my own advice and get the facts. So, I mustered up the courage and dialed Erika's number and here I was, just two days later, standing at her perfectly painted red door. How ironic, a mistress with a red painted door.

"It's fine," I was able to say.

"Please come in." She invited me inside her ranch style home. I almost hesitated, but that was the reason I had come in the first place. So, I put one foot in front of the other and stepped inside. There was a spacious room to the left of the door. I assumed it was the living room because it had an inviting atmosphere, neutral colors of ivory and light gray, nice sofas, and artwork. "Have a seat wherever you feel comfortable. Can I get you something to drink?"

I reluctantly sat down and gave her a stern look that said *get to the point*. Did she forget why I was here? I hadn't come for small talk, coffee, and donuts. "Erika, I didn't come over to break bread. You said you had things you wanted to explain. Please . . . the time is now." My tone and body language conveyed a mix of curiosity and clarity. She nodded. Her expression was serious as she took a seat across from me.

"Okay, and you're right. I didn't invite you over here for small talk either. I wanted to explain everything to you first . . ." She took a deep breath. Her tone now matched my urgency. "For three years . . ." She looked down briefly but immediately turned her attention back to me. "For three years or so I've been seeing Andre. I've been in a relationship with him, or so I thought."

To hear her say that again, I could feel the knot forming in my throat and the heat rising on the top of my scalp, giving me a huge headache. I listened attentively.

"In the beginning, I did not know he had a wife, didn't have a clue he was married. In time he told me as if it were no big deal. In a way it wasn't. I was in love with him, even when my head told me to leave him alone. My heart told me differently. It told me that he was worth it. Six months ago, I gave birth to a baby girl, right here in my very own home." A gasp escaped my lips, and I had no control over it. I quickly gained my composure.

"Are you okay?" she asked.

"Of course, I'm fine." I was offended by her alleged concern. A rush of anger overcame me. I pushed it back. "Go on." I raised my head back on my shoulders, prepared to listen.

"When I gave birth, Andre and I had both decided that we would use a midwife. I wasn't planning to be a mother because I wasn't married. I'm no saint, but in my mind marriage should bring forth children. But I do understand that things happen. So, if I was going to have a baby, I wanted things to be as natural as they could be. That's how I envisioned childbirth. It's what I wanted, and Andre agreed. On the day of the delivery, the midwife I'd seen throughout my entire pregnancy came to the house as planned. We'd worked on this for eight months to be exact, because I found out pretty early that we were pre . . . excuse me, that I was pregnant."

She cleared her throat. "But things were just like we planned. Things were going pretty well. There had been no red flags of anything being a concern with the pregnancy." She threw her right hand up nonchalantly and it landed softly back onto her lap. Her eye sockets suddenly filled with water, and the painful emotions were written all over face.

"Suddenly"—she seemed to choke back the memory, and it was evident that it was a painful one for her— "suddenly, there were complications." Her voice was full of sorrow. "The midwife was trying to assess the situation. Soon she knew it was the baby's heart, then my blood pressure spiked. And suddenly a host of things progressed fast." A tear escaped her eyes, displaying the depth of

MY HUSBAND'S MISTRESS IS DEAD / 65

what she was feeling. "Then the pain . . . the pain was getting severe. I mean it was a natural childbirth so I knew there would be pain, and I was prepared for that. But this pain was different. It was so intense until somewhere along the line, I blacked out."

She paused and took a breath to compose herself. I waited. "When I woke up it was a week later. During that time Andre had brought in a private doctor to care for me. Once I was alert for one full day and I guess they assumed I was strong enough, they sent the good doctor in to speak with me. He explained to me that the placenta separated from the uterine wall, *blah, blah, blah,* I'd given birth, but she didn't make it. It was so unbelievable to me that I couldn't, or wouldn't, comprehend what had happened."

The weight of her words hung in the air, the tragedy of losing a child evident in the room. Erika's pain was clearly obvious in every word, and I could tell the experience had left a lasting impact on her.

"Anyway, I was completely distraught, totally inconsolable. But Andre, the good man that he is, had thought of everything and taken care of it as well. The burial was set up, I didn't have to do anything. And in that moment, I was so thankful for him. Here this man was going through the worst pain of his life. But he had sacrificed his pain so that I could grieve the loss of my child properly. God, I loved him so much in that moment."

More tears had fallen from her eyes as she continued to recount her story, but she sniffed them back as much as she could. "But I don't think that my baby is dead. I tried to accept it. But I don't believe it, nope." She shook her head as she went off into a trancelike state.

"What do you mean, not dead?" My body seemed to shift to the edge of the couch at the horrors that were coming out of her mouth. "You just said there was a burial," I reminded her, not hiding my disbelief at her words. I thought she was lying so fast, she couldn't remember what she'd said ten minutes ago.

"Yes, there was a burial, but I never actually saw my baby. I never once laid eyes on her. When we arrived at the chapel, the baby was already in a small casket that was sealed. I was told it had been sealed after three days. And since I had been unable to make any decisions, Andre, the next of kin, the father, had made the call to close the casket for good, all of which was legal."

"Are you saying that you think Andre . . . and a professional doctor, who took an oath to uphold medicine, are lying?" My tone was full of sarcasm on purpose. I wanted her to hear me so she could know just how outlandish she sounded.

"I know it sounds farfetched. But yes, I do believe they are lying to me. As a matter of fact, I believe he paid that so-called professional doctor and that midwife to lie for him and keep his secret. Andre has enough money that will persuade people, even though they have taken oaths, to not do the unthinkable. And I think, sadly, this is one of those times."

I had to rub my forehead on that one. It seemed like a lot for someone to fabricate. And not for nothing, what would Andre's motive be in trying to pull this off? "Erika, I think the whole world would also think this is farfetched. Besides, why would Andre lie about something like that? We're talking about his child, his own flesh and blood," I pointed out.

The one thing I knew for sure, but would not share with her, is that Andre loved children. It was the one thing in this world that he wanted and did not have. He would never get rid of a child. I just couldn't believe that.

Erika released a light chuckle, but her lips had no curve

that would indicate a smile. "I'm not smart, and even I know the answer to that. It's simple. Andre did not want you to find out about me or our baby. That much was clear. Out of the blue, soon after the birth of the baby, he broke it off with me. Before that . . . the pregnancy, I mean, he had claimed he loved me so much that he had to be with me. Suddenly, he wanted to be at home with his wife. Me, being the side piece, had to step off. Be gone like I never existed, just like that." She connected her thumb with her middle finger and snapped.

I was dumbfounded by the constant lies that easily slid out of her mouth. There was no way any of this hogwash was true. It was almost laughable. "You said you had complications during the birth, pains that were so bad you blacked out. If you were going through all that pain, something was clearly amiss. Why do you find it so hard to believe the baby died? How do you know she is truly not dead?" I just refused to believe her stupid allegations.

She stood up, paced a bit, and considered my words. Then she sat back down in front of me and looked straight into my eyes. "Look, as much as I despise Andre for how he has done me, I tried . . . I mean really tried, to get this all out of my head. But something just doesn't add up, I can feel it inside of me. I carried that baby inside of me for nine months. There was a bond before she even entered this world. I felt the kicks and heard the heartbeats. She was mine, and I was her mother. Call it instincts, but a mother knows. She's out there . . . Since this happened, I have lost everything. I can't work because I can't focus, knowing my baby is out there somewhere with strangers, I'm sure." More tears cascaded down her cheeks.

There was too much running through my mind. What was really going on? But there were a few burning questions that I didn't understand. Why was I here? "Why did you seek me out? Why me, Andre's wife? Why not just call the police if you think your baby has been taken from you, let them do their job?"

She slapped her knee and chuckled out loud. "Why do you think?" The half grin on her face belonged to that of a madwoman. "I haven't been to the cops because of Andre . . . your husband is rich. What do you think he will do when I start running around telling people he fathered a baby with me, and the dead baby is still alive? No, he would pay people off to lie for him, just like he did with the doctor and midwife. Then I would look like a lunatic. No one would dare believe me over him. Hell . . . you don't even believe me." Her truth hit me in my face so hard, that it nearly slammed me backwards into the sofa. "No, they will all think I'm crazy. And write me off as so."

"Erika, that still doesn't explain why I am here. Why would you come to the wife of the man you've been sleeping with?"

"As you said, you are his wife. You live in the same house as him. Surely, you can find facts, things he is hiding, like my child. Where is she? What did he do with her? Is he hiding her in your home? I don't know."

This time I was the one who chuckled. She was talking crazy. Maybe she didn't really know Andre, maybe she had googled him. "Lady, your child is not in my home. While it is a mansion, if a child was in it, I would know. Nothing in my home could be hidden from me this long, especially not for six months." I shook my head with disgust at her lies and attempt to ruin me and my family.

"Listen . . ." Her eyes took on a slight bulge with a begging gaze. "I know you are probably thinking I'm after something. Money maybe, that's usually what people with money think everyone wants from them. But all I want is my baby, and I promise once I have her, I will go away from here. However, I can't leave this place without my baby. I know you are trusting your million-dollar husband. But I know better than to do that. Because I have seen the other side of him. So, for my sake, will you please, please not mention the baby, if you confront him. Please!" she begged. "I know I have no right to ask anything of you."

I was stunned and speechless. I felt as if I had been cemented to the spot I sat in, my legs were heavy, my mind shaky. I had to be in some type of shock. How could I begin to process all I'd just heard? This was nonsense. That much was coming clear to me, and quickly. I should not have come. Coming here and entertaining this was pure madness. I had to put an end to this.

Somehow my legs flexed, and I stood straight up. "Look, I'm not sure why you really reached out to me. But I can't help you. Andre Perry is not the type of man you just described to me. You don't know him . . . He's my husband of six years. I know him."

I was adamant. It was time I defended my husband. How could I let some stranger tear him down? I should have stopped her when she first accused him of hiding her baby. Only a monster would do that; not my Andre. With the key to my Porsche gripped tightly in my hand, I was prepared to put Erika and her phony allegations behind me for good. Before I could leave, she jumped to her feet, her face displaying desperation.

"No, you don't know him. The things he did to me. He beat me after the baby's burial services because I questioned him about my concerns. He burned me with a CIGAR!" she yelled; frustration was riddled on her face. Her face was wet with tears.

Her words were like a punch in my gut. But I was fed up with her baseless accusations, and ready to relieve myself of her. As I was leaving, I stepped past her, not caring about her tears. Hell, I was the one who should have been crying and hurt. "I'm out of here and done with this fiasco. I don't want to hear any more of this." My back was to her and so was this situation. I reached for the doorknob so I would be free.

"Aggghhh!" Erika screamed out loud. "And that woman he calls a mother. I will bet you my bottom dollar that bitch knows where my child is."

I stopped and turned to face her; she had once again captured my attention. "Vivian knows?" I asked. My heart raced with curiosity and apprehension. It was disturbing to think Vivian might be aware of this, and unease swelled in me.

"Vivian always knows, those two are thick as thieves. Anybody who knows them, knows that. Trust me, that lady knows where my baby is. And yes, she knows all about me. When I first found out I was pregnant, he told her. He tells her everything . . . and I do mean everything. I can't believe you don't know that." She eyed me with confusion.

"Well, she didn't like it when she found out, and to prove it she hunted me down while I was on a job. She told me if I didn't get my bastard baby aborted, that she would hit me in the stomach with a bowling ball to help me out. Then the nasty bitch spit in my face. And that's the person who raised Mr. Andre Perry." She hissed his name from a pit of hate, and I felt it. I turned around, twisted the doorknob, and without a word made my exit.

Chapter 10

By the time I got home from my meeting with Erika, I was battling nausea and feeling physically sick. I ascended our massive staircase in record time. My heart raced so fast I could hear its loud echo as I reached the top. I touched the double doors that led into our bedroom, and they seemed to fly open. The air felt thick inside, as if it might suffocate me. Inside the bathroom, my body gave way as I doubled over and was met by the heated tiled bathroom floor. A burst of explosive emotion spilled out from inside of me into the toilet. I hocked up my insides repeatedly, before falling into deep breaths and tried to calm myself so that I could catch my breath. "AGGHH," I grunted as more came out. I was disgusted over the things I had been told, and the contents coming from my stomach were proof of that.

Thoughts of Andre and Vivian made my stomach even queasier. The idea of Andre being violent was a complete shock to me. I had known him to be a bit edgy when he was upset about something, which wasn't often. But being downright violent was a side of him I had never seen before. Vivian's face, which most often seemed to be set in stone, flashed in my mind. When I pictured her face, it was hard like Joan Crawford from *Mommie Dearest*, when she went berserk over those wire hangers. Everyone who knew Vivian, or ever had any encounters with her, was familiar with the fact she was a force to be reckoned with. She was not known to be friendly, nor inviting. She came off as hard, uncaring, and did not have one ounce of empathy in her. But the threat she had allegedly made to Erika, *to hit a pregnant woman in the stomach with a bowling ball*, even I was startled that Erika had made that accusation. And quite frankly, I thought it was a bit of a stretch.

After throwing up what felt like a piece of my lungs, I felt weak. I gathered the strength to lift myself off the floor, undress, and step into the shower. I welcomed the warm water as it cascaded down my face, with the hope that it might cleanse away all the ugliness that I'd heard about my husband. I'm afraid that wouldn't be the case. Out of the shower, I moisturized my skin, dressed, and went to my closet to put away my shoes.

"There you are, baby; I was looking all over for you." Andre's gentle voice cut across my shoulder like a blade. In that moment an anger burned in my belly as if it had been ignited by a match. My hand gripped the shoes that I was holding so tightly I thought blood might come seeping through my fingers.

"Liar! . . . Liar! . . ." I screamed at him and threw the shoes that were in my hand at him. My jaws were clenched tight as I abruptly turned and reached for another pair of shoes to toss at him. My emotions—a whirlwind of anger and hurt—were all over me.

"Babe . . . Brooke . . . Wait," Andre called out and ducked a shoe that was inches away from hitting his left jaw. I'd made two long strides across the room and was in front of the island, where I grabbed the Saint Laurent bag I had been carrying for the day. I reared back.

"BROOKE . . . PLEASE DON'T . . ." Andre dropped to his knees and covered his head in a protective manner.

I paused midair with the bag in my hand. My chest pumped up and down, my heart raced so fast. "Andre Perry, you a liar and cheater," I huffed, breathing hard.

Andre's forehead seemed to crumble along with his sunken body. "What? Why would you say that?" He hesitated at first, but then slowly stood up, his eyes still focused on the Saint Laurent bag. He was concerned I might still throw it at him.

"Don't play dumb with me." I shook my head with disappointment. "I know all about your mistress, so cut the shit."

"Babe. It's not . . ." He was about to lie, and that would send me back over the edge.

"Don't lie to me, please." My hand went up again with the Saint Laurent bag, ready to smash it against him with all my might.

"Brooke . . . don't . . . please just put that bag down." He held his right hand up and tried to conceal his face. "I will tell you the truth, okay. Just please stop throwing things at me. Let's talk like civil adults."

I chuckled but it was from pain, not laughter from the heart. My face was somber from mixed emotions. "Adults? Is that what you think you are?" I asked him sharply, my tone full of anger. I knew I would not like his truth and was certain I would not be able to handle it like an adult.

"Please, just let me explain how this all happened," he pleaded. His voice had a hint of desperation in it.

"Andre, what is there to explain? You're a married man with a mistress." I could not hide the bitterness in my tone. "Let's see, what's her name again?" I pretended not to remember as I tapped the temple area of my face with my forefinger. "Erika Jones, yep, I think I got it right. Ms. Erika Jones is your mistress." I locked eyes with him, my stare cold as ice.

"Listen, I know how this looks and I'm sorry. But you know how I feel about you and would never do anything to intentionally hurt you."

"Are you insane? Or just plain stupid?" I was getting fed up with him. "Stop with the weak *I care for you* crap and go ahead, explain your lies."

Andre dropped his head, then slowly held it back up to meet my gaze. "Yes, it's true. Erika has been in my life," he admitted. To hear him say those words made me feel nauseous and it once again rose to my throat. I had to breathe through it so that it would not spill all over me and onto the floor of my closet.

"It all started back when we were going through the loss of our first baby. We were both grieving, and I don't know how much you remember about us at that time. But our relationship, it was strained." I could feel the sadness that was in his voice. "You were so hurt that you became distant. Not sure if you remember, but we've talked about this before."

I breathed in and rolled my eyes into the back of my head. Was he blaming me for his affair? "So, it's my fault that you cheated? Is that where you think it's safe to go with this?"

"No . . . no, please." He shook his head. "Babe, this is in no way your fault. I would never blame you for something I did. Just please hear me out. We were distant back then. We both were hurt and suffering. I needed someone to talk to, it was never my intention. But I just happened to meet this woman. She was nice, easy to talk to, which led to us laughing together. That made my grieving bearable at a time I really thought I might break."

My Husband's Mistress is Dead / 75

I could see he was reliving it.

"Babe, I was hurting so much . . . I was hurting so bad." Tears started to flood his face. "Brooke, I never told you this." He choked up and swallowed hard. "I thought about suicide . . . I contemplated killing myself. That's how deep I was suffering. I couldn't save myself and I couldn't save you. I didn't know how to pull you out of the sunken hole that you were in because I was drowning too."

The hurt and pain etched on his face and in his body language ripped through me like fresh wounds. It triggered the memory of the pain I endured at the time. Oh, how I had suffered. I shut myself off from love. I didn't want to love anyone, and I didn't want to be loved because my grief over the loss of our baby completely consumed me. I stopped thinking, I stopped hoping, and I stopped eating. I lost ten pounds on my already slim frame. If wasting away was truly a thing, I had secretly made plans to follow through with it to the very end. I had a secret pact to destroy myself.

No, I didn't consider Andre and his pain, just looking at him hurt me even more. I feared I'd let him down. I destroyed his future of having the family he always dreamed of having. I concluded I was less than a woman for not being strong enough to hold his child. So, I punished him with coldness, hoping this would give him his out and force him to be rid of me. But day after day, he was always there. But I'd pushed all of that out of my mind. And now I remembered. With a face full of tears and sorrow, I deeply regretted the way I'd neglected him—my devoted, loving husband.

The warmth and safety I felt as Andre's arms suddenly pulled me in was what I needed. "I'm so sorry for hurting you, Brooke." He apologized while kissing me all over my face. We embraced tighter as we both cried. Our pain soon turned into passion as we made love intensely. Andre also knew in that moment, without my having to say it, that I too was apologizing for denying him my love and support when he needed it most. I, too, had failed him as a wife. But the love that was like an electric current running through him to me, confirmed that whatever wrong I had done to him, he forgave me. And for that I was thankful. But what about the baby? I had purposely not mentioned her in the beginning. And in Andre's confession, he hadn't either.

Chapter 11

I stood in front of the huge window of my office and gazed down at the bustling streets as people hurried to their destinations, all with an eager look on their faces. The sun was shining hard; I imagined I could feel it on my skin. I felt like I was in a fog, and the urge to be outside loomed large in my consciousness. The honking of an unknown horn snatched me back to reality and I sighed with frustration. I had this foreboding feeling that something was wrong, that my happiness was being tampered with. And I knew exactly where that feeling was coming from. I was not feeling settled, there was this unrest within me. But it was Monday, and I really needed to focus on work.

I heard a tap at my door. I turned to see Leah on the other side of it. "Come on in," I said. I pulled my chair out and sat down at my desk. Leah pushed the door open and stepped inside.

"Here is the file for the Linear account. Janae left it at my desk for you. Remember she will be out until Thursday."

"Yes, I remember. I hate it but I remember." I smiled. Janae and Leah were my right-hand people; I considered them indispensable. And I couldn't help but pout in a good way. I loved having them on my team. Both of them were ambitious, reliable, and ready to tackle any challenge that arose.

"Oh, *tink, tink*," Leah teased me like she always did. "Oh, by the way, Mr. Hanks just asked to be put on your calendar for two o'clock today."

I closed the Linear file and looked up, feeling slightly concerned, not in a bad way. My curiosity was piqued though. Anytime the partners asked for a last-minute meeting it was worth a second thought. Would I be made a partner today? Or would I be expected to give a speech? "Did he give any reasons?" I quizzed.

"Well, according to Rachel, Mr. Hastings wants to meet with Mr. Hanks."

I rolled my eyes with frustration at the mention of Mr. Hastings. Today was just not the day for his nonsense. Erika Jones was at the forefront of my mind, no matter how hard I was fighting to force her toward the back of it. Now I had to deal with Mr. Hastings, without forty-eight-hours' notice. I grunted with frustration on the inside but said to Leah, "Okay, hold my calls this morning unless it's urgent. And do not put anyone on my calendar for any late meetings or consults."

"For sure." Leah bounced out of my office and shut the door behind her.

I logged into my computer and typed in *Hastings*. My cell phone, which would usually be put away, was still sitting within eyesight on my desk. So I saw Reese's name as it lit up on the screen.

"Hey, Reese," I spoke, with no emotion in my tone. There was no response, and it was quiet on the other end. I was about to end the call, thinking maybe she had butt-dialed me, which happened sometimes.

"Umm . . . hey." Reese's voice finally appeared. "Can you hear me?" she asked. "I think my signal is not good."

"Yes, I hear you now."

"Why haven't I heard from you? You, okay?" She fired away at me. I had not phoned to update her yet on how the meeting with Erika Jones had gone. Actually, I hadn't even told her that I went.

After the whole incident with me confronting Andre, then him admitting to the accusation of a mistress, we had discussed how the whole affair was able to unfold. Then we spent the entire weekend together, trying to reconcile and figure out our marriage and how to save it. With all of that going on there had been no time to reach out to Reese.

"I'm sorry," I apologized. We were used to talking at least once a day or every other day if we were both busy in our careers. Sometimes she'd be on twenty-four-hour shifts at the hospital, and with my fourteen-hour workdays we'd just miss each other.

"I was so busy this weekend, I just chilled and re-grouped. Did you miss me?" I teased, hoping to make light of my absence. I knew my best friend, and now was not the time to tell her about Erika or Andre and his confession. She would not be impressed by his confession. His shot at being honest and open would just not go over well with Reese, that much I was sure of.

"Ahh," she sighed. "You are a hardworking woman, so I guess I forgive you. But can you do lunch today?" I instantly felt bad when she asked that because I would have to turn her down. I had to prepare for the meeting with Mr. Hanks that likely included Mr. Hastings.

"Actually, I can't. And before you bite my head off, I have good reason," I started to explain. "I have a meeting with Mr. Hanks. He has this asshole client that is coming in to see him around two today, and I was invited to attend. And I really must prepare for this. How about dinner?" I suggested. "You can pick the place."

"Sounds like a plan, I'll text you the spot. Are you sure you good, though?" she asked for the second time.

"I'm fine," I assured her. That would have to do for now. I would bare my soul to her at dinner.

"Alright, well, that's all the time I have to spare. I'm a resident at this hospital. If I ever wish to be a doctor, I better get back on this floor," she declared with a gruff chuckle. We ended the call. I had work to do as well.

Mr. Hastings, our potential client, and Mr. Hanks were seated around the long triangular mahogany table that dominated the center of the conference room. The triangular shape of the table added an air of sophistication to the room, complementing the modern décor and the view of the city skyline that was visible through the large windows. I entered the room three minutes behind schedule, according to Leah's instructions relayed by Mr. Hanks's assistant, Rachel. I had no idea why I was supposed to arrive late, but I was sure Mr. Hanks had his reasons.

"Brooke, come on in, and have a seat." Mr. Hanks lifted his chin in my direction with a huge welcoming smile, as I entered through the glass door. The room was bathed in natural light, casting a warm glow on the polished wood surfaces and the plush leather chairs surrounding the table. The atmosphere was charged with anticipation. I, too, was eager but took a moment to compose myself.

"Mr. Hanks, Mr. Hastings." I acknowledged them as professionally as I could. My body language and energy were both welcoming. But it was evident that my mere presence was a shock to Mr. Hastings, and the twitch on his forehead said I was unwelcome.

My Husband's Mistress is Dead / 81

Mr. Hastings shifted his weight in his seat and faced Mr. Hanks with a loud huff. His sudden discomfort upon my entrance was betrayed in his body language. "I had assumed this meeting would be amongst the partners of this firm." He grunted; his words were more of a demand than a question. Despite his discontent, I maintained my calm composure, ready to be addressed directly.

Mr. Hanks cleared his throat. "Of course, that's why I'm here. Walter is not in, as I'm sure Rachel made you aware of when you requested this meeting. And in any case, correspondence with potential clients is always done with the assigned financial manager, which is, as you well know, Brooke Perry." Mr. Hanks nodded in my direction with approval.

Mr. Hastings didn't acknowledge that nod. He continued to stare through Mr. Hanks. The man exuded dominance and was equally overbearing and impatient, qualities that had become all too familiar to me since overseeing his finances. The atmosphere was uneasy, but I held on tight to my professionalism and remained silent.

"Now, you requested this meeting today, and as you told Rachel, it is urgent. How can we help?"

Mr. Hasting cleared his throat, leaned forward, placing his hands on the table, his posture like stone. A sure sign that his need to be on defense was evident. "Well, for starters I would like to know what my status is. What is going to happen with my finances? I came to this company because Walter and Hanks are beyond a doubt one of the best accounting firms in the entire state of California. But I do not feel I've been treated with the respect a man of my stature deserves. I don't feel as though me and my business here are being valued at all. I feel like I'm being given the runaround, or worse, ignored, as if I was some common person." Not once did he even look in my direction. He ignored my presence. It was as if I wasn't even in the room, more evidence of his resistance and objection to my being there.

"Mr. Hastings, let me first apologize to you if you feel that things have not progressed at the speed you might have hoped they would. But I can assure you that we value every potential client who walks through our doors regardless of stature. And—"

"Are you sure about that?" Mr. Hasting cut him off with the wave of a hand. "Now, when I came here I was under the assumption that, with the caliber of my reputation, my company would be represented by a partner of this firm." He cut his eyes at me with a snide growl. "No offense." I would have been a fool if I had believed that he did not mean to offend me. He had said what he meant, and he would have a good laugh when he replayed it in his head later.

"Mr. Hastings!" Mr. Hanks grabbed both of our attention; it was clear his tone had changed. "Sir, Brooke Perry has an excellent, one-hundred-percent resolve history at this firm. And you can be sure that you are not only lucky but are in the very best hands. As a matter of fact, Brooke can give you an update even as early as today. Brooke, if you please."

Mr. Hanks gave me the floor. It was clear that Mr. Hastings had offended him with his statement about being represented by a partner. The tension in the air was so thick one would need a butcher's knife to hack through it.

But I would not let Mr. Hastings know that I wanted to grip his throat with both of my hands and squeeze tight. No, instead, I held my head high on my shoulders and pulled open the file that lay in front of me. Unlike Mr. Hastings, I kept my composure and gave him my undivided attention. "While I understand the benefits of a firm like Walter and Hanks taking on a client of your *caliber*, Mr.

Hastings"—I wanted him to know that I was listening to his *I'm the shit* speech—"after conducting a thorough analysis of the financial records provided by you and your company, it has become evident there are significant discrepancies and red flags that warrant further investigation. Engaging with a client whose financial practices are not transparent and may potentially be ethically questionable, could pose a risk to our firm's reputation. Upholding our commitment to integrity and ethical standards is paramount, and I fear that representing Mr. Hastings's company may compromise these principles."

I snatched my gaze from Mr. Hastings and placed it onto Mr. Hanks. "With that said, Mr. Hanks, I would like to make a recommendation and go on record that I don't think it is in this firm's best interest to represent Mr. Hastings and his company at this time."

"Why I never . . . Bob"—he called Mr. Hanks by his first name—"do you mean you're going to sit here at let this . . . this girl talk to me in this way? She's insulted my company—a company that's been in the family for generations. And she sits on her high horse and calls me a common criminal. I won't stand for it." He shot me a look that said *die*. But I didn't blink or flinch, I kept my professional composure. Nothing he could do, short of coming across the table and slapping me, could change that. And I dared him to do that. Because if he did, every foster-care trick for holding my own that I had hidden away would resurface and he would not survive it.

Suddenly the room was too quiet, except for Mr. Hastings's panting. For the first time I became concerned that Mr. Hanks had not said a word about this decision, even though it was *gotcha* for Mr. Hastings on my end. I was a professional when it came to making decisions. I always truly gave the opinion on what I thought was best for this company. Walter and Hanks was my future, at least that was my hope. But I would not risk the company taking on, as he said, *a common criminal* like Mr. Hastings. So, my opinion could be detrimental to my career here at the firm. If in fact it was not an agreeable decision for Mr. Walter or Mr. Hanks, I could be looked over for partner, depending on the damage, if my decision was wrong. I could be fired altogether. My heart sped up and I felt a bit of nausea from nervousness. My facial expression remained confident because not only was I, as Mr. Hanks said, sitting on a *hundred percent resolve history,* I would not give Mr. Hastings the satisfaction.

"Hastings, I feel compelled to say that this company, as Brooke said, understands the benefits of taking on potential clients of your company's caliber. But in addition, it's crucial that we maintain the high standards that our firm is known for. Accepting a client whose values do not align with ours may lead to a strained relationship, affecting our ability to deliver our services effectively. With that being said, I stand a hundred percent behind Brooke's decision."

A subtle frown appeared on Mr. Hastings's face. "I'm appalled that this company would jeopardize its reputation by allowing a high-strung teenager fresh out of college to make a decision on a Fortune 500 company's future, with no validity or hard proof. You can believe you'll hear about this when you lose clients," he threatened, but still had not budged from his seat.

"Mr. Hastings, please have a good day." Mr. Hanks stood up and showed him the door. I breathed a sigh of relief as Mr. Hastings exited. But Rachel burst in right behind him.

"Mr. Hanks, I have Mr. Walter on line one. He says it's urgent he speak with you."

"Of course it is." Mr. Hanks smiled. "I'll take it in my office." Rachel shook her head and rushed off to update Mr. Walter. "Brooke, I'm sorry I must rush off. Thanks so much for today. Sorry it was last minute that I asked you here."

"That was not a problem, Mr. Hanks. Anytime," I assured him. Mr. Hanks exited the room, and I sat in my seat and breathed a sigh of relief. I'd had no idea how this meeting would go. When I had come down with the report, I figured things would not go well. I had known for a week that Mr. Hastings's future with this company was not looking good. I had started the report to crunch everything together, prepared to share it with Mr. Walter and Mr. Hanks at our meeting next week. But Mr. Hastings had put a rush on it by demanding his off-the-cuff meeting. I, for one, was glad that part was done with. But I wasn't out of the woods yet. Mr. Hanks agreed with me because he trusted my judgments, but he would still go over the report with Mr. Walter. My hope for making partner was still top tier, but at this stage there was no word yet.

Chapter 12

"It's cocktail time!" Reese sang out while shimmying her shoulders as soon as we were seated.

"Yes, please. I must have a drink now." The waitress approached our table, ready to take our order. "I will start with a shot of Don Julio first, and you can follow that up with a Casita cocktail with an extra shot of tequila, please."

I was still a bit flustered after the meeting with Mr. Hastings and was glad Reese and I had dinner plans because Andre would be working late. Thankfully, Reese had chosen Casita, which was one of our favorite Mexican cocktail bars. Casita had the most tasteful margaritas around, and tonight I was in dire need of a strong alcoholic drink.

Reese ordered her drink, then fixed her attention on me. "What's with the Don Julio shot on a weekday?" she quizzed.

"Oh, girl, please let me fill you in." I rubbed my brow and went on a rant about Mr. Hastings's rudeness, entitled attitude, and downright nasty behavior. Our drinks had arrived during the rant, and I couldn't wait another second so I downed my Don Julio shot. The burn hit my throat, dumping its way down my esophagus and immediately revived me.

"His ass has a strong case of racism," Reese groaned as soon as I was done. She rolled her eyes to emphasize how much she was irritated by Mr. Hastings's actions.

I sucked my teeth with a new aggravation and disturbance at the thought of that foul man. "You know, I had originally considered that to be an issue too. Here I am, a young Black female, making decisions about his million-dollar empire. Well, now he can go find another company, which I highly doubt he'll be able to do. Only a desperate fool would want to deal with his arrogant entitled ass." That much I was sure of. And once word got out that Walter & Hanks had not got into bed with him, any respected, prestigious firm in the city of LA would not dare touch him. Walter & Hanks is very well respected and looked up to. No, Mr. Hastings would do well to tuck in his shirt, figure out a way to pay his debts, and clean up his act. Because if he keeps going the way he is, sooner or later he's going to end up behind a locked cell.

Reese raised her margarita glass into the air. "How about we toast to one assed-out million-dollar man?"

I was tickled and could only laugh as I raised my glass. It felt good to have a good laugh with my friend. These were the times that I cherished the most. But the pit of my stomach quivered once again as I remembered what I had to discuss with Reese, and my laugh soured as my face hardened with uncertainty.

Reese's cheeks sunk into a concerned expression. She knew me. "What's up? I know that look, so go ahead and spill it." She wasn't asking. It was more of a demand. I broke it down as best as I could without missing any details because none of them were small. Reese's mouth closed and opened several times while I went on and on.

"Damn, Brooke, that's a lot of information for anyone to absorb." She sat back in her chair, surprised, gripping her temples and forehead.

The waitress arrived to see if we needed anything else. We both ordered another margarita because it was needed. "Well, do you believe her? I mean, what are you planning to do?" Reese tossed questions at me one after the other. I was about to speak but her eyeballs nearly bulged out of their sockets. She slapped the table with great force. "And Andre, you have to confront his ass now."

"I already did," I told her. "After talking to Erika . . ." I swallowed, just remembering what I'd been subjected to listen to from this woman, Erika Jones. "I just couldn't hold it in any longer. So, when he came home, I was distraught, yet full of anger, and confused. I attacked him . . ." Again, I paused for what I was about to share. "He confessed."

"He actually confessed?" Reese's voice boomed, yet it came out sounding confused and stunned at the same time. An angry scowl immediately appeared on her face. She sat up straight in her seat. "That fucking narcissist confessed to being guilty of having a mistress and a child?"

"No, actually, I left the baby out of it. I never brought that part up."

"Why?" Her left eyebrow arched high in disapproval.

"I'm not sure. She did ask me not to mention the child. But I'm not even sure if that's the reason why I didn't mention it."

"You believe her, don't you?"

Reese's question brought on a feeling of mixed emotions I didn't even realize were rising to the surface until I felt the breeze on my cheeks, and I knew tears had fallen.

"I don't know," I admitted. "Something held me back from mentioning the child. But . . ." I picked up the napkin from the table and dabbed at my tears. "I mean, Reese, really . . . why should I believe a man who has loved me, put me first in everything he does, and treats me like a queen, would be so vindictive and vicious? To tell a mother that her child is gone when it really isn't . . . I mean, to go through with planning and executing a funeral." I shuddered inside just from the thought of the coldness, cruelness, and hate someone would have to be capable of to do such a thing.

"Hey, I agree. No normal human being could do such a thing and walk around as if nothing happened. As much as I think that Andre is a narcissist piece of shit that I can't stand, I agree with you that it seems like a long shot he could be capable of those things. But Vivian . . ." She tightened her lips into a ball and shook her head left to right. "I believe she did that shit. That woman is evil. I can see her in action right now."

"Evil, Reese." I chuckled at her dramatics.

"A Chucky doll!" She giggled. "She could easily be on the shelf at Target being sold as a Vivian Chucky Doll." We both burst into gut-wrenching laughter. Reese was hilarious. A few customers glanced in our direction. They probably wanted us to stop interrupting their dinner.

"For real, though, you need to have someone look into it so it can be proven or disproved, once and for all," she insisted, waving both of her hands.

"But who would I get?" I definitely needed her advice on that because I was clueless.

"Oh, you know, I got you on that. I'm going to text you the contact information for a trusted PI."

"A private investigator!" My tone was surprised. I had not even considered that. "Umm, how can I do that to Andre?" I was apprehensive about that piece of advice.

The last thing I wanted was someone spying on my husband. "Yes, he made a mistake, but we were going through a rough patch . . . I was distant and emotionless when it came to him, after the first miscarriage. I forgot that I wasn't the only one in pain and grieving our great loss. My husband was too, and I couldn't see it. I was selfish in a lot of ways."

"No, Brooke, that wasn't being selfish. What's selfish is that Andre is willing to allow you to believe his infidelity is your fault. And what's more, he violated your trust. You had a right to grieve, as did he. How dare he make you feel like because you couldn't sugar tit his needs, that's why he was unfaithful. That *asshole*!" She sneered as she picked up her iPhone, did a few scrolls with her forefinger, then followed up with a little typing. A notification text came through on my phone. I glanced over and read: **PI information**. She was not playing.

"Reese?" I said, getting ready to protest, but she held up the palm of her hand and extended it toward me. That meant she didn't want to hear it, and she was done with that conversation.

"Now, Brooke, would you like another drink?" Like a kid who had been scolded and put in line by their mother, I nodded yes to the drink. There would be no more disputing that situation.

The alcohol had begun to take effect, numbing the sharp edges of my emotions and allowing a temporary relief from the tumultuous thoughts swirling in my mind. Reese and I continued to chat and laugh, the weight of our serious conversation momentarily lifted. However, as the evening wore on, the reality of my situation crept back into my consciousness like a dark cloud overshadowing the momentary absolution.

Reese leaned in, her expression serious. "Brooke, I know

we've been joking and trying to lighten the mood, but we need to talk about what you're going to do next."

I sighed, the weight of everything crashing down on me once again. "I know, Reese. I just . . . I don't know where to start. I feel lost."

Reese reached out and squeezed my hand. "You're not alone in this, okay? We'll figure it out together. First things first, we need to gather more information. That's why I suggested hiring a private investigator."

Her words struck a chord, and I knew she was right. I couldn't continue to live in uncertainty and doubt. It was time to face the truth, no matter how painful it might be. With a renewed sense of purpose, I finished my drink and stood up, ready to face whatever challenges lay ahead. As we left the bar and said our goodbyes, I felt a mix of apprehension and resolve building within me. It was time to confront the truth and take control of my life once again. Or was it really only the drink talking?

Chapter 13

"Hello." Reese's voice burst through from the other end of the phone. I had called her while whipping through the ugly traffic in LA that everyone with good sense hated. I happened to be one of those people, but since there was no getting around it, I just paid attention, prayed, and stayed in my lane, all the while hoping no one forced me to jump out of my car and go ballistic on them.

"What's up, Mrs. Brooke-eee?" Reese chanted.

"Girl, not much. I left the office early today. I'm out in this disrespectful LA traffic to meet Vivian at Neiman Marcus." I knew that anything involving Vivian was going to unnerve Reese. "She insists that I have a pair of pearl earrings to start my own family tradition of having a family heirloom to pass down."

"Where does she get this crap? Did she just wake up with the idea? Don't get me wrong, I understand some families have family heirlooms and that's cool. But you married her son; if she wants you to have a family heirloom why don't she start passing it down to you?"

My Husband's Mistress is Dead / 93

That had been my very thought when Vivian had dragged me from under my warm sheets to tell me basically, I had no family and no rituals. Then she insisted on setting up this mandatory pearl-earring shopping spree. "I think that's how it is usually done in loving families but . . ." I veered off the interstate while still navigating my way through traffic.

"But you had to go marry into a family of pit fire bullshit, run by an egotistical, stuck-up individual. Ugh," Reese stated.

"I just ignore it," I said. The Neiman Marcus parking lot was packed. I pulled into a parking spot between two parked cars and turned off the ignition. I had arrived. I looked into my rearview mirror and happened to catch a shadow of a woman holding the hand of a little girl.

"Oh, I wanted to ask. How are things going with Carson? He really is a great PI, and I know it's only been three weeks but . . ." Reese said.

"Carson is legit, that's why I'm glad you called. We've both been so busy with work. I want to sit down with you to sort out a few things."

"Hey, for sure, but I'm pulling the night shift at the hospital for the next two days. Umm"—I could hear her sucking her teeth—"how about the day after tomorrow?"

"Sounds good. Let me go in here and get this over with," I grumbled.

"Good luck with that." Reese giggled and we ended the call.

I slid my Tom Ford sunglasses on and reached over in the passenger seat to grab my Saint Laurent bag. My red-soled heels clicked and clacked on the concrete as I made my way to the entrance of Neiman Marcus. The heat was suffocating. I reached for the door handle and a brush of cold air immediately hit me in the face. I stepped inside and sighed with relief to be out of the heat. I started toward the jewelry department, which is where I had been instructed to meet Vivian.

"Brooke." I heard my name and found Vivian approaching me from my left.

With my attention now on her, my lips stretched into a smile. "Vivian," I responded.

Now close to me, she reached and gave me a slight hug and smooch to both my cheeks. It was the sure sign of a snob, but I did everything I could not to think that of Andre's beloved mother. Upon release I thought Vivian held a snide look on her face. I never could read Vivian's face for the most part, but looking at her in the moment she put me in mind of the bougie version of Angela Bassett in the role she played in *Jumping the Broom*. Vivian was just a bit thinner and taller. I blinked to get the running thoughts out of my head and forced another smile.

"I swear," seeped from Vivian's lips. My breath caught in my chest, where I held it, waiting for the criticism. "Brooke, you are an agreeable girl, pretty, even." Her eyes appraised me with uncertainty. I waited with curiosity. "But those legs, I think they call it bowlegs, in low-income areas."

I blinked at the words "low-income." The word hung in the air like the plague. I was stunned, intrigued, and tickled at the same time. I sucked in my breath to keep from laughing. Never had I heard of bowlegs being a low-income thing. Normally I overlooked her silliness, but I felt compelled to address this. "Vivian, I don't think my walk or bowlegs has anything to do with being low-income. It's likely genetics," is how I laid it out.

Vivian's eyes lit up and suddenly an unrestrained laughter bubbled from deep within her. She was laughing so hard her shoulders shook. My attempt to explain things had amused her and I was annoyed with her and her ugly laugh. She stopped suddenly. "Oh dear, you grew up in foster care. You wouldn't understand these things. I'm sure someone told you it was cute. But we can have those fixed."

My mouth flew open to speak but she held up her hand and cut me off. "Anyway, dear, let's not waste time. Time is pearls and we must get you to understand family values." Once again, she insulted me without a hint of care for my feelings. I sucked in a gulp of air and remembered Erika Jones's claim about how Vivian had threatened her. Right away, I tried to shake that thought from my mind. Now was not the time to think about that. Vivian was just being Vivian.

An hour and twenty-five thousand dollars later, beautiful pearls and the urge to strangle Vivian came over me. I was anxious to get out of Neiman Marcus, but Vivian had a kidnapping grip on me and would not allow me to leave until I promised to help her clean her attic. For nearly thirty minutes, I tried every excuse I could come up with, but nothing worked. She was adamant that she needed my help. In order to be released I agreed, and with the sales slip in my hand and the promise from Neiman Marcus that the pearl set would be delivered under armored guard, I bolted.

The hot air outside Neiman Marcus felt like a curse from the cool atmosphere inside. I hurried toward my car; the thought of the hefty price tag for the pearls weighed on me. But I waved that off, Andre being rich, and that money would be coming out of his bank account, not mine. As I settled into the driver's seat and took a moment to breathe, I couldn't shake off the unsettling encounter with Vivian.

I dialed Reese's number, needing to vent and seek some trace of normalcy after the ordeal. She picked up after a couple of rings, her voice greeting me with warmth. "Hey, girl. How did it go with Vivian?" Reese asked, her concern evident.

"It was . . . interesting, to say the least," I replied, my tone tinged with frustration. "I ended up spending way too much on pearls and had to promise to help her with something else."

"What? That woman never ceases to amaze me," Reese exclaimed. "What did she rope you into this time?"

"She wants me to help her clean up her attic," I explained, shaking my head at the nonsense of it all. "I tried to get out of it, but she wouldn't take no for an answer."

Reese chuckled on the other end of the line. "Well, at least it's not something too serious. But knowing Vivian, she'll find a way to make it an ordeal."

"I wouldn't put it past her." I sighed. "Anyway, I needed to call you to calm my nerves after Vivan.

"Ah, yes. I told you the lady could turn a devote Christian." We laughed.

After ending the call, I started the car and navigated my way through the busy LA traffic once again. Despite the chaos around me, I felt a sense of determination growing within me. I had to take things one step at a time.

Chapter 14

Ding dong! The sound of the doorbell echoed throughout the house, announcing that someone was at our front door. In the kitchen pouring myself a nice cold glass of Tropicana orange juice, I put the glass down.

"I'll get it!" I shouted. I pulled open the double doors and came face-to-face with a Black female who looked to be in her early forties, and White male who looked to be about the same age. They both were dressed in business attire with a look of seriousness and suspicion written all over their faces. "Can I help you?" I asked.

"Are you Mrs. Perry?" the female asked.

"Yes, I am," I answered, suspicious of who these two peculiar people were.

"Is Andre Perry in?"

Now they had my attention for real. "Can I ask what this is about?"

"Mrs. Perry, I'm Detective Nicole Kruz and this is Detective Ron Wize." Each of them produced a badge from thin air. I should have known they were cops by the cheap suits, and cocky smiles on their faces.

"Ma'am, we work for LAPD in the homicide division." Detective Wize spoke up for the first time since I answered the door.

"Homicide?" I repeated. "Who died?" My heart rate was racing.

"We need to speak with your husband," Detective Kruz instructed.

"ANDRE . . . ANDRE!" I yelled over my shoulder. "Sue, can you please get Andre?" I asked her. She was now in the hallway. "We will be in the den."

"Certainly," she answered and was off.

"Please come in," I offered and stood to the side until they were inside. I shut the doors and headed toward the den just as Andre appeared.

Andre's curious gaze fell from me then toward the detectives. "What's going on?" He paused in mid stride.

Detective Kruz seemed to step beside me swiftly. I could smell the cheap JCPenney all over her black polyester suit. "Are you Andre Perry?" she asked him.

"Yes, I'm Andre."

"Mr. Perry, I'm Nicole Kruz and this is my partner." She kind of moved to the side so Detective Wize could step closer.

"I'm Detective Ron Wize, and we are with the LAPD homicide division."

"Wait, who died?" Andre seemed to follow my lead with the same confusion and concern. I took a step forward and stood next to him; now we both faced the detectives head-on for whatever they were about to throw our way. "Is my mother okay?" Andre asked; his tone held anxiety.

Detective Kruz glanced at Detective Wize, then focused back on Andre. "Sir, we are not here about your mother. But we are here about Ms. Erika Jones. Are you familiar with her?"

I'm not sure if it was just me, but I was getting the feeling the detective wasn't asking him but stating a fact.

Andre's head dropped a bit; he seemed to be thinking about the question. "Yes," he grunted and cleared his throat. "Yes, I know her. Why?" he asked, looking at both detectives head-on.

"Mr. Perry, Ms. Erika Jones recently died in a house fire," Detective Wize said with a bit of apprehension.

Everything seemed to fall quiet around us as what he said settled in. Andre's eyes seemed to widen, shock and disbelief etched across his face. "Umm, wow," he stuttered. His tone of voice conveyed that he felt saddened by the news.

"When did this happen?" I asked. It seemed as though everyone looked at me as if they had forgotten I was even there.

"A few days ago," Detective Wize answered, then it became quiet once again.

"Well, you asked for my husband when we were at the door. He has no blood relation to her. Why come here?" Once it was out of my mouth, I knew it didn't sound very compassionate and that had not been my intention, but I stood behind my question. Detectives Wize and Kruz glared at each other; it was clear they were not expecting me to ask that kind of question so bluntly.

"Ahem." Detective Wize cleared his throat. "As we said, we are from homicide. We think it's very possible the fire was an accident, but there are things that need answered, so we are continuing the investigation. We are speaking with anyone who might have known Ms. Jones. In doing so it seems Ms. Jones does not have any friends or family. However, we came across you, Mr. Perry, as a constant person in her life."

"Exactly what was the nature of your relationship with

Ms. Jones?" Detective Kruz jumped right in as if she had been tagged.

"I told you I just knew her. We were merely acquaintances." Andre was so nonchalant about it.

Detective Kruz shifted her weight and gave a slight sigh. "I'm going to try this again . . ." she said kinda under her breath. "Mr. Perry, what was your relationship with Erika Jones?"

This time her tone was pushy. It was clear she knew something and wanted his validation. Andre looked to his left at me, and I could see the apology written all over his face. I nodded that it was okay for him to be honest. "We . . ." He paused. "We had a romantic relationship," he admitted, and the pit of my stomach churned. Even though I knew the details, hearing it was like him admitting it to me for the very first time.

Detective Kruz nodded her head in an agreeable way. She folded her arms across her chest. "And just to clarify, was it sexual?"

A palpable silence settled over all of us. The sting of the question seemed to hang in the air, burning in my chest until a tear escaped my eye, but I sucked it back. "What do you think, Detective Cruz . . . would you like every freaky detail?" Andre was becoming upset. There was an invisible tension in the air that would not hold much longer.

I stepped in. "Andre, calm down."

"Now, where were you two nights ago—that would be Tuesday night?" Detective Wize asked.

"Tuesday night . . . let's see, I came home from the office. I had dinner with my wife. I got a call from my mother. She needed my help with financial papers. Then I came back home."

Detective Kruz started to pace; her forefinger was now roaming her chin as if she was contemplating his response.

"So, let me get this straight: Your mother is your alibi?" I instantly didn't appreciate her sarcastic tone. Everything about it and her body language was accusatory.

"Detective, you asked me where I was, correct? Well, being at my mother's and in her presence happens to be the place I was at."

"Hmm, okay," Detective Kruz said, her tone full of skepticism. "What is your mother's name and contact information?" She turned the page on the little notepad she had taken a few notes in. Andre gave her the information she asked for.

"Mrs. Perry, can you give us an account of your whereabouts?" Detective Kruz turned her attention to me.

"Yes, I was home." I was short and to the point.

She sucked in her lip and considered my answer. "Can anyone else verify that?"

Detective Kruz was now starting to unnerve me as well. But I tried to keep in mind that she was just doing her job. I shook off the frustration. "Well, when Melva and Sue ended their shift, I was here in the house."

"And exactly who are they? And can I get full names, please," she continued.

I gave her their full names and explained they were both our housekeepers.

"Oh, so you have employees in the home?" Detective Kruz asked. For some reason, she seemed surprised, and her tone was critical and judgmental. The sarcasm sat on her face like a huge zit that needed to be popped. Clearly, she couldn't see this big mansion she had stepped inside of. "Mr. Perry, you do own a brokerage firm, correct?"

Andre sighed. "Yes." He was clearly tired of the baseless questions.

"So, you're quite wealthy?" She glanced at Detective Wize, and I was almost certain I'd seen a smirk.

"You can say that. Now, do you need anything else?" Andre asked.

Detective Wize turned to Detective Kruz, then faced us. "Actually, Mr. and Mrs. Perry, I think that will be all. But we may need to reach out to you again. Here is my card and Detective Kruz will give you hers. If you happen to think of anything or have any questions, or hear anything, please don't hesitate to call."

Andre took the cards swiftly. "Thanks, we'll do that. I'll see you both to the door." He gladly led the way for the detectives. Both of us were left in a state of oblivion over what we'd just heard and what had happened.

"I can't believe it," Andre returned. "Erika dead . . . in a house fire." He looked at me, his eyes showed shock.

"How unfortunate," I remarked. "Does she really not have any family?"

"She never mentioned having a family to me. That was something she never wanted to talk about. And she didn't have any friends. She was a loner at best." He rubbed his forehead with frustration. "But what do you think about that Detective Kruz? She definitely has a chip on her shoulder."

"Either that or she's just passionate about her job. They certainly had their questions lined up, but they did say it seemed to have been an accident. So, hopefully they have what they need." I sighed with relief that they were done and gone. I held up my left wrist and gazed at the time on my Louis Vuitton watch. I sucked my teeth. "Aww, I have to get going. I have a meeting in an hour. See you later, babe." I walked over, kissed him on the cheek, and rushed off to grab my bag and keys. A crazy start to my day— finding out that my husband's mistress is dead.

As I drove to my meeting, my mind was still reeling from the unexpected visit from the detectives. The news of Erika

Jones's death in a house fire added a layer of complexity to an already tumultuous situation. I couldn't shake off the feeling of unease and suspicion that lingered after their departure.

The meeting I had scheduled was with a potential client that had been referred to me through Andre's brokerage firm. Despite the lingering thoughts about Erika's death, I focused on maintaining my professional demeanor during the meeting. The client seemed impressed with our services and expressed interest in moving forward.

After the meeting concluded, I returned home to find Andre in the living room, deep in thought. His expression was a mix of sorrow and contemplation.

"Andre, are you okay?" I asked, placing a gentle hand on his shoulder.

He looked up at me, his eyes tired yet filled with a sense of resignation. "I don't know, Brooke. This whole situation with Erika's death, it's just surreal. I never expected something like this to happen."

"I know, it's a lot to process," I replied, sitting down next to him. "But we have to stay strong and focused. We'll get through this together."

He nodded, but I could sense the weight of guilt and confusion weighing heavily on him. We sat in silence for a moment, both lost in our thoughts. I couldn't help but wonder about Erika's death and the circumstances surrounding it. The detectives' visit had left me with more questions than answers.

"I think I'm going to go for a drive," Andre said suddenly, breaking the silence. "I need to clear my head a bit."

"Sounds like a good idea," I replied, giving his hand a reassuring squeeze. "I'll be here when you get back."

As Andre left for his drive, I took the opportunity to

check my phone for any updates. The events of the day had left me emotionally drained.

As I waited for Andre to return, I couldn't help but wonder what the future held. Erika's death, and the ongoing investigation, added an unexpected layer of complexity to our lives. But I was determined to face whatever challenges came our way, together, with Andre by my side.

Chapter 15

"Girlie sounds a bit jealous or something to me." Reese picked up a hot wing and dipped it into blue cheese sauce. We were at a restaurant close to my office. I had asked her to come down and meet for a quick lunch so I could catch her up on the detectives stopping by about Erika Jones. The main topic of the conversation was Detective Kruz and her over-the-top antics.

"Maybe, I don't know what her deal was, but the attitude was a bit much though. And I can't even explain how unprofessional and uncouth she came off. Andre wanted to have a one-on-one boxing match with her, but since she was a woman, he didn't have a choice but to chill."

"Andre was probably scared she'd knock the narcissist out of him. Matter of fact, I wish Vivian would have been there too, so she could've enjoyed the back of girlie's hand."

I chuckled out loud. "Reese, you are awful, stop. You ain't no stand-up comic." We both laughed. "But for real, do you think they will come back? They made it clear they might revisit us." The thought of that made me anxious, because I was in no hurry to see either one of them again, especially that pushy Detective Kruz.

Reese opened a pack of wipes to clean the sauce from her fingertips. She smacked her mouth from the hotness. "I doubt it. If they suspected him of anything, they would have taken him down to the station to ask their questions, not spared him the comfort of his own home. Rest assured they are doing just as they said, talking to the people she knew."

"I hope so." I exhaled. "I have too much going for this shit to be happening now."

"Listen, I got you," Reese cut in. "Besides, you two have nothing to worry about. Andre is rich. You said the detective even pointed that out. Trust me, they will not badger him with something they think is an accident. Money normally gets rid of them and fast." She picked up her Diet Coke and sucked down a large gulp. I knew she was trying to get rid of the spicey taste that now owned her tongue. "Now, isn't today the day your firm announces who made partner?" She grinned.

"Yes, the meeting is in two fucking hours and I'm a wreck," I admitted. I had been all morning long. I left the house with no keys until I couldn't start my Porsche. At work I made it all the way to my office and realized I left my briefcase in the car and had to go back to get it. I had almost broken into a sweat twice before lunch.

"Why do they wait until the end of the day to tell you guys? Couldn't they have done so in a meeting this morning?"

"Normally, yeah, but Mr. Walter's plane just landed this morning at ten o'clock. He's been in Dallas for two days, so the meeting was pushed to the afternoon. I'm just ready for it to be over and done with, so I can breathe the fresh air the way I used to before this partnership invaded my life."

Reese chuckled and picked up another hot wing. "Listen, in two hours you will have all the right reasons to celebrate. You can count on that." She had so much confidence in me that I didn't need to have any.

"Whew . . ." I sighed. "Chile, I certainly hope so or I'll be one pipe-smoking junkie." We joked. We laughed, but the nervousness was real. "Aww, Reese, I've worked so hard for many nights, staying awake with little or no sleep, all to realize my goals."

Reese slid her hands across the table while gesturing for mine. She held them and said, "Brooke, you worry way too much. You are on a fast track to success. Those sacrifices are to be reaped today with your best reward. In two hours, you will be a partner at Walter and Hanks. Now, what champagne do you suggest for the celebration? Matter of fact, eighty-six the champagne, we will do Hennessey shots all around."

The thought of that made me giggle. "Girl, can you imagine pulling out a bottle of Hennessey in front of Vivian? She is liable to go into pure distress and pass out." If she had thought my bowlegs were a low-income issue, who knows what she'd think about a bottle of Hennessy.

"Reese, no, even worse. I think she might call the cops and try to have me arrested for having what she would consider illegal drinks. You know she thinks anything the lower-class uses is bound to be an illegal substance." We exited the restaurant full of laughter.

As the elevator climbed to the top floors of the building, my mind raced with a mix of anticipation and anxiety. Reese's words of encouragement had added a new sense of confidence in me that I didn't have before. But the gravity of the partner announcement still weighed heavily on my shoulders. I couldn't get the what ifs out of my mind. The doors slid open to the executive floor where the air buzzed with an obvious tension. Colleagues exchanged nervous glances, and the sound of muffled conversations filled the hallway leading to the boardroom. It was evident that everyone was on edge, awaiting the pivotal moment that would define the path of someone's career.

But I would never allow anyone besides my best friend to see me sweat. So, as a rule of thumb I held my head high and walked in with a sense of purpose, my heels clicking against the polished marble floor. As I approached the boardroom, I could hear bits of discussions about quarterly reports, client acquisitions, and strategic plans. The atmosphere was charged with ambition and determination, a testament to the hard work and dedication of everyone present.

Taking a deep breath, I pushed open the doors to the boardroom. The room fell silent as all eyes turned toward me. Mr. Walter, a distinguished figure with gray hair and sharp eyes, stood at the head of the table. He nodded in acknowledgment as I took my seat, signaling for the long-awaited announcement.

The minutes ticked by slowly, each second feeling like an eternity. My heart pounded in my chest, and I stole glances at the clock on the wall, willing time to move faster. Every passing moment was a mixture of excitement and apprehension, the culmination of years of relentless effort and unwavering determination.

Finally, Mr. Walter cleared his throat, capturing everyone's attention. "Thank you all for being here today. As you know, we are gathered to announce the newest partner at Walter and Hanks Accounting firm."

A hush fell over the room as he paused for dramatic effect. My pulse quickened, and I clasped my hands together, trying to contain the nervous energy coursing through me. I was certain I caught a glimpse of Mr. Hanks glaring at me.

"It is our pleasure to welcome Brooke Perry as our newest partner."

A loud round of applause erupted, and I felt a surge of emotions wash over me. Relief, joy, pride—a whirlwind of feelings flooded my senses. I stood up, my face breaking into a wide smile as I accepted the congratulations and well wishes from my colleagues.

Chapter 16

The city lights filled every inch of me with energy and excitement as Andre and I cruised along the skyline in our Bentley. The night air had a brisk feel to it that I could suck up for the rest of my life. There was a sense of excitement that had been bubbling up in my chest since the big announcement that I had been made a partner at Walter & Hanks. I was still on cloud nine, and who knew when I might come down. Erika Jones still periodically invaded my mind, but I was fighting to keep her at bay. While I knew I had not heard the end of that situation, I wasn't going to allow that or anything else to get in the way of what I had worked for. Andre and I were on our way to celebrate my partnership and we both were feeling and looking good.

I could feel Andre's eyes on me. I looked over at him. God, my man was handsome. This man loved me, it was written all over his face. "So, how are you really feeling about this new reality?" he asked me.

My smile slowly faded, not from sadness but from the realization of my truth. I gazed out of the window. "You know I've worked from day one with the goal in mind to be as successful as I can be. Just successful." I paused as I thought over this fact. "Becoming a partner wasn't in my mind yet. But it didn't take long for it to become my goal. But to have it be true . . ." I could feel my emotions about to spill over. Before that could happen, I paused to push them back. I gazed out of the window at LA's beautiful night lights and then looked back over at Andre. "It's unbelievable," I finally said. It was the only way I knew how to describe it.

"Well, believe it, sweetheart, and nobody deserves it more than you." He reached for my hand, and I gladly gave it up. "I know things have been crazy the past few months. But they will get better and I'm going to continue to do everything I can to make sure of that."

"But are you happy? Even with the obvious . . . no children." This was probably not the best time to ask this question that constantly loomed inside of me. Yes, I was successful in my career, but what about in my marriage? I had not and probably would never give my husband a child. The very thought that he might have a child out in the world weighed heavily on me.

We were at a red light when Andre lifted my hand and kissed it so lovingly with his soft lips. Love and concern for my question was in his gaze. "Sweetheart, as long as I have you, I will always be happy. *I love you, Brooke Perry!*" I could only grin like a schoolgirl knowing his words rang true.

"I love you too, Mr. Perry!" My tone was above a whisper, but the excitement was the same. I just felt too emotional to use my normal tone of voice. Fighting back the tears to keep my makeup intact was a must.

We pulled into San Laurel, one of LA's most sought-after reservations and hottest restaurants. It was a who's-who kind of place that wasn't easy to get into. "Oh, Andre!"

I squealed with excitement. I had been wanting to get reservations at this restaurant for the longest time. "You must have made these reservations months ago? How did you—"

"How did I what?" He cut me off. "I always knew you'd make partner," he said just as a valet opened my door. I could only exhale to keep from crying. I swear it was becoming a job keeping the tears at bay.

I held on to Andre's arm as we stepped into the upscale restaurant. The first thing I noticed was the beautiful artwork, the atmosphere so inviting. Then I noticed the sound of light jazz music being played in the background.

"Good evening, Mr. and Mrs. Perry." A guy who I assumed was the maître d' appeared. For the first time, I noticed no one else was in the room. That's when I realized the restaurant seemed to be empty. I leaned into Andre and whispered, "Are they open for business?"

"*Surprise!*" I heard screams from all over and suddenly a host of friends, family, and colleagues appeared out of nowhere. My heart nearly exploded from fear and excitement. They had scared the shit out of me. But as I put names to the faces, I couldn't help but smile. There was Reese, Vivian, Janae, Leah, Andre, Walter, Hanks, and many more.

I could no longer hold them in. Tears escaped my lids. "I rented the place for this special night in your life. I'm a millionaire, remember," Andre whispered in my ear. I could only chuckle at his playful arrogance. For some reason, I seemed to forget that all the time. Never had I focused on Andre's money and the material things he had. It wasn't the thing that attracted me to him, and it wasn't the thing that kept me in love with him.

"Congratulation on your promotion, Brooke-eee," Reese sang as she hugged me tight.

"I guess you can keep a secret," I whispered to her.

"Girl, I nearly died hiding it from you." She jumped back and held her chest. We both laughed at her dramatics.

Walter and Hanks made their way over with their wives in tow. "Thank you both for being here," I said.

"We wouldn't have missed it for the world. We are excited and honored to have you as our new partner," Mr. Walter said.

"Now, the sky is the limit," Mr. Hanks threw in, lifting his glass in the air. "And tonight, we drink on Andre's tab." We all laughed, as the jazz music turned into singing from the live band Andre had hired. I hadn't been able to see the band when we first entered. The band members were in dark silhouette at first; then the stage was brightly lit once the surprise was revealed.

"Oh, Brooke, I'm so excited. I'm now the junior assistant of a partner. I'm feeling so stuck-up now," Leah boasted with a grin and a wineglass in her hand.

"I bet you are. Have you gone to a car dealership to start looking for a new car with that new salary raise you are sure to get?" I asked her.

Leah had been wanting to get a new car for a while but swore it was not in her budget. I assured her the day I became a partner she could go to the car lot, because I had plans to give her a substantial raise. I had in mind to take her from fifty-five thousand a year to eighty thousand.

"Brooke, you are the best." She hugged me.

"Congrats, Brooke," Janae said, now in front of me. "This is so nice." She gazed around. "Welp, I have to say I have enjoyed being your assistant. But now I'll be assigned to someone else."

"Over my dead body," I expressed it with pure dramatics. "You, my dear, are mine. Pack up your office next week, because you will be moving with me and Leah. And yes, there will be a healthy raise." I had a great team with

114 / *Saundra*

Leah and Janae, and I did not plan to lose them. No, I was going to make sure to keep us on top. I'd already spoken to Walter and Hanks about it.

"I can't believe it." Leah's free hand covered her mouth as she cried.

"Hey, stop that crying. Tonight is a night for celebration, remember. Now both of you go drink, eat, and enjoy."

I noticed Vivian coming my way and she blew into me like an unwelcome wind that I had no choice but to accept. There was no smile or emotion on her face. "I take it those girls are from your old neighborhood," were her words to me. No *Congratulations on your promotion, Brooke.* Nothing, just this odd statement, which confused me.

"Can I ask as to what old neighborhood you speak of?" I asked.

She blinked and pursed her lips together. "Listen, dear, you must learn to take care. I know you like to remain—what word would I use—*down*. But you have a different life now. If you wish to have social class, you must surround yourself with such."

I glared at Vivian, then shut my eyes for five seconds. I really was not in the mood for her nonsense talk, and certainly not for insulting good, hardworking women who didn't deserve her criticism. "Vivian, those young women are not from any old neighborhood. They both have college degrees and work with me in a respected firm, as you know, Walter and Hanks." For once, I was going to set her straight.

She sort of peeked over my shoulder and with a slight glance behind me I could see Leah and Janae talking to other guests. "Are you sure they went to college? A thorough background check would clear that up." I nearly choked on my own spit. She just wouldn't quit. This was why I ignored her instead of wasting the good air in my lungs to address her. I smirked.

MY HUSBAND'S MISTRESS IS DEAD / 115

"Anyway, Brooke, I came over to congratulate you on your promotion." And there it was, a sign that even she could come off her pedestal and see someone else beside her son.

"Thank you, Vivian," I said from the heart. I knew if I gave her time, she would show me she was good.

The snide, pursed look on her face never changed. She just looked as though she was looking through me. The band was singing in the background, but to me it was an eerie silence. Had I given her credit too soon? I feared that I had. "You should have worn your pearls." Her words came out normal, but to me it was in slow motion. "It's warm in here." She wiped at her brow and without even a goodbye brushed past me like the wind she had brought with her. I was baffled and astonished.

"Brooke . . ." I looked up to find Andre standing directly in front of me. I had been so blanked out over Vivian, I had not noticed him approach. "Babe, I want you to soak up this night. It's all for you." He pulled me into his embrace, and I felt safe in his arms. I shuddered on the inside as I shook Vivian off. That woman was one hard pill to swallow.

"Thank you, babe." I breathed into his chest. I wanted to lie there for a minute, but I had a party and a host of guests to attend to. I would not allow Vivian to ruin my night. My life was on the right track. Yes, recently I had hit some stumbling blocks in my life. But who hadn't? No one was perfect and I was learning that things could be corrected and put into their place. I was on my way to making those things happen and everything in my life would be made right. Because every piece of the puzzle was fitting into place right before my very eyes. There was no doubt all would be well.

Chapter 17

I was a bit nervous as I stood and prepared to do my presentation, giving my insights of how we would move forward as a successful accounting firm. The nervousness was the simple fact that I was no longer a financial advisor, but a partner. And the partners were in the room, all eyes on me. My slide show was up, and it was game time.

"Good morning, all! I'm delighted to present with you today as one of your new partners. Thank you for having me." I smiled as everyone nodded. "In this pivotal chapter of this firm's journey, allow me to present how we will dive into the strategic capitalization and client targeting strategies that will indeed boost our firm into new heights. This is what I like to call our road map to success." The partners were deeply engaged; I had their attention.

"I will begin by revisiting our firm's mission and vision. Our commitment to excellence and client satisfaction is the cornerstone of our success. As we embark on this chapter it's crucial we keep our core values at the forefront of our minds. Market analysis shows a growing demand for specialized accounting services in sectors such as technology, healthcare, and renewable energy. These are ripe areas for us to explore and dominate." Before long there was not a nervous bone in my body. For the next hour, I worked the room like I did on a daily basis. Not once did I lose everyone's attention. They were on board—hook, line, and sinker. I wrapped it up. "Together let's seize the opportunities that lie ahead and elevate our accounting firm to new heights. Thank you."

Back in my seat, Mr. Hanks took over and thanked me for such a great presentation, in addition to welcoming me as partner and reiterating, as they had done since they announced my partnership with the firm, that I was the prime pick. Everyone was leaving the room as I stepped out of the door. Leah nearly bumped into me.

"Good, you are done. There are two detectives here to see you. I told them that you were in a meeting, but they were adamant they would wait." She tried her best to speak in a whisper.

My anxiety accelerated to full speed. Two detectives could only mean one thing, Kruz and Wize. What other detectives would be here to see me? It had been three months with no word. I was almost certain I wouldn't see them again. "Where are they?" I tried to sound calm. I didn't want to alarm Leah that I was unnerved.

"Well, I didn't know what to do with them, but I didn't want them roaming the building. So, I sat them in your office."

Normally, I would have been furious if she let someone in my office without my knowledge, but on this one occasion she had made a good choice. I did not want homicide detectives roaming around my place of work, for God's sake. I could only imagine who already knew they were here.

"It's okay, Leah. You did good. I'll head in to see them. Hold my calls." I gave her a forced smile and tone of reassurance that all was well. Not hesitating, I headed for my office to get whatever was going on over with. Even though I was now in a much bigger, more exquisite office since I had made partner, it was still see-through glass. And I could see Detectives Kruz and Wize sitting comfortably in my office.

"Detectives," I greeted as I made my way inside. Their backs were towards me. Upon hearing my voice, they turned their heads.

"Mrs. Perry," they said in unison.

"We were just sitting here admiring your office. And please let me congratulate you on your promotion." Detective Kruz gave me a grin that I did not care for.

"Thanks, now how can I help you two?" I sat down at my desk and intertwined my fingers.

Detective Wize spoke up to answer my question. "As we said, we might need to speak with you and Mr. Perry again."

"Yeah, I remember—that was what, three months ago?" I pointed it out on purpose.

"Give or take, but these things take time in thorough investigations before they can be tossed out or closed," Detective Kruz added.

"Well, what exactly can I do for you today?" I didn't care for her sarcasm.

Detective Kruz pulled out a notepad and pretended to read over her notes. At least that's what I assumed she was doing. Wize just glared at me. "Why don't we start again with your husband's alibi," Wize said.

That twisted my brow. They had already talked to Andre about his alibi, why ask me about it again? I had not been with him when he was out. "As he told you, we had dinner. His mother called, he went to see her and then came back home. By the time he got home, I was in bed."

He shook his head, then pulled out his notepad. "Mrs.

Perry, I know your husband admitted in front of you when he spoke with us about his romantic relationship with Ms. Erika Jones. But did you know about their acquaintance beforehand?"

I was surprised Kruz was so quiet, but I was glad of it. "Yes, I knew." I shrugged my shoulders in a somewhat nonchalant matter. "Just as Andre informed you." I sucked my teeth.

Detective Kruz jumped back in. "So, where were you again on the night in question?"

"As I said, I was home."

Detective Kruz looked at Detective Wize and they both stood up. I gazed up at them, wondering what was next.

"Well, thanks for your time today, Mrs. Perry. Please give us a call if you remember anything that might be helpful." Detective Wize handed me another card. That was the same speech they had already given me. I nearly snatched the card out of his hand. Had they really just come all the way down to my office to ask me the exact same questions they asked at my house?

"This really is a nice office." Detective Kruz looked back at me. Her face held a grin but a suspicious one. They both exited. I could see them talking as they walked away.

I picked up my office phone. "Leah, please make sure they get on the elevator and leave this floor." I hung up. Then I picked up my cell phone.

"Reese, you will not believe this shit. Those detectives just showed up at my job and asked me the same questions they asked when they came to the house. That investigation is not over."

"What? Damn . . ."

"Will you be home later?"

"Yep, I'm leaving the hospital in the next hour."

"Good, I'll bring dinner by. Andre is working late." We hung up and I called Andre to inform him, but he was in a meeting. I gathered my things and prepared to leave for the day. I couldn't believe these detectives had shown up at my job. I could have answered those questions over the phone. What really was their motive?

As I left the office, my mind was buzzing with questions and frustration over the detectives' unexpected visit. It felt like a disruption to my newfound sense of achievement as a partner. Reese's words of encouragement echoed in my mind, reminding me to stay calm and composed despite the situation.

Resse was waiting for me when I arrived at her house with dinner. We sat down in the living room, and I recounted the events of the day, including the detectives' visit to my office.

"Girl, they are really trying to dig deep, aren't they?" Reese remarked, shaking her head in disbelief.

"Yeah, it's like they're not satisfied with the answers they got the first time. And what's with showing up at my workplace? It feels like they're trying to intimidate us or something," I replied, frustration evident in my tone.

Reese nodded in understanding. "Well, you just have to remain calm and collected. They can't pin anything on you or Andre without solid evidence."

"I know, but it's just unsettling. I thought we were done with all of this." I sighed, feeling a weight of unease settle over me.

"Let's not let it ruin our evening," Reese suggested, trying to lighten the mood. "How about we indulge in some guilty pleasure TV and forget about detectives for a while?"

I couldn't help but smile at Reese's attempt to lift my spirits. "Sounds good to me. Let's relax and unwind."

We spent the evening watching mindless reality TV, laughing and enjoying each other's company. It was a much-needed distraction from the stress of the day.

The next morning, I woke up determined to focus on

MY HUSBAND'S MISTRESS IS DEAD / 121

work and put the detectives' visit behind me. As I arrived at the office, I could feel a sense of routine returning. I greeted my colleagues and delved into the tasks at hand, trying to engage myself in work to keep my mind occupied. However, the nagging thought of the ongoing investigation lingered in the back of my mind. I couldn't shake the feeling of being scrutinized and watched, even though I knew I had done nothing wrong.

Throughout the day, I received a few curious glances and whispered conversations from colleagues. It was evident that news of the detectives' visit had spread, adding to the unease I felt. During a break, I stepped out of the office to get some fresh air and clear my head. As I walked through the hallway, I bumped into Mr. Hanks.

"Good morning, Brooke. How are you settling into your new role?" Mr. Hanks greeted me with a warm smile.

"Good morning, Mr. Hanks. I'm adjusting well, thank you," I replied, trying to maintain a professional demeanor.

"I wanted to check in and see how you're doing after yesterday's visit from those detectives. I hope it wasn't too disruptive for you," Mr. Hanks said with a concerned expression.

I appreciated his consideration and honesty. "It was unexpected, but I'm handling it. Thank you for asking."

"If you need anything or have any concerns, please don't hesitate to reach out. We're here to support you," Mr. Hanks reassured me before continuing down the hallway.

His words offered some comfort, reminding me that I had a supportive team behind me. I returned to my office with a renewed sense of determination to focus on my work and not let the investigation distract me.

The days passed, and life at the office gradually returned to normalcy. I threw myself into my role as a partner, working on new projects, collaborating with colleagues, and contributing to the firm's growth. Despite the lingering uncertainty caused by the detectives' visit, I refused to let it hinder my progress or dampen my enthusiasm for my new position. With each day, I grew more confident in my abilities and more determined to succeed.

As time went on, the investigation seemed to fade into the background, and I focused on building a successful career and a fulfilling life with Andre and Reese by my side. Whatever challenges came my way, I was ready to face them head-on, knowing that I had the strength to overcome anything.

Chapter 18

I rang the doorbell to Vivian's Hollywood estate and waited for her butler to open the door. Of course, Vivian would have a butler. She wouldn't dare open her own front door. That job was for Benson and believe it or not that was her butler's real name. Benson was content to be at her beck and call just as the rest of her staff. For this house alone she had two maids and a chef who cooked for her seven days a week, regardless of what property she was at. Vivian owned several homes in the Los Angeles area, even one out in Bel Air, where she hardly ever spent a night. She and Andre owned a house out on the beach in Malibu, not to mention Vivian owned a house with a nice piece of land out in Martha's Vineyard. No one could accuse her of not flaunting her wealth.

"Mrs. Perry." Benson, who was tall and sleek, with a bald head and smooth chocolate skin, greeted me. To see this grown man answer the door dressed in a butler suit and a hand tucked behind his back always tickled me. But he really was nice.

124 / Saundra

"Hi, Benson, and please, please call me Brooke," I all but begged him again. I'd done told him a thousand times.

"Okay, Mrs. Brooke." He grinned, and I smiled. "Mrs. Perry is expecting you." He started to lead the way as if I didn't know how to find her. This property was about thirteen thousand square feet, with like ten bedrooms, and I couldn't even count the bathrooms. The walls were adorned with intricate artwork and tapestries, all telling a story of Vivian's wealth. It was beautiful but, just like my and Andre's home, in my opinion, it was too much.

"Brooke, I see you arrived." She stepped out of a corner. I was sure she had to be hiding with the objective of scaring me out of my wits.

"Vivian . . ." I paused as my right foot was in midair to take another step. My right hand went to my chest as I held my breath. "That was scary."

"Oh, Brooke, you and that sense of humor." She waved me off as a dramatic crazy person. "You are about ten minutes late, but I'm glad you came." Here I was, taking free time out of my day off to help her trample around in her attic, and she had the audacity to point out my ten-minute tardiness.

"Welp, I'm here to help. Whatever you need," I said, instead of addressing her negative comment. "How can I help again?"

Instead of answering me she turned on her heels—and I do mean literally, her feet were decked out in a pair of Christian Louboutin red bottoms. She had on a pair of tight-legged designer pants and a fitted designer shirt. She sure wasn't dressed to pack up an attic. Here I was in a pair of Nike shoes and sweatpants, and a fitted tee. I wasn't sure if I was underdressed, or just badly dressed in her eyes. We climbed the sweeping staircase, holding on to the wrought-iron railing that led us to the upper levels of the third floor. Though elegant, none of Vivian's houses gave the ambiance of warmth. I always felt a slight sense of discomfort visiting them. But I continued to follow her as she led me down a long hallway where we passed several rooms. Then we made a turn where a ladder sat waiting for us to climb up into the attic.

Vivian pushed open the attic door, then climbed through first. My eyes quickly adjusted to the darkness, followed up by what seemed to be clouds of dust as I climbed inside. Vivian was across the room in no time. She pulled back the velvet curtains that covered a window. The sun rushed in, and I saw nothing but boxes and what looked to be a treasure trove frozen in time. I was in awe. I gazed up at the slanted ceilings that seem to create cozy nooks and crannies. Right away I could point out antique furniture and things that were surely family heirlooms.

"You have some really nice things here," I commented.

"Things . . ." she repeated, her tone of voice gruff, as if I had offended her. "Brooke, these are not things, they are precious heirlooms that have been passed down from generation to generation. They can't be bought and are not ever"—she gazed at me with a stone face—"to be sold."

"Yes . . . I see." I nodded. "With these things being so important, why didn't you have a professional person pack these up?" I asked her as I had before about paying someone or helpers to do this.

"It's simple, dear. I don't trust these so-called *things* to be handled by just anyone."

"Sure," I said as if I understood. I was ready to get on with what she expected so I could leave.

"Here, let's start with these boxes." She pointed to some boxes that were stacked up to my left. Clicking over in her heels she pulled up the flaps of the box on top. She rifled through it carefully. "Get closer, dear . . . nothing in this box bites," she ordered and made fun of me at the same time. I gazed around quickly and noticed a majestic grandfather clock sitting quietly in a corner. The air inside the attic was tainted with a musty scent that evoked a sense of history. I stood over the box Vivian had been rifling through and there were beautiful pieces of intricately crafted silverware. Soon we had put our hands on box after of box of Perry family history.

To my surprise, Vivian continued to help out, standing and bending in those heels like she had been born in them. I tried to keep quiet to be sure that she remained the same. So far, my strategy was working. I looked at the time on my phone.

I heard the *tsk, tsk,* and realized it was Vivian sucking her teeth, which could only mean one thing. Quiet time was over. "That girl . . ." She was finally released. Since she had not revealed what girl she was speaking of, I thought it might be smart not to ask. I continued with my task at hand. I was now wrapping some broaches that were still beautiful.

"I told Andre you have to leave the gutter in the gutter. Erika Jones . . . *tsk* . . ." She sucked her teeth again. And just like that, the mystery had been solved. *That girl* was, indeed, Erika Jones. I still remained quiet. "All of this uproar involving her, having the police show up at my son's house and questioning him as if he is a criminal. Humpph!" she tossed out. "Her kind is uncouth. She was probably having an affair with some other woman's husband. And if she was murdered, that other woman is probably to blame. So, the police should go badger them and leave Andre alone." Still, I kept quiet.

"People of her lot always get what they deserve. So, I believe she got what she deserved." That statement was more than I could stand. Had Vivian just said that Erika

Jones's death was a well-deserved one? The woman had slept with my husband and possibly conceived a child, and even I had not said or thought such madness. What decent person would?

"Vivian, no one . . . and I do mean nobody, deserves to burn to death." I could no longer keep my mouth closed.

I watched as Vivian never took her eyes away from the antique jewelry box in front of her. She picked up the box and wiped away any dust that was visible. "Dear, some people deserve exactly . . ." She squinted her eyes at the piece in her hand as if seeing a small particle that didn't belong there. "And I do mean exactly what they get." She repeated it again and this time I could hear a coldness in her voice. Those were her feelings from her soul, nothing but pure contempt.

"Did you know about Erika Jones and Andre's affair when they were messing around?" I asked her, playing dumb to the fact Erika had already told me that Vivian knew.

"Actually, no, I did not. Didn't have a clue. But Andre did tell me about it once those detectives got involved."

It didn't surprise me one bit that Vivian knew all about the detectives coming to the house and even to my job. Andre told her most things. So that is the precise reason I believed she was lying about not knowing about Erika Jones. I knew that she would keep that secret because Vivian always covered for her beloved son.

Suddenly I thought of Erika Jones and could see her face as she declared that Vivian had threatened to kill her baby. Erika's face held a sincere concern that the threat was real. Erika was more than convinced Vivian was capable of such an act. Vivian's words were ice-cold, disconnected, and downright cruel. I couldn't fathom Vivian believed that Erika Jones deserved to be burned and dead.

My conscience now questioned, *Was Vivian capable of murder?* That question haunted me as I listened to Vivian.

"Andre's father was an adulterer, and yes, I knew about it. Well, at least as you did, I came to know of the disagreeable situation. But I also learned that men being men has nothing to do with where their loyalties really lie." She looked over at me. "Andre is his father's child. But he is honest and good. He's a loyal and devoted man and husband. Infidelity, like most offenses is forgivable, especially when one is under pressure." Vivian's speech was baseless, tactless, heartless, and poorly timed. I was not impressed. As usual, she wanted to wipe Andre's slate clean. But she didn't understand I didn't need her for that. But I did need answers.

Chapter 19

I pushed open the doors to the police station and was immediately greeted by what I would describe as a fluorescent-lit environment. It was so bright I couldn't help squinting. I could hear my heels clicking on the polished tile floors as I maneuvered through the building. I immediately noticed the strong, overwhelming scent of disinfectant; if it had been any stronger, I would have gagged.

I approached the reception desk. "Hi, I'm here to see Detectives Kruz and Wize. My name is Brooke Perry." I balanced my Chanel bag on my right wrist and tried to lower it to my side. I felt as if the young uniformed, red-headed, green-eyed police officer was eyeing it and not listening to me.

"What was your name again?" she asked.

"Brooke Perry."

"Just one second." She picked up the phone on her desk and spoke with Kruz. "Go ahead and sign in here. They will be out in a minute. You can have a seat over there." She pointed behind me.

I was about to dig in my bag for a pen, but her judging

eyes pushed my hand toward the germ-filled pen that was lying on top of the sign-in sheet. I scribbled my name, then stepped away from the counter. There was a contactless hand sanitizer pump on the wall. I ran my hand under it twice so that it could dump the chemical into my hand.

I made my way over to the waiting area. I could hear nothing but buzzing phones and the constant clatter of feet as people moved all around. Officers were meeting with some civilians right out in the open, and other people were just standing around waiting to be helped. I noticed some magazines scattered on a table that was close by. But I wouldn't dare touch them for the fear of them being covered in germs. Not only that, but I also had a bit of a quiver in my abdomen. I had no idea why I was here.

I had just gotten into the office when I got a call from Detective Kruz requesting I come down to the station. It was clear they were still investigating but I didn't understand why they were calling me. However, what I didn't want was for them to show up at my job again. So, I decided to come on down and get it over with. Further observing my surroundings, I noticed the wall was covered with framed posters displaying information about community safety and crime prevention.

"Mrs. Perry." I faced the voice that came from Detective Wize. "Thanks for coming down." He extended his hand. I accepted. "If you can follow me, please."

I stood up reluctantly and wandered behind him. Soon we were walking down a hallway. The more steps we took, the more I wondered if I should have called Andre. I knew he was probably in a meeting and the last thing I wanted to do was cause him to worry. I mean I was certain there was nothing to worry about. But being in a police station gave me second thoughts. Detective Wize stopped in front of a room on the long hallway stroll. He opened the door and gestured for me to go in. I didn't like the look of the cheap beige paint on the walls and the standard table with chairs.

"Please have a seat."

I hesitated but pulled out a seat. I was about to ask why I was there, but before my butt was firmly in the seat, Detective Kruz entered. "Mrs. Perry, thank you for coming down."

"Listen, today is a workday for me, and I have a lot on my plate. Can one of you please tell me why I'm here?" I was tired of the small talk.

"Let me apologize for interrupting your day." Detective Kruz pulled out a chair and set the file that she had in her hand on the table before sitting down. "Mrs. Perry, where was your husband on the night Erika Jones was found dead.?"

My temples instantly started to throb, and I was sure I was red in the face with frustration. Had I had no self-control I would have screamed. I could not believe this woman had the nerve to ask me that question for the third time. "Detective Kruz, I have been asked this exact same question three times . . . three." I held up three fingers. My irritation was apparent, and I would no longer hide it. "Tell me this . . . is Andre a suspect?"

"Calm down, Mrs. Perry." Detective Kruz played the victim and made me sound like the aggressor. "What we are doing here, the questions that are being asked, are only procedure in cases like this." She still did not answer my question. I watched Detective Wize; as usual he said nothing. The show belonged to Kruz.

"What about Jessica Perry?" Detective Kruz scooted closer to the table and crisscrossed her hands. She tightened her lips and stared at me. For a minute, I didn't even catch the name. "You do know who that is, right? Andre Perry's first wife." Once again, I was sure there was a smirk on her face.

"Of course, I know his first wife's name." I was baffled. Why was she being brought up now? What was the angle? "Why?" I asked.

Kruz twisted her mouth and shrugged in a nonchalant matter. "What do you know about her?"

Again, I looked at Detective Wize. Now his gaze was on me. "Andre's first wife. Umm, she was sick for a time and then she died." I kept it simple, and like Detective Kruz, I shrugged nonchalantly.

I watched as Detectives Kruz and Wize looked at one another in a suspicious manner. Whatever game they were playing, I was not on board.

"She was sick for a time then she died," Detective Kruze quoted me. I waited. "So, is that what you were told?"

"Yes, because that is what happened," I assured them. Like I said, I was not about to play this game they were piecing together. I was on to them.

"Hmmph," Detective Kruz grunted. I knew that was to bait me. But one thing I knew for sure and that was I trusted my husband. And I would not let them play with him in front of me.

"Do either of you have anything to add to that?" My chest was out, and I was wearing my confidence like the scarlet letter.

"Mrs. Perry, I'm not sure what you and your husband have discussed concerning the late Mrs. Perry's death. But this department, which is homicide, was investigating her untimely death. That case concerning the late Mrs. Perry is still very much unsolved."

My mouth opened to speak, but no words would come out. Both detectives continued to speak but beyond that point everything was muffled. I heard nothing. Detectives Wize and Kruz walked me out to the lobby, and I left in a daze. What had I just heard? Were they accusing my hus-

MY HUSBAND'S MISTRESS IS DEAD / 133

band of murdering his first wife? Did they believe he had murdered Erika Jones?

I was in no mood to work after leaving the police station. I had Leah confirm I had no appointments then went home, where I popped two Excedrin pills and fell into bed. I was mentally exhausted. I woke up to a dark house and no sun coming in through the windows. I had slept for hours. Climbing out of bed, I quickly discovered Andre was still not home and it was midnight. Where was he? Downstairs, I visited the bar and poured me a shot of Don Julio. I wanted something strong.

"There you are." I looked up and Andre was standing there. "I've been looking all over for you."

I just looked at him for a second. The police station lighting, the shiny floors, the stifling scent of disinfectant, all crept back into my mind. Detective Kruz's words found a space to speak. *So is that what he told you.* I poured another shot.

"Babe . . . are you okay?" he asked.

Was he oblivious to the time? It was midnight and he was asking me if I was okay. "Andre, where are you coming from at midnight?" Since I had to ask, clearly it wasn't at the top of his list to tell me.

"Oh, sorry, babe. Didn't you get my text? I was at the office, I had so many meetings that ran over to the next. I sent you a text around ten o'clock, but I figured you were asleep."

I would have responded to the fact that he sent me a text at ten o'clock at night instead of calling me, but I moved on to my interesting day. "Well, today I was summoned down to the police station and questioned once again about your whereabout on the night of Erika Jones's death."

"Wait, what? Why didn't you call me?"

"I would have, but I thought you were in a meeting. And you know, Andre, that is beside the point." I suddenly became angry. "They just keep pounding me with the same question. *Where was Andre on the night of Erika Jones's death.*" I mimicked them. "Why would they keep asking me the same shit over and over again?" I shook my head. "Andre, do you have any information about Erika Jones's death . . . anything?" I demanded to know.

"No . . . of course not. What would I know about that? I wasn't involved with her then. I swear, sweetheart, I don't have anything that could help them."

I nodded and shook my head before downing my second shot of Don Julio. "I hope not, Andre. Because since this fiasco started, I have been scrutinized and put under a microscope. And it's all because of your lies and infidelity!" I stressed with gut-wrenching pain.

"Brooke, babe . . ." He tried to come close, but I stepped out of his reach. I was not in the mood to be embraced by him. "Brooke, I swear to you, I don't know anything about what happened to Erika Jones. I honestly believe the detectives are just doing their jobs. But I can put a stop to them contacting you. I can call the attorney. Perhaps I should have done that from the beginning."

"No . . . no!" I shouted. "As you said, maybe they are doing their jobs. It might be best to just cooperate, and this will be over soon." I reached for my forehead. The throbbing headache and exhaustion from earlier had returned with a vengeance.

"Are you okay, sweetheart?" Again, he reached for me. I held up my hand to block him again.

"I'm fine. I'm going to lay down for the night. Excuse me." I stepped around him and exited the room. Now was not the time to get the attorney involved. As much as I was in distress, I had not mentioned what the detectives had said about Jessica. Andre had always been adamant about his love for his first wife, and talking about her was a touchy subject. He'd shared with me that she had been sick, and she'd died. Because she had been his first love, he suffered a lot from that pain. He said he thought he'd never find love again and had no desire to be married, until he met and fell in love with me. The last thing I wanted to do was renew his pain with some trumped-up assumptions from two detectives who seemed to really have no angle. They were fishing to make a name for themselves off the millionaire brokerage-firm owner. That had to be it, right?

The next morning, I woke up with a lingering sense of unease from the previous day's events. The conversation with Andre had left me feeling conflicted, and I couldn't shake the feeling that there was more to the detectives' line of questioning than they were letting on.

As I got ready for work, I tried to push aside my worries and focus on the tasks ahead. However, my mind kept wandering back to the police station, the detectives' probing questions, and the mention of Andre's first wife, Jessica. Arriving at the office, I tried to focus on my work, but it was challenging to concentrate. The constant buzzing of my phone with emails and notifications only added to my stress. I needed a moment of peace to gather my thoughts.

During lunchtime, I decided to take a walk outside the office building. The fresh air and change of scenery were a welcome relief. As I strolled along the sidewalk, I couldn't help but replay the events of the past few months in my mind. The detectives' visit to my home, their questions about Andre's whereabouts, the mention of Jessica Perry—all of it felt like pieces of a puzzle I couldn't quite solve. Was there a connection between Jessica's death and Erika Jones's murder? Or was it just a wild theory concocted by overzealous detectives?

Chapter 20

The private investigator Reese had referred me to, answered his phone. "Carson here."

"Hey, Carson, it's me, Brooke," I said, my voice coming out low but steady. It had been two days since the detectives had called me down to the station, and I still was sort of uneasy about the conversation. I had taken an extra day off because there was something I needed to do.

"Hey Brooke, how are you?" Carson was upbeat.

I pushed the phone closer to my ear, a bit apprehensive but sure of what I was doing. "Listen, I know I told you that I didn't want that address but . . . I've changed my mind."

"Oh, okay . . . you alright?" he asked.

"Yeah, I'm fine." I really didn't want to talk about it.

"Okay, listen. I'm going to text it you, but please be careful and don't be obvious," he warned. I thanked him and hung up.

It took me about an hour in traffic, but I reached my destination, I parked good distance out of the way. Making sure to take Carson's advice to stay out of the way so I wasn't obvious. I sat in silence as my stomach churned with nerves, my heartbeat pulsing with anxiousness, and my eyes read truths that were beyond my understanding. "Why the lies?" I mouthed, as I gripped the steering wheel so tight my hands felt as if they might bleed.

I wasn't sure how long it had taken me, but I arrived at Reese's house. I climbed out of the car. The neighborhood was quiet as usual, except for her neighbor's landscaping company. I had called before I arrived. Reese pulled the door open before I could knock.

"Hey, come on in."

"Please pour me a glass of wine." I walked past her and headed for the den.

"Here you go." Reese handed me a glass of wine. I nearly sucked it down in one gulp. "Well, damn," she uttered. "Guess I better fill your glass again."

"Yes, please," I mouthed and extended my glass toward her. Leaning over, she reached for the bottle of Merlot, and the sound of the glass filling calmed me. "So, today I did it. I called Carson and I made the drive."

Reese's eyeballs bulged to the edge of their sockets. Her hand was in midair to place the wine bottle back onto the table. "Did you get out?" she asked, her shock turned to concern.

I lifted the glass to my mouth and this time sipped and took time to savor the taste. "Of course not . . . I can't." The feeling of anxiousness that I had earlier returned as I pictured it in my mind. Then Kruz and Wize popped in my head, and anger creeped in on me. "Ughhh!" I groaned. "Damn, Reese, I'm going mad with this shit." I suddenly stood up. "I got called down to the police station the other day." I had not wanted to tell her.

"*The other day?*" Reese yelled.

"Yes." I looked away.

"Why in the hell did you not call me?" I knew she would be upset, but I had just not been in the mood to discuss it. And I knew she would be ready to crucify Andre.

"I know . . . I was just overwhelmed, and too exhausted in my thoughts." I turned to face her and sat back down on the couch.

"Tell me what happened."

I started from the beginning of getting the call and spilled. "But weirdest shit was, they brought up Andre's first wife." I was still unnerved, and unsure about why they had done that.

"Really?" The lines that were etched on Reese's face showed her disbelief as well. "What did they want to know exactly? I mean, what would her death have to do with all of this foolishness?" Her disbelief turned to concern.

I sighed at my own distress, and it was surely mirrored in her eyes. "I don't know. They basically questioned how she died. I told them she was sick." I shrugged.

"That is what happened, right?" Reese leaned into me with a serious expression on her face.

"Yes, of course it is. I'm not sure why they would bring her up. Anyway, they just told me to contact them if I have any information on Erika."

"Sheesh." Reese rubbed her forehead. "Why don't they close this damn case already."

"I know," I agreed. "When I left the police station, I got home frustrated, so I jumped into the shower thinking Andre would be in soon and we could talk. But he didn't show up until midnight. Midnight, Reese," I repeated. "I was beyond pissed."

Reese shook her head and gave a slight grin. "This guy. Where the hell was he?"

"Working." I clenched my teeth, still aggravated about it.

MY HUSBAND'S MISTRESS IS DEAD / 139

"Hey, his brokerage firm is in the top ten." She smirked, and I knew she was trying to joke.

"Not right now, Reese." I was emotional and not in a laughing mood. I had been more bothered about Andre's working hours than I wanted to admit to myself. "What if he's cheating again? I mean, he did it for years . . . right under my eyes."

"Wait . . . not that . . . has he shown any signs?"

"Signs . . . what are those? Hell, I didn't see the other ones, remember." I rolled my eyes at my own stupidity.

"You know you shouldn't do this to yourself, Brooke. See, the problem is, you are all work and no play. Fuck Andre and his bullshit. Let's hit Plush tomorrow night. It's a Friday and you don't have to work on Saturday. Let's go shake our asses till two in the morning like we used to do. Leave Andre's ass home alone for a change. We'll say we're celebrating your promotion, on me." She chuckled.

I shook my head at Reese and her devious ways. She was always getting us into something. "You are so messy." I smiled for the first time in days. And it felt good, and Reese was right. I never did anything fun anymore. Who knew, maybe I should take her up on her spontaneous outing. It could be fun.

The idea of a night out with Reese filled with music, dancing, and laughter, did seem like a much-needed escape from the mounting tension in my life. I nodded, a hint of a smile playing on my lips. "Alright, Reese. Let's do it. Plush it is."

Reese's eyes lit up with excitement. "Yes! It's been too long since we've had to make up for lost time. Get ready to tear the club up then shut it down!" She cheered.

As we discussed our plans for the evening, my mind shifted away from the troubling thoughts that had been consuming me. The idea of dancing away the stress and enjoying a carefree night brought a sense of relief.

Chapter 21

I opened the huge double doors to enter the house and immediately felt the allure of comfort. The day at the office had been long but productive. The tranquility I felt once I got home was one which no other emotions could compete with, especially after being stuck in the LA rush-hour traffic jam. I could almost kiss the marble floors.

"Hey, Brooke." Sue emerged wearing a smile and carrying a bouquet of floral arrangements that she was on her way to put in the den. Fresh floral arrangements were put out in the den at least twice a week at Andre's strict request.

"Hi, Sue," I returned. "Those are beautiful."

"I know," she concurred. "I made some finger sandwiches and picked a fruit and veggie tray. So, make sure you go grab a snack."

"Thanks, Sue, I'll be sure to do that. I must get out of these heels first." We kept petty cash in the office that Sue and Melva shared. This way anything needed for the house that was small and reasonable, they could just run out and get it. Melva was in charge of balancing petty cash to be sure it added up and reconciling all of the receipts, and she did her job quite well.

"Oh, you're here." Melva's voice came from behind me.

I was just about to climb the first set of stairs. I paused and turned. "Hey, Melva."

"Hey, I was hoping to catch you. We need to review a few of the landscape plans for the new season, so I can go over them with the landscaper. Can you spare a quick minute?"

As much as I wanted to race up the stairs and jump out of these shoes, I knew that Melva also had a job to do. And I didn't want to hold that up. "Sure." I retreated back down the marble floors and followed Melva to her office.

Inside the office, Melva retrieved the blueprints from a file on her desk. "So, these are for the summer season." She handed it to me.

My eyes scanned the blueprint, and I instantly fell in love with the vibrant, appealing design. "Just as I pictured when we last had spoken about it. Give him the go-ahead." I returned the blueprints back to her.

"And here is the quote Dexter sent over for the cleaning of the pool," Melva added.

I looked it over and signed off so she could also get that started. I loved to swim, so having a pool up to par was always a must. I was an avid swimmer throughout high school and college. I even won some medals in competitions. I started working at Walter & Hanks right out of college and kind of slowed down. But I had plans to start swimming more often soon. To be sure I got back at it, I had reached out to a personal trainer to start in the summer months.

"Don't forget I have that personal swim trainer starting right after school gets out for the summer. She is going to start the first week in June. I want you and Sue to bring Marcia, Marilyn, Alva, and Pez, so they can learn how to swim." I referred to each of their granddaughters.

I continued. "They are past beginner's age in the swimming world. The twins are like, what, seven now?" Melva's granddaughters were identical twins. "And Alva and Pez are like five and six?" I asked. I was a cheerleader for kids learning to swim by the age of four at least.

Melva gave me a smile. "Yep, you got it. You have never forgotten any of their ages." I could see the pride on Melva's face.

"Of course not, I love those girls. Now please, don't forget. And you can tell Ashley to call me if she is scared." Ashley was Melva's daughter and mother of Marcia and Marilyn and was very protective. On the other hand, Sue's daughter Maria was excited about the swimming lessons.

"I will." Melva chuckled. "You know how Ashley is, but the girls will be here."

I nodded, then excused myself. I needed to relax before I started to get ready. And a hot soak in bubbles was calling to me and it had my undivided attention.

I stood in front of the full-length mirror and couldn't help but admire the outfit I had chosen for the night. The Helena white skinny jeans fit my curves like a glove, topped with a white silk cami top with V-neck spaghetti straps, paired with Balmain rouge colored patent leather pumps. It was clear I wasn't leaving anything to chance. My outfit sang *bad and bougie* with no debate. I was sure Vivian still wouldn't approve, even though I was wearing over three thousand dollars' worth of clothing. And that didn't even include the diamond stud earrings that decorated my earlobes.

"Umm, umph . . . Damn, you look good, babe." Andre appeared in my mirror, his eyes trolling my body with hunger in them. "Where are we going?" he asked.

"I am going out with Reese," I shared with him. I had purposely not told him that Reese and I had made plans to go out.

"You and your girl Reese. Where to?"

"Plush." I gave myself one last look of approval and a slight wink.

"Oh, I see." I detected a hint of saltiness in his tone. "What if I had plans for us tonight?"

I turned toward him so quickly that I felt a brush of wind at my neck because that question had baffled me. What was he playing at? I know he was not playing the "being put second" card. "Andre, please, you never have plans for us. You work every night." My tone was matter-of-fact and sarcastic on purpose. My response had stunned him. I could see it etched on his face. His mouth opened to speak, but we both knew there was nothing he could say to counter the fact I had just delivered. I didn't have time for his pettiness. I strutted over to the bed where I had laid my diamond-studded crossbody shoulder clutch.

"Don't wait up for me." And I was out.

Chapter 22

Reese scoped out my outfit as she strode around me, giving me a once-over inspection. "Look at you. I guess you really are letting your hair down tonight." She approved and I could only smile at her dramatics.

"For sure. I figured I might as well be outside. Since I'm outside," I joked. Tonight was my night, and I meant to enjoy it.

"Okay . . . okay, I'm here for it." We had made it inside just as Rick Ross's "Hustlin'" blasted out of the speakers. It sounded so good to my ears. "This used to be my jam."

"Mine too."

We both started chanting along, "*WHO THE FUCK, YOU THINK YOU FUCKIN' WIT? I'M THE FUCKIN' BOSS!*" We looked at one another and started laughing.

"Let's get that first shot going, so we can really get this party started." Reese was hyped and I agreed.

"What the hell. Why not?" I threw my hands in the air and continued to sing the lyrics as we made our way toward the bar.

"Okay, we down it on three." Reese held up her shot of

tequila that was going to be our first shot of the night. She had suggested Don Julio for our first shot, and I flat out refused. I wanted to start out slowly, so I could make it through most of the night. The good thing is we didn't have to drive home. We had both ordered cars; they would pick us up then drop us off.

"*One, two, three,*" we counted, then downed our shots.

The warm, fiery liquid burned my chest after it traveled down my throat. It gave me a good headbutt and made my eyes widen. I shook my head and rubbed my chest. "Aggh," I gasped, from the heat. "Oh my, whew." I sucked my tongue. "That was hot and hard."

As the self-proclaimed champ of shots, Reese's face held pure satisfaction. She gave a triumphant smile as she savored the taste, smacking her lips. "Ummm . . . that was good."

I gave a sheepish grin. "You are something else," I said, as Chris Brown's "Party" came on.

Reese grabbed my right hand without warning and pulled me to the dance floor. Soon as our feet were planted, we started dancing. I was really enjoying myself, the music, the people, all of it was a celebratory vibe. Two more songs came on and we danced without stopping.

"Come on, Brooke, it's time for that second shot," Reese said. We started toward the bar.

"Reese," someone called out. We looked up and there stood a tall, handsome chocolate-colored guy. I soon realized exactly who he was.

A grin suddenly stretched Reese's face, and her cheeks blushed. "Anthony," floated from her lips. "What's up?"

"Reese, Reese." Anthony's eyes ate Reese up from head to toe. "Still beautiful." He smiled so hard his cheekbones arched back until he produced a dimple.

Anthony finally noticed I was present. "Hey, Brooke."

"Hey, Anthony," I responded.

146 / *Saundra*

"What are you two ladies doing out alone?" The question was delivered to both of us, but I knew it was really directed at Reese.

"We are celebrating Brooke's promotion. She's just become a partner at the firm she works for."

"Oh, okay. Congrats on that promotion, Brooke. Are you still with Walter and Hanks?"

"Yes, I am," I replied proudly.

"That's what's up. Hey, why don't you both join me and some colleagues in VIP?"

Reese looked at me for the answer. Honestly, I didn't care one way or the other. I just wanted to continue to enjoy myself. "Why not?" I shrugged.

"You sure?" she asked.

"Why not . . . we outside remember." We nodded and we both laughed.

Anthony was glad to lead the way through the crowd. The atmosphere changed once inside VIP. The dim lighting made the setting more intimate, and the music was more pronounced. Whenever I went out with Andre, he always reserved us a spot in the VIP section. Being inside revived that feeling for me. Anthony introduced us to his friends and colleagues, Terrell and Raymond along with Claire and Regina. The glittering LED lights caused an alluring glow on everyone's faces.

"So, Anthony, is this the Reese you've told us about who encouraged you to become the cardiologist that you are today?"

Anthony gazed at Reese then shyly looked down at the drink in his hand. Reese's mouth widened. I could tell she was surprised, yet proud.

"OMG, Anthony, you finished? I thought . . . I thought—" Tears filled Reese's eyes. I watched as she blinked them back.

"Yes, I realized you were right, and I didn't quit. All thanks to you." He gazed into her eyes; both seem to have

MY HUSBAND'S MISTRESS IS DEAD / 147

forgotten we were all in the room. Reese looked at me and I smiled.

The bottle girls stepped in the VIP area with lit sizzling bottles of champagne on ice.

"Okay, enough of the mushy stuff," Anthony joked. "Tonight, we celebrate our boy Terrell here, who was just promoted to chief of surgery." Terrell, like Anthony, gave a shy grin as everyone roared and clapped.

"Come on, enough of that," Terrell waved off. "Let's pop these bottles," he said in an encouraging way. Beyoncé and Megan Thee Stallion's "Savage" ripped the club up.

"Come on, girls." This time it was Claire, whom we had just met, who pulled us to the designated area for dancing in the VIP space. Anthony made his way over and approached Reese from behind. She started doing her moves on him. I continued to dance along with Claire and Regina, but on the next song made my way over to the leather couches and sat down.

"Come on, don't tell me you're tired." Terrell was sitting as well.

"Listen, I'm out of practice. It goes away after a while." We both chuckled.

"Okay, okay. I confess too, that's why I'm seated here. I'm a bit rusty." We both laughed again. A waitress who had entered with shots for everyone approached us.

"No thanks, I think I've had enough," I said, as Reese was making her way back.

"Oh, come on, Brooke. Have one more for the night. We are celebrating, remember?" Reese said.

"What are you two celebrating?" Terrell questioned.

"We are celebrating my girl here; she was just promoted to partner at Walter and Hanks."

"Wait . . . the financial firm?"

"Yes," I confirmed proudly.

"They are the hottest in the city." Our firm's reputation

preceded it. The firm was the who's who that everyone in LA talked about.

"Damn right they are," Reese said, then tossed back her tequila shot.

"Congratulations to you," Terrell said politely.

"Thank you. But it's not like I can save lives."

"Sure, you save lives, million- to billion-dollar lives, financially speaking."

We both laughed some more. We sat and talked as I was done dancing for the night. I learned that he was from Arizona, single with no children. I shared that I was married but never mentioned children. The very thought of kids forced Erika Jones back into my mind. I had tried so hard to push her out.

"Oh, it's two thirty," I looked down at my phone. "This place closes at three thirty." I looked over to see Reese booed up with Anthony. As much as I hated to break up their good time, I was ready to go. Anthony walked us out to our waiting rides.

As we pulled away from the club, I called Reese's cell phone. "Hello," she answered.

"Girl, Anthony is looking good, and he is still stuck on you."

"Yeah, he always was." Reese's tone was nonchalant. "But remember we were both players, and he couldn't handle my player side."

"Yeah, I remember."

"What about that Terrell with his fine ass. I mean he's too light-skinned for my taste. But ummm . . ." she joked.

"Reese, why you always forget that you yourself are mixed." I constantly reminded her. If a guy was not dark chocolate or at least milk chocolate enough, she wasn't interested. She would not even glance at a light-skinned guy. But nearly every Caucasian man she met was smitten with her. But no matter their status or how fine they were, she

My Husband's Mistress is Dead / 149

wouldn't give them a second glance. It wasn't because they were White. The real reason was they were not dark enough.

"I know . . . I know, but you know I like them double dipped. I can't help myself. I get it from my mother."

Reese's mother was fully White and only dated Black men. They had to be chocolate colored. What could I say, they liked what they liked. "But for real, Terrell is fine though, light or not. And he's into you."

I gasped at her insinuation. "But you forget one thing."

"And what's that? Madam, set the record straight," she teased me.

"I am married, DUH!"

Reese snorted. "Oh, that situation." Her tone was dry.

"You are not a comedian. So, stop." My driver pulled up to my house. "Well, I've arrived home, text me when you get in."

"Will do. Enjoy the lowlife while you still can," she trilled into the phone.

"Good night, messy." I giggled.

The night at Plush was everything I needed and more, but the thought of being home still excited me. As I stepped into the house, the quietness seemed almost eerie compared to the vibrant atmosphere of the club. The house felt different in the late hours of the night, a sense of loneliness and reflection settling in. I climbed the grand staircase. I craved my bed and Chanel sheets. I scarcely recalled when I could party all night at the club then come home and stay up for hours. This was not one of those times. I was exhausted but felt good and tipsy.

To my surprise, I found our king-sized bed empty with no Andre in sight. I rolled my eyes. Was he really feeling some type of way about me going out with Reese? I set my heels down and turned to head down the hallway to one of Andre's favorite guest rooms. I opened the door. Still, no Andre. I sighed with annoyance. This house was huge. There was no way I was going to walk around looking for him. A text would have to do.

Me: **Where are you?**

I headed back to our bedroom so I could start to undress. By the time I stepped out of my clothes, there still was no return text from Andre. I slid into a tight, short nightgown and still no reply from Andre. I looked at the time and it had been ten minutes since I'd texted him. That was alarming. Andre normally answered texts in his sleep.

Then suddenly the alcohol in me started to kick in from beyond just feeling tipsy. I needed to lie down. I pulled the covers back and prepared to climb in when a text came through.

Andre: **Ended up doing a late business meeting, should be home soon.**

I could feel my blood pressure instantly rise. To say I was pissed was an understatement. Work was all he thought about. The alcohol was weighing on me more and more with each passing second. As much as I wanted to respond to Andre, I allowed my head to hit the pillow. And I was out. I wasn't sure of the time, but I stirred and realized Andre was in bed. My body was so heavy I couldn't bother to open my eyes completely or look at my phone for the time. I was out again.

The next morning, I opened my eyes to a slit of sunlight coming through the window. The curtains were not closed all of the way. "Aggh," I groaned. My right hand went to my forehead as I had a pounding headache. The tequila shots were showing their effects. I turned to Andre's side and noticed he was already up. I reached for my phone to look at the time. Right away I noticed I had a text from him.

I know it's Saturday, but I have another meeting. Let's do dinner tonight.

Chapter 23

I was so appalled that I read Andre's text over and over again. Had my husband, who wasn't even home when I arrived at three o'clock in the morning, not even stick around until I woke up before heading off to another business meeting on a Saturday morning?

I threw my legs over the edge of the bed. My head was still pounding and I needed to take some Excedrin to silence the ache. I massaged my temples. But suddenly Erika Jones's words were in my head. *I had no idea he was married. In the beginning he never told me.*

Brooke, I love you. Andre's sweet words followed up.

He's a FUCKING NARCISSIST! Reese's words invaded like a storm.

All the voices hit me like a ton of bricks and the headache increased tenfold. Lifting myself from the bed, I made my way into the bathroom and retrieved the Excedrin. I popped two into my mouth, sucked down some water and sighed. Twisting the shower knob, I slid off my nightie and climbed inside.

After my shower, I dressed in something comfortable

and jumped on the elevator instead of taking the stairs. I could feel the headache subsiding but not my thoughts as I drank some orange juice. No matter how hard I tried to regroup, questions and doubt staggered into my mind. Was I blind? Could I really trust Andre? Was he really in a meeting on a Saturday morning after arriving in the wee hours of the morning? I was tired of wondering. I snatched the keys to my Range Rover, one of my three vehicles, from the key hanger.

"Are you leaving?" I heard Melva say from behind me. I stopped in my tracks. I had almost forgotten she was there. Sometimes she worked on Saturdays.

"Yes," I replied without turning around. I opened the double doors that led to the front door. I had driven my Range Rover all week, so it was parked in the circular driveway.

I drove in silence and seemingly with no thoughts of what I was doing, but soon pulled up in front of Andre's office building. I parked and treaded inside, straight to security. John, who manned the door, knew me, so I didn't need to show him any credentials. I climbed inside the elevator once the doors opened and punched the button for the sixteenth floor.

As the elevator doors opened on the sixteenth floor, I felt a surge of nervous energy course through my veins. I felt as though I could hear my footsteps on the polished floor. I noticed Heather, who was Andre's secretary, right away. It was quiet but I could see a few other people were in. I was charged with anticipation and uncertainty and couldn't shake the uneasy feeling that my unannounced visit might prompt an impression of there being problems at home. But I couldn't turn back now.

"Mrs. Perry, hi." Heather spoke.

"Hi, Heather." I did my best to sound upbeat and normal. "Umm, how much longer before Andre's meeting is out?

Which boardroom is it in?" My eyes darted around, hoping to catch sight of Andre.

By the subtle look on Heather's face and the uncertainty that flickered in her eyes, I knew she had been caught off guard. "Uh, meet . . . meeting," Heather stammered. "Umm . . . Mr. Perry is not here, ma'am."

A knot instantly tightened inside my stomach. I also felt a hint of nausea as her words, *not here, ma'am*, replayed in my head over and over again. I was totally dazed and confused.

"I'm sorry, but I can try him on his phone for you." Heather's words interrupted my haze.

"You will try him? Heather, he's my FUCKING HUSBAND. I HAVE HIS NUMBER!" My voice boomed; I shook my cell phone at her. I was angry and annoyed.

Heather's eyes widened and her face seemed to drain from the shock of my outburst and behavior. I had never been anything other than nice and respectful when I visited the office. "I'm . . . I'm sorry. I . . ." She tried to apologize, and I immediately felt horrible. What was I doing?

"No, Heather. I'm sorry, you didn't deserve that. Listen, I will call Andre, and thanks so much for your help." I took a few steps backward before turning toward the elevator. Thankfully it opened as soon as I turned around. Someone stepped off and I rushed inside, ready to be out of sight.

Inside the comforts of my Range Rover, my emotions were all over the place. I was pissed, confused, unsure of what was going on. I jumped on the interstate and sped home. When I got there, there was still no sign of Andre. I stood still in the middle of our bedroom, and it became clear to me. "He's cheating and I'm going to catch him in the act," I mouthed to myself.

I rushed from my room and tore open the doors that led into his walk-in closet, which was almost as big as mine. A surge of anger came over me once I was inside the space that had once felt intimate and familiar. Now it just felt suffocating. The cologne scent that filled the closet had once been comforting; now it was a reminder of the trust that I feared was unraveling. My eyes scanned the room before I started aggressively pulling his designer suits from hangers, checking the pockets. Turning my focus to his sock and underwear drawers, I emptied them, in an attempt to find a stray receipt or hidden note or any sign of his infidelity.

Immense frustration was roaming throughout my entire body. I stopped cold. "WHERE THE FUCK IS THE PROOF!" I yelled. "FUCKING BASTARD!" I continued. My eyes suddenly zoomed in on the safe tucked away in a corner. Upon contact, I started pushing numbers, any sequence that I thought Andre might use, but nothing.

"Brooke." I heard my name and stopped. I turned to find Andre standing in the closet doorway. A look of confusion and worry was etched on his face.

But the sight of him enraged me even more. It was like some invisible force pushed me to my feet. "WHO THE FUCK IS SHE, ANDRE!" I screamed.

"Who? What?"

"Oh, don't you play innocent with me. You are FUCK-ING some new BITCH and I'm going to find out. And I know the proof is here." I shook my head to confirm my own suspicion.

"So, is that why you have destroyed my property?" Andre's eyes roamed the room then fell back on mine. "Looking for proof of another woman."

Here I was telling him that I knew he was once again dishonoring our marriage, and his only concern was his property. "Fuck your property, Andre. And you know what, FUCK YOU! Don't do that narcissist shit with me today. All you do is lie, day in and out, this big meeting this or that. But not today. See, I went to your office. And I know Heather has called you and informed you." I shook my head up and down. "What, you think I'm stupid? You get home close to four in the morning, and then you rolled up in here from a so-called late night to go to an early morning meeting after only getting a few hours of sleep. What is it really? You can't take a break from your mistress?"

"Brooke, I'm not lying," he said. His voice was calm and serene. "I had a meeting this morning with the Dubois Brothers, but they decided they wanted to do it over golf instead of the office. Sorry I forgot to update Heather of the changes. Then after the meeting I went by Mom's."

The mention of Vivian hung in the air like a fog. I groaned. "Here we go with that shit. Is Vivian your alibi again?" I threw my right hand up and slapped it against my leg in frustration. "You know what, Andre? I'm over this crap. I want a divorce. You have ruined my life with your cheating and your lies. I have detectives questioning me about your mistress as if it's normal that I know about her. You have single-handedly humiliated me." My emotions boiled over and I felt weak as I dropped down to my knees. I cried from deep within. This was not supposed to be happening to me.

Andre immediately bent down and slowly crawled over to me. "Brooke, baby, I am so sorry. You have every right to be upset, every right to lose trust in me. But I promise you the late nights, early mornings, and weekend meetings are not about a mistress. I feel so awful about what I did to you with Erika." His voice trembled with remorse. "And I will never do anything like that again." He reached his hands out to embrace me; I could see the regret in his eyes. I pushed him back, still filled with anger and sorrow. Unwilling to give up, he reached out again. This time I crumbled into his arms and cried.

"I swear to you, babe, we are going to get through this," Andre whispered in my ear, but I wondered if the damage was irreparable. "We need some time alone, no work, no interruptions. I had Lionel fuel up the jet. Let's fly down to Vegas for dinner, some gambling, and just us time. You know, like old times."

I gazed into his eyes and could only see remorse, regret, and true love. He placed his lips on mine, and we kissed deeply. He was my husband, and I trusted and loved him. I couldn't believe I was allowing my paranoia to turn me into a weak, insecure woman. That was not me. I had a husband who adored me, and he showed it in everything he did. I had to forgive him for his mistake that was hardly his own fault.

Chapter 24

The day-and-a-half getaway to Vegas had been wonderful; neither of us had realized how much we needed a reset. It had really given us a minute to address some of the issues that were straining our marriage. Enjoying our Presidential suite in Vegas, we sat on the couch, the conversation shifted to lighter topics. We reminisced about our early days together, the moments that made us laugh until our stomachs hurt, and the adventures we had embarked on without having a care in the world. It was refreshing to relive those memories, to remember the joy and connection we once shared so effortlessly.

With each story, we laughed, and the tension from earlier seemed to dissipate. It was like we had found a bridge back to each other, a reminder of why we fell in love in the first place. Andre's smile, the way his eyes crinkled, really melted my heart. After a while, Andre suggested we watch a movie together. It was a simple gesture, but it spoke volumes. We snuggled up on the couch, our bodies fitting together comfortably as the movie played in the background. There was a sense of happiness in the air, a feeling of being truly present in each other's company.

As the movie neared its end, I leaned my head against Andre's shoulder, feeling a sense of peace wash over me. Despite the challenges we faced and the moments of doubt, we were still here, still choosing each other.

When the credits rolled, Andre turned to me, his gaze soft yet determined. "I'm sorry for letting work take over too much lately," he said, sincerity lacing his words. "I want us to make more time for us, for our relationship."

I nodded, a small smile on my lips. "I want that too," I replied. "Let's make a conscious effort to prioritize each other, no matter how busy life gets." We knew that realistically there was not enough time to really tackle our issues, so we agreed to take another big trip soon, where we could really reconnect.

In the meantime, we agreed to schedule regular date nights, to have open and honest communication, and to never lose sight of what truly mattered—our love for each other. As the night drew to a close and we headed to bed, I felt a renewed sense of hope and commitment. Our journey together wasn't always smooth sailing, but it was worth every moment, every challenge, to be with someone who understood and supported me.

As we cuddled under the soft blankets, I whispered, "I love you, Andre."

He pulled me closer, planting a gentle kiss on my forehead. "I love you too, more than words can express."

With those words lingering in the air, we drifted off to sleep, knowing that no matter what tomorrow brought, we would face it together, stronger than ever before.

We were back in Los Angeles too soon, but we had to get back to the basics. Back at work I felt a sense of contentment and satisfaction. I was emotionally rejuvenated,

My Husband's Mistress is Dead / 159

and I could feel it inside and clearly it resonated on the outside.

"Hey, you seem to be in a great mood today," Leah remarked as we rode the elevator together.

I chuckled, feeling genuinely happy. "Yeah, I guess I am. Sometimes a little time away can do wonders."

"Away? You've been on a trip I don't know about?"

I smiled. "Vegas for two days. Andre surprised me."

"Fill me in later." She grinned.

The elevator doors opened, and we stepped out onto the busy floor. The familiar hum of productivity surrounded us, and I dove back into my work with a renewed sense of enthusiasm.

Throughout the day, I tackled tasks with focus and determination, the sense of contentment from resolving things with Andre translating into my professional life. I felt more confident in my decisions, more open to collaboration and more appreciative of the opportunities I had.

As the day progressed, I received positive feedback from Mr. Walter on a project I had been working on, further boosting my spirits. It felt good to be back in the groove, to be contributing meaningfully to the team and the organization.

During a lunch break, I caught up with a colleague who'd been promoted to financial manager recently. We discussed work projects, shared ideas, and laughed about some office anecdotes. It was a simple moment, but it reminded me of the importance of connection and camaraderie in the workplace. Before heading back to my office after lunch I had a taste for Starbucks, so I decided to run downstairs to the first floor to grab some. It was always a pleasure having a Starbucks so close by, at our disposal.

"Mrs. Perry." I paused at the sound of my name being called, just as I stepped off the elevator and rounded the corner. The voice that I was becoming familiar with un-nerved me. I was about to turn around but before I could, Kruz and Wize were both standing beside me.

"Do you guys ever schedule appointments?" I asked. I was about at my wit's end with this behavior. They could not show up at my job whenever they felt like it. I was about to address it, but Kruz shared with me that they needed me to take a ride down to the station with them. And she made it clear that it wasn't an invite but a demand. I tried to ask questions but was afraid of making a scene in front of colleagues, so I went along with it.

Back at the station I was delivered to an interrogation room and left alone, sitting in the lonely space filled with silence—a mix of emotions swirling around me. The silence amplified my anxiety. Something about this visit was different. My mind started to race with thoughts of what might unfold. Either way I was ready. The door opened and both Kruz and Wize entered.

Kruz sat and placed a file in front of her. She said nothing so I spoke up. "Why am I here again? Why do you continue to pop up at my place of employment?"

"You know, Mrs. Perry, you have a lot of questions," Kruz started to say. She didn't take her eyes away from me. "But let's not do questions, let's do facts. What if I tell you that we know about the heated argument between you and Erika Jones at your place of employment."

"Listen, we understand." Wize spoke up and my eyes darted toward him. He had his fingers intertwined, which bothered me for some reason. "You were upset when you found out about—"

Kruz cut him off. "Yeah, when you found out about Andre's infidelity you flew into a rage, you couldn't help yourself, you could no longer control your anger."

I felt as if they were just throwing stuff at me. Their eyes burned holes in me as they stared. "Yes, I was angry . . ." I admitted. I thought back to Andre, when we stood in our room, his face sincere as he bared his soul. "Who wouldn't be upset, but Andre and I talked about it. He was truthful about the affair. He didn't lie about it. And I understood . . . as his wife I understood." I slowed down; my emotions were igniting my nerves and causing me to shake. "Things were different. We had been going through a rough patch."

"Do you know where Erika Jones lives?" Wize asked.

I sniffed back tears. "No," I lied.

Kruz leaned forward and placed her hands firmly on the table. She used her sharp eyes to convey her authority. "We have two eyewitnesses who saw you leave Erika Jones's house the day before the fire."

A thick knot formed in my throat so quickly I thought I couldn't breathe. My right eye blinked. "That . . . that can't be true." Bile rose to the top of my throat, and I felt as if I might be sick.

"Mrs. Perry, the time for you to *stop the lies is now*!" Detective Kruz's right hand smacked the table. She instantly stood up, walked around the table and stood over me. I gazed up at her as she reached behind her back, and I saw cuffs come out. "Brooke Perry, you are officially under arrest for the murder of Erika Jones." I hadn't even noticed Wize had come around the side of the table.

Wize reached down and helped me stand up. Kruz placed my hands behind my back, and I felt faint as the cuffs gripped my wrists and clicked. "We will take you down to be processed, now," Wize said.

"No . . ." I found my voice. For a second it had disappeared. I had wanted to speak while I was being handcuffed but no words would form. "You can't arrest me for this murder. You *just can't*!" I screamed.

Detective Kruz narrowed her eyes at me. "We have a scorned wife, eyewitnesses to an argument between the victim and the suspect. Not to mention the suspect leaving the victim's home less than forty-eight hours before the murder. I assure you we can, and we will charge you with murder. And all your husband's money won't change that."

The room fell silent at the mention of Andre's money. It struck a nerve, and my jaws started to tighten with a mix of emotion and indignation. How dare she insinuate privilege? "Is that what bothers you? My husband's wealth."

Detective Kruz released a hearty chuckle, but I knew it was fake. She didn't appreciate me calling her out. But I had more to say. "You can't and won't charge me with me murder, because Erika Jones is not dead!"

Chapter 25

The click of the handcuffs echoed throughout the room as I rejoiced that the restraints freed my wrists. I massaged them one after the other with each free hand. The brief confinement had been stifling. I dropped back down in my still pulled-out chair as Detectives Kruz and Wize returned to their seats. The room was charged with anticipation as they glared at me and I them.

"I know you both have been at this awhile, but things are not always as they seem," I declared. Detective Kruz watched me intently. I felt as if her gaze had penetrated me. "Erika Jones did come to my office a while back. One day she burst into my office declaring she'd had an affair with my husband, just out the blue," I added. Because that part is how I vividly felt about her showing up as if it was a normal day.

"We met up afterward, I went to her home. While there she once again admitted the affair, then proceeded to tell me she had a child with Andre. Then she told me the child died. At least that is what she herself had been told."

The stunned looks on Kruz and Wize's faces were priceless. Kruz looked as if she had been gagged. Wize looked as if he had been drained of all his blood.

"But then Erika tells me she didn't think her child was dead . . . she thought the child was alive. All of this of course coldcocked me. The story itself was outlandish. I didn't want to believe any of it. But I confronted Andre about the affair, and he admitted it . . . however, I never mentioned the child. Even to this day, he doesn't know that I know."

"But—" Kruz tried to cut in but I wouldn't let her.

"Please, Detective, let me finish . . . please."

Kruz waved her hand, giving me the floor back.

"I didn't want to believe Erika. I mean why would I? She was a mistress, so I hired a PI because I wanted to find out if Erika was lying. In fact, I wanted to prove that she was lying. After a few agonizing weeks of anxiety, I received a call from Carson, who is my PI. I had been so anxious to hear from him, but I was also very worried. The day I got the call, I arrived in his office. I sat across from him with shaky knees and I was so thankful his desk concealed them. It had been two weeks since I contacted him." My mind rolled back to that very day.

Two weeks after private detective hired

"Brooke, come in and have a seat," he said to me as soon as I entered his office. Right away my stomach twisted into a knot so tight I felt faint. Maybe I was tripping but I thought I saw sweat on his forehead even though the office was ice-cold. Was he nervous? I thought to myself, this is bad, which rattled my nerves to the core.

"Carson." I gave him a weak smile as I sat down in the chair, my insides rattling with fear. I

MY HUSBAND'S MISTRESS IS DEAD / 165

swallowed softly as I crossed my legs. "What do you have for me?"

"Well"—he cleared his throat and that annoyed me—"Erika Jones has nothing bad on her that I can find. She doesn't have any family that I can find and no friends to speak of. She's from Georgia. But she seems to have been adopted by an older lady who is now deceased. Because she has no friends or family, I haven't been able to prove she was pregnant though. The last company she freelanced for said that she gave her notice and left suddenly. So, no one knows why the sudden departure."

I was a bit shocked by this information. For a brief second, I felt sorry for her. Her life sounded a lot like mine when it came to having no family. That saddened me. "So, you have no information about a baby?"

"Well, while checking on Erika, I found Andre of course. Andre has an estranged sister, and he has been visiting her a lot."

This part about Andre having a sister did not shock me at all. Andre had long ago told me the stories of his father, Watson, having an illegitimate child by his mistress: his older sister, Kara. According to Andre, Vivian would have nothing to do with Kara and all but forbid him to, as well. But it did shock me to hear that Andre was visiting her. He had not told me about this. Why was it a secret? I had encouraged him to see his sister many times. I'd even been willing to meet her, even though Vivian had strongly forbidden it.

Carson must have noticed the puzzled look on my face. He sighed and then went on. "Kara has a six-month-old baby. But what I can't seem to find is any record of her being pregnant, having a baby, or adopting one."

That shocked me. Right away I wondered if this was Andre's and Erika's baby. That would explain why he was visiting her so much and possibly why the visits were kept secret from me. But I couldn't assume. We couldn't assume. So, I told Carson to investigate it some more. I had to be sure. Carson promised he would.

Only a couple of days had passed since I had met Carson and I was just sick with uncertainty. Hiding this information from Andre was no small matter for me, him still thinking everything was okay. Inside, my resentment for him was growing. He was a liar and a cheat, that much I kept in my rear-view mirror. Yes, he had admitted to the affair but never mentioned this so-called child. Hell, he hadn't even mentioned the relationship he had with his own sister. Who in the hell hides that? But things got even crazier two days later when Erika called me.

"Hello." Sitting at my desk, I answered the call. I had no idea who it was. Erika had given me her number, but I had not saved it. And I had never given her my number, so I was stunned to find her on the other end of the line.

"Brooke, it's me, Erika . . . Erika Jones." Her voice was shaky, yet it was loud. I ignored the dramatics.

"Why are you calling me? How'd you get my number?" I asked her instead.

"Please . . . don't hang up . . . you have got to help me." I was learning quickly that she ignored my questions. "Please, please, you got to help me. Andre has threatened to have me killed if I don't leave

town. I knew he would be angry about me telling you. These last few weeks I've been pretending like I'm not home. I hid my car but last night he kicked my door in. And he he . . . OH MY GOD! He threatened to kill me. I don't know what to do. I have no one."

In shock, I just held the phone. I mean, what was she doing? Why was she calling me? Was I her new point of contact?

"Erika, I don't believe you, okay. Don't you get it? Can you understand? Andre is my husband. Now, will you please stop fucking calling me?" I started to hang up.

"Noooo . . . Brooke, please, you have to help me. He beat me . . . bad. I think my arm is broken. I have no one."

Again, that part tugged at my conscience. I knew that overwhelming feeling of loneliness and power-lessness. I grew up with it for too long. With hesitation, I went to her house. Sure enough, she had a swollen cheek and purple eye. I just couldn't believe my husband had done this to a woman. For some reason I felt compelled to help her, but I didn't know how. So, I shared with her about the child and Kara. Erika was shocked because she never knew Andre had a sister. I told her we had to prove it first. In the meantime, we had to do something with her. She was afraid to be alone. She said Andre told her he would be back. She believed the only way Andre would leave her alone was if he thought she was dead. I left there, promising her I would be back.

The very next day, Carson came by my office and confirmed Kara had no child. The baby she had was reported to be in her care only days after Erika claimed to have given birth. Then Carson pulled out a picture of the baby, who looked exactly like Andre. I felt so betrayed that I was ill. At that moment it was clearer to me than ever. I had no idea whom I was married to. So, with the help of a dear friend, we plotted Erika Jones's death. The bone fragments in the fire were from the morgue and returned to that same morgue where things were in place for a paid cremation of the already mostly ash bones.

Chapter 26

A heavy silence hung in the thick air with what I assumed was disbelief as Detectives Kruz and Wize stared through me, their eyeballs bulging in confusion. The silence became so unnerving I started to feel as if the dimly lit room was closing in on me. I hadn't felt the wetness from the tears that had cascaded down my face until I felt a drop hit the top of my right hand that had been sitting atop the table as a kickstand to keep me from falling over.

The sudden tapping of Detective Wize's fingers on the table filled the room and eased the quietness that was so choking. He appeared deep in thought as he leaned back in his chair. Detective Kruz was her usual composed self, but I could read the puzzled look that covered her face as she stared me down for any proof of deception.

She leaned forward as if to get a closer look at me. "So let me get this straight. Are you telling us that Andre has a child and that you know that it went missing? And that Erika Jones is alive? Her tone was full of sarcasm, balefulness, and accusation.

"Yes," I said simply.

"You mentioned that we found bone fragments. That was never shared with the public." Detective Wize said.

"Like I told you they were purposely placed there so it would look like Erika Jones who lived in that house had perished in the fire. But the bones were from the morgue." Kruz shook her head at Wize; they knew I was being truthful.

"Okay so . . . if Erika is alive, then where is she now?" Detective Kruz squinted her eyes as if she was waiting on my lie to be delivered.

I squirmed in my seat and cleared my dry throat. I was really in need of a drink of water. "I stored her away," I revealed.

"Is Erika somewhere safe? What plans do you have for the baby?" Wize had finally jumped back in the conversation and threw questions at me.

"Right now, we are still trying to figure that out. The best thing I've come up with is kidnapping the child. I mean it wouldn't technically be kidnapping though, since the child is hers and is supposed to be deceased and what's more no one has custody of her." I shrugged my shoulders. "I mean not even Andre has obtained any documentation such as a birth certificate on the baby yet. I do believe he might be trying to give her an identity. So, this means if the baby is kidnapped, who would he call? The cops?" This time I was sarcastic in tone, but I was dead serious. Who could Andre really tell? "If I'm correct he can't report a kidnapped child that he hasn't even reported as being born?" My statement was more of question. Both detectives eyed each other in silence.

Detective Kruz's eyeballs seemed to roll around in their sockets. It was clear she was considering my plans.

MY HUSBAND'S MISTRESS IS DEAD / 171

"Okay, you're saying you are going to kidnap this baby, but then what?" What is going to happen to Erika and this baby?"

"I don't know exactly yet. Like I said, I'm still working on that. Perhaps I'll get them out of town so they can have a new start." I laid out my possible intentions.

Detective Kruz nodded at Wize and on cue they both stood and excused themselves. Once alone in the room I felt the weight of the decision I had made to reveal the truth. I had this looming feeling as to what might happen now. The room now void of Kruz and Wize felt empty.

The door opened and both detectives reappeared. I could feel the atmosphere shift in the room. I read Kruz's lips as she said they had a proposition for me. Her words clogged my ears and rattled my brain. What did she mean, *We can help get Erika's baby back and there will be no kidnapping involved.*

"Brooke, Andre will never believe someone just kidnapped his child. It's like you say Erika said, he's rich. We all know that his wealth makes him sort of powerful. He will find out what happened. Then he will hunt down whoever is responsible, and that will lead back to you." Kruz stood up as she laid out her thoughts. I had to look away in order to soak in her words.

Wize jumped in. He was sitting across from me but sideways in his chair. "There is a safer way that Erika can get a clean start with her child. Then she would never have to look over her shoulder." I listened but was still unsure of the part I would play to help them. Everything they said made sense. I hadn't even thought of Andre looking for the kidnapped baby. Maybe I assumed he would just forget about it since it was a secret he was hiding.

"Listen, I won't lie. What you say makes sense. Actually, I hadn't even thought of some of what you've said.

But . . . but I don't see how I can help . . . I mean what would you need from me?"

Kruz stopped pacing and I was thankful. I was getting dizzy watching her bounce back and forward. She pulled out the chair that was next to Wize and dropped into it. "We need your help to implicate your husband for murder."

I nearly gagged at the shocking nonsense that Detective Kruz had just spilled out to me. My eyes widened and jaw dropped. There was a mixture of shock and disbelief as the weight of her words sunk in. Then anger erupted.

"Detective Kruz, why do you keep insisting that my husband is some monster? Andre Perry is no murderer . . . yes he took the child, which was wrong, but maybe he was worried about something. I'm still having a hard time trying to figure out what to believe. But Andre, he is a good, caring, and loving man." I was adamant, as I asserted his innocence. My chest heaved up and down, I was full of emotion. I sucked in a deep breath in an attempt to calm myself down. "Now, for the last time, his wife was sick . . . okay, she was sick, then she died." I defended him and would keep doing so. My husband was no murderer.

"Brooke, I can respect the impassioned plea you have made here today for your husband. The man you exchanged vows with. I get it, okay. But I can assure you we wouldn't be discussing this if there wasn't more to it. Jessica Perry wasn't sick and just died. Her official cause of death was drowning while she was apparently sick. Did Andre tell you that?"

That revelation froze me momentarily. I had never heard that Jessica drowned, only that she was sick. Was this even true? "I ummm . . . no matter, I still don't believe Andre . . . is a . . . murderer." I stammered, and for the first time pondered over my words.

Detective Kruz grunted and twisted her shoulders. She

seemed aggravated and squinted her eyes at me. I'd seen this look before. "Brooke, I'm not sure why you are having such a hard time seeing who your husband really is. Here is a man with a living child he had out of wedlock, who comes home every night and sleeps with you. He hasn't mentioned the child once. Even though you know about the mistress. Why hide it?" The truth in what she said made me feel nauseated. Embarrassed, I looked away.

"Mrs. Perry." I heard my name. The tone was gentle. I looked up knowing it was Detective Wize. He opened the file that had been sitting on the table the entire time. He picked up what appeared to be Polaroids. He slid them across the table in my direction. "Here are the pictures of Jessica Perry. And this is the report." He slid those over too.

I held my head in the air and looked at the ceiling for a moment; I was reluctant and did not want to see the pictures. I didn't need to see them.

"You need to see them." For the first time the tone in Kruz's voice was tender. I shook my head side to side, and let out a long, loud sigh. Was I betraying my husband by listening to all this gibber jabber about his character?

I turned my gaze downward at the spread of pictures and fixated on the images. Emotions of shock, disbelief, and sadness flooded my entire body as my eyes scanned the Polaroids. The pictures of Jessica's bruised and battered-looking body were sickening. Suddenly, there was an internal struggle to reconcile my preconceived notions about my husband.

"Agghh!" I cried out. "What would my role be, helping you . . . huh?" I was hurt, upset, and confused.

"You live with Andre. He loves and trusts you. You can get him to confess. Get him to at least admit that he was in the house when Jessica allegedly drowned," Kruz said as if she was talking about getting ice cream and it was no big deal.

"Oh my God!" I cried out again. My right hand massaged my forehead as a banging headache was taking over. This was just unreal.

"Listen, you can do this. If you can get him to confess, he will go away for a long time and Erika Jones can just walk into Kara's house and get her child. She will never have to hide again," Kruz went on.

This woman was crazy, and I was over it. I jumped outta my chair and pushed it back. "Why . . . why . . ." I balled up my fist and hit the table with so much force my hand ached as I continued to cry. "Why should I care about Erika Jones, huh?" I screamed. I thought about the wrong she'd done me. Why had I even come this far with this bullshit? Why had I helped her in the first place? "You sit here and talk about sending my husband to jail like you're ordering a meal off a menu. This is my life you guys are talking about. Why should I turn my back on the man I made vows with for his FUCKING MISTRESS?" My voice boomed so loudly I could hear it bounce off the walls.

"That's right, get angry. You should be angry. When you talk about that husband of yours remember his infidelity, remember he still is a liar who holds secrets. A man who keeps a live child that he has told the mother is deceased a secret is a dangerous man, Brooke. Possibly even a murderer." Her words were harsh, but I couldn't help but hear her loud and clear. "Why should you help your husband's mistress? Welp, because it was you who told her you would help. You who helped her fake her death. Hell, it was you who constructed that plan. Now ask yourself that question that you asked us. But you know what I think: I think it's because you are a decent person."

With the images of Erika revealing to me that she was my husband's mistress and that they bore a child together, followed up with ones of me sitting in Carlson's office as he revealed this baby possibly really did exist, and the nausea that turned my stomach at the pictures of Jessica's battered and bruised body, which I would never forget, I agreed to help. But Andre wouldn't admit anything. He knew nothing of the murder of Jessica. Because Jessica wasn't murdered. That much I was certain of.

Chapter 27

My life had truly spiraled out of control after agreeing to help the detectives with their little investigation. I had returned to the office after leaving the police station, and I was in shock at how things were unraveling. I had driven there because I was unable to face Andre. For some reason, even though he was the one who had cheated and turned our life upside down, I still felt a twinge of guilt. I didn't know how I could face him knowing that I was part of a plot to set him up. So, I figured my office could be a haven for a few more hours before I went home. I had no idea that my life was about to get systematically worse.

Of course I was wrong about how things could get even worse. As Walter and Hanks entered my office, I could feel the tension in the air. Their expressions were a mix of concern and disappointment, and I knew that this conversation was going to be difficult. I was simply embarrassed and wanted to slide under my desk and never come out. But I put on my professional partner hat and looked them straight in the eyes.

"Jack, Norman, please have a seat," I said, gesturing to the chairs in front of my desk. I was also still getting used to calling them by their first name since I'd become partner they both insisted I use their first names.

They exchanged a glance before sitting down, their expressions unreadable. I took a deep breath, steeling myself for what was to come. "I understand why you're here," I began, choosing my words carefully. "And I want to assure you that I never intended any of this to happen. It's just that . . ."

Walter raised his hand, cutting me off. "We know about the situation with Andre and the detectives," he said gravely. "And while we empathize with what you're going through personally, we have to consider the impact on the company as well."

Norman Hanks nodded in agreement. "It's not just about the scandal or the potential fallout. The detectives' constant presence, no matter how unintentional, is distracting and puts us in a difficult position."

I felt a knot form in my stomach. I had considered how my actions could affect the company, my colleagues, and our reputation. Guilt washed over me once again, mixing with the already overwhelming emotions. "I'm truly sorry," I said, my voice barely above a whisper. "I never wanted any of this to happen. I'll do whatever it takes to make it right."

Walter sighed, his expression softening slightly. "We know you're a valuable asset to the company, a partner, and we don't want to lose you. That's why we're suggesting you take a leave of absence until things settle down."

Mr. Hanks added, "It's for your well-being too. This situation is stressful, and you need time to focus on yourself and your personal life."

I nodded, feeling a sense of resignation. As much as I

wanted to protest, I knew they were right. My life had spiraled out of control, and I needed a moment to regroup, to figure out how to navigate this mess I found myself in. "Thank you for understanding," I said, mustering a small smile. "I'll take the leave of absence and do my best to rectify the situation swiftly as possible."

Walter and Hanks stood up, their expressions softening with understanding. "Take care of yourself, Brooke," Walter said with a nod.

Hanks added, "We'll be here when you're ready to return."

As they left my office, I slumped back into my chair, feeling a mix of emotions—relief that it was over, sadness at the state of my personal life, and determination to find a way to set things right.

By the time I made it home I was livid, to say the least, about being put on leave for something that was hardly my fault and had everything to do with Andre and his deceit. I vowed that this was the final straw. I walked into the house in complete outrage, as I revealed to Andre in the loudest voice, that was beyond screaming, everything that had happened to me that day.

From me being arrested, to the questions about his first wife, to being put on a leave of absence from a firm where I had worked my ass off to become partner. The only parts I left out were being charged with murder, and of course me agreeing to work with the cops. I still had not mentioned the baby nor had Andre manned up and told me this secret of his. With all my misfortune I made it clear to Andre that I needed my space, so I packed my bags and moved out.

As I stormed out of our shared home, emotions were roiling inside me like a tempest. I couldn't shake the feeling of betrayal and frustration. How could Andre keep such crucial information from me? How could he expect me to continue living under the same roof, pretending everything was normal, when our lives had been turned upside down? Despite the turmoil, I couldn't shake the nagging feeling that there was more to the story than what I knew. Andre's silence about Erika's child gnawed at me, leaving me with unanswered questions and a sense of unease.

Chapter 28

The ringing of the doorbell startled me momentarily and my heart skipped a beat. It had been two weeks since I moved back into my old home. Thankfully, I'd never sold it when Andre and I married. Had I done so, I would've had to rent an apartment or move into a hotel, and neither sounded pleasing to me. The comforts of my home in this time of unhappiness were crucial to my mental health. I rushed to the door and pulled it open. As much as I wanted to be strong, I couldn't hide the mix of relief and vulnerability that was written all over my face.

"Hey," Reese said, concern on her face. She reached out and gave me a hug.

"Come on in." I reluctantly let her go and stepped inside so she could come in. I tried to smile and hold back the tears that I'd been crying all day. I knew I must've looked disheveled. I had on an oversized Bulls jersey and some biker shorts. My hair was straggly. I had an appointment to get my hair braided, but I'd missed it on account of being too upset to go out.

"Ah, Brookie, how have you been holding up?" She gave me a sympathetic smile.

"It's been hard," I admitted.

She knew I had been arrested, that I'd been placed on leave and moved out of Andre's house. Other than this, I had not given her the details. There were things I needed to tell her that I wanted to say face-to-face. She'd been on call at the hospital for the past two weeks. Today was her first day off that shift and as the true friend that she was, she had come.

"Well, I'm here now."

"Thanks for coming, friend. I know I look a mess."

"Just like a lost puppy, but we'll find you," she joked. "I brought us a pick-me-up." She reached inside her oversized Coach bag and pulled out a bottle of wine.

"Yes, yes, I need that. I haven't been to the store in a week. I've been shut up in this place sulking in my own miseries." I gave a light chuckle. Inside the kitchen I grabbed flutes and Reese popped open the bottle and then we kicked back into the den.

"I just can't believe Walter and Hanks put me on leave. That was just the worst. But what else could they do? You can't have a partner being arrested at work," I rationalized, as much as it hurt. I understood their position.

"Yeah, but damn, this ain't your fault, none of it. That fucking Andre." Reese shook her head, then sipped from her glass. "How long before they take you off leave?"

"Until this blows over." I hunched my shoulders. "I still can't believe I was arrested at work."

"Did they put the cuffs on you?"

"No, but they escorted me out, so it was clear I was being taken, and not voluntarily. They did allow me to take my own car but they followed close behind me."

"I swear those two detectives are so out of pocket. They know you are innocent of any crime."

"Well, they know now. The reason I wanted you to come over is because I had to tell you face-to-face . . ." I paused. "I had to tell them about Erika being alive and that her death had been faked. They needed to know how I pulled it off and I told 'em."

"OMG, you told them?" Reese scooted to the edge of her seat with one leg on the floor and the other folded on the couch.

"Reese, I had no choice. They were about to book me on a murder charge. They had two witnesses who saw me days before the fire. I had to tell them." I started to cry again.

Reese came over and hugged me. "It's okay . . . it's okay. I understand."

"I'm so sorry. I just didn't know what else to do. Then they brought up Andre's wife Jessica again. This time they showed me pictures of her dead body. Reese, they believe he murdered her. They think he drowned her, to be exact."

"What? No way. Never." Reese's mouth hung open.

"I don't want to believe that either. Andre always told me she was sick. Vivian said the same thing. And I had no reason to believe otherwise. There just must be some other explanation. I know. But this time they showed me pictures." Tears stung at my eyes as I replayed the images in my mind. "Reese, she was covered in bruises. Just all over."

Reese's eyes widened with concern. "Well, okay . . . but she was mixed, her skin tone very light. Is it possible she fell?" Reese shook her head up and down as if to confirm instead of it being a question. "I'm just asking?" She shrugged her shoulders.

I hadn't considered that when I first saw the pictures but now, I thought it was plausible. I just had too much running through my mind. "I don't know. I just don't know at this point what's fact or what's fiction. He never told me she drowned. Till this day, he is adamant she was sick. I've been married to the man for seven years. Would I really not know if he was capable of murder?"

Reese exhaled and shook her head again. "Brooke, I'm just speechless. I just honestly don't know what to think either. What we do know is that Andre is capable of hiding things. But even that don't make him a murderer. Just makes others question your character."

I could only nod in agreement. That sounded familiar to me. It was the same thing Detective Kruz had said. "They are willing to help Erika get her baby back and us off the hook for faking her death. They want me to get Andre to admit that he was at least home when Jessica died. According to them when she died, he claims he wasn't home. They are thinking if he lied about being home then maybe he knows more about how she died. Oh, Reese, I feel so guilty for even considering setting up my own husband. I mean, how am I going to get him to confess to something I'm sure he didn't have anything to do with? And if not, how will we be able to get Erika's child back? I mean, why has Andre not told me about this child? Why?"

"Brooke, that is a good question. That's what you need to keep in mind. He has hurt you so bad with infidelity. And still, he looks you dead in your eyes, knowing he has this secret. But you will figure it out, I believe that."

As I sat there contemplating the weight of the situation and the tangled web of lies and secrets surrounding me, a newfound determination surged within me. I couldn't let fear or guilt hold me back anymore. If I wanted answers, if I wanted justice, I had to be willing to confront the uncomfortable truths head-on. All the while proving to detective Kruz and Wize they were wrong about Andre.

Reese sensed the shift in my demeanor and placed a comforting hand on my shoulder. "Brooke, whatever you decide to do, just know that I'm here for you every step of the way."

Her words of support bolstered my resolve. "Thank you, Reese. I appreciate you more than you know."

And that was the one thing I had to do. This crying was not going to resolve anything. I was stronger than that. It was simple, I had to get my shit together because I was no fool. I sucked back my tears and declared a drought from now on and then drained my flute of wine. "Yes, I must, and I will figure this out. My reputation and my life depend on it."

Chapter 29

Benson opened the door for me when I arrived at Vivian's home. I had come over to finish up her request of preparing the final boxing and labels for the heirlooms to be shipped off. She had called to tell me something had come up and she had to fly out to New Jersey, therefore I would have to tackle the job alone. That was a relief for me, since I wouldn't have to be bothered with her and her nonsense. I had enough going on and didn't need pestering.

"Mrs. Perry told me to make sure you got into the attic," Maxine, one of Vivian's maids, informed me as soon as I was inside. I fell in step behind her as we ascended the staircase. On the third floor I gazed around; the house always had an eerie feeling. I never quite felt welcome in Vivian's home.

"Here you go." Maxine unlocked the door to the attic. The door swung open and there came the familiar smell of the attic. Maxine moved to the side so I could enter. "Please let me know if you need anything." She stuck her head inside, then was gone.

I started right away, I only had two boxes that needed

to be properly boxed up. The rest just needed the labels put on them. I reached for one of the brown folded boxes and a plank in the corner of the floor popped open. "Oh shit, Brooke, what have you broken?" I asked myself. The last place I needed to be breaking stuff was Vivian's house.

I turned around carefully, measuring the space with my body to be sure I didn't knock over anything else. I placed the big box on top of the other already sealed boxes that still needed to be labeled. Stepping over another box and a few things that were sitting on the floor, I bent down and carefully attempted to push the plank back into its place.

Right away it became clear to me the plank was being stubborn. "Come on, plank, please cooperate." I continued to talk to myself. "Ugh." I grunted and gave it another slight shrug. To my surprise this time it popped in. I smiled from pure relief. "Whew, thank God for small miracles," I celebrated. Then I stood up and nearly fell as the heel of my shoe stepped on something hard. I just couldn't win in this booby trap of an attic.

I looked down at my feet. There was something colorful there and I proceeded to pick it up. In my hand, I held a journal. Again, I smiled. "Humph, Vivian's secrets. This must be a treasure, must be something special." I gripped the journal in my hand. A mischievous feeling came over me and I decided to take a peek and read some of it. Stepping carefully over the rubbish, I located my Burberry bag and slipped the journal inside for safekeeping. Soon I was in the groove of putting on the labels. I wasn't sure how much time had passed. I jumped at the sudden knock at the attic door. Vera, one of the maids, stepped inside. "Mrs. Perry," she called out.

"Vera, please call me Brooke," I reminded her as I always had to.

"I'm sorry, I always forget," she replied as she always did,

MY HUSBAND'S MISTRESS IS DEAD / 187

and that annoyed me. "I'm about to be done for the night and Maxine is gone. Is there anything I can get for you?"

"Actually, I'm just wrapping up in here. I'll walk down with you." As we made our way toward the staircase, I saw another room sitting off in a corner that I was certain I'd never seen before. "Vera, I swear this house is too large."

"Oh, that it is." She smiled.

"That room over there"—I pointed—"I've never noticed it was even there. Is that another guest room?"

"Oh no, that was Mr. Perry Senior's room, or at least that is where he stayed while he was sick, up until he died."

I swallowed to keep from revealing how eerily surprised I was to hear that. "How sad. What type of man was he, Vera?" I asked.

"Mr. Perry Senior, oh he was a nice man. Thoughtful and fair. We miss him around here." I noticed the sad, strange gaze on Vera's face. I wondered if she had more she could share. Vera was one of two employees out of the six who lived here full-time on the property. I could only imagine the things or secrets she might know.

"Wish I could have met him," was my simple reply. As much as I wanted to be nosey and pry for more, I decided not to. I shut the door to my Range Rover and a chill went up and down my spine.

That unexpected revelation sent my mind racing with surprise and curiosity. Was this another hidden story in the family? I was under the impression that Mr. Perry Senior had a sudden heart attack and died. This version of what had happened to him had been confirmed by both Vivian and Andre. But Vera had just said matter-of-factly that he had a designated sick room inside Vivian's mansion. Why would Vivian and Andre lie about that?

* * *

The insistent trill of my cell phone jolted me awake from the depth of my dream. I was so close to the edge of my bed, had I not been nestled so tightly beneath my cozy sheets I would have fallen to the floor. Still groggy, I sat up and reached for my phone while navigating myself back to consciousness. I squinted at the screen, the harsh glow nearly blinded me as I read Vivian's name. I contemplated not answering it; it was too early to have to deal with her nonsense. Reluctantly, I swiped to answer.

"Hello," I said.

"Brooke, I hope it's not too early. A woman should never sleep past eight."

Had my eyeballs not been tired I would have rolled them. I took the phone from my ear and glanced at the time. It was ten o'clock. "Oh no, I'm not in bed. I just got back from a five-mile run," I lied and hoped it explained the exhaustion in my voice.

"Good, a girl must also stay in shape." She gave me advice that I did not need. I wondered why she was calling me. She didn't call often unless it was to complain, give me advice I did not ask for, or flat out ridicule me for simply being me. "I wanted to thank you for finishing up the boxes and labels for me. Everything was picked up at eight this morning, as planned."

"Oh, you don't have to thank me, it was my pleasure." I tried to sound upbeat. Vera's statement about Mr. Perry Sr. dying popped into my head. I'd come home with that statement fueling my curiosity. Vivian was a closed book; she didn't discuss her business. So, how could I ask her about Mr. Perry Sr. without her noticing? "I enjoyed looking over your family heirlooms. I noticed some of the things Mr. Perry Sr. purchased for your family, timeless pieces. I can tell he loved you very much. It's things like this that make me wish I'd met him. It is so sad to know he died suddenly of a heart attack." I purposely put emphasis on *heart attack*. The silence was thick as I waited for her reaction. Vivian said nothing, so I tried again. "Heart attacks can be tricky." Now I sounded like I was making the remix of a heart attack song.

"Well, we all have a date, no matter the cause." Vivian's voice was cold as ice, with no emotion.

I nearly gasped at her cold response and for what she did not say. Twice, I had mentioned Mr. Perry and a heart attack. Twice Vivian never corrected me. Was Vera right? Was he sick? Or had Mr. Perry Sr. died from a heart attack? I started to feel as if I was getting hot. I pushed the blanket off me, welcoming the cold air.

"Anyhow, I just wanted to thank you." The silence came out of nowhere as it was clear she'd hung up. She hadn't even said goodbye. Just ended the call, never giving me a chance to respond. A nervous feeling crept into my abdomen and squeezed. I gazed off to my right and my eyes landed on Vivian's diary. What was inside? I set my cell phone on the bed and stood up to retrieve the diary. My phone beeped with a notification. I reached back onto my bed, picked it up and paused. The number Erika used lit up. I had burned the number into my brain so I could easily put her name to it.

Chapter 30

"Didn't I tell you not to text me unless this place was burning down? This place don't look to be on fire to me." I looked around with aggression and attitude. "I told you when the time came, I would come to you. You really must learn to follow directions." I had driven nearly an hour to the location where I had hidden Erika. The orders were for her to stay silent and stay put. She was only to get in contact with me in case of an emergency.

Erika's face was full of curiosity, but I could see traces of fear. "I just wanted to know what was going on." She gazed at me wide-eyed.

"We have to be careful, Erika. You wanted to do this, remember? What if I'd been with Andre or even worse, his mother?" I shook my head with frustration as I thought of being caught by Vivian and the scandal it would cause.

"Listen, I understand all that, but out here day in and day out, I'm going to start going crazy being cooped up in here. I have no sense of certainty at this point. I need to know what's going on. Have you seen her . . . have you seen my baby? Do you know yet where he is hiding her?" Desperation seeped from her eyes; I could see the water filling them. "Does everyone really believe I'm dead?" She threw more questions at me.

"No, I have not seen your baby, nor do I know where she is, but I'm waiting on some information that is promising." I lied, knowing where the baby was. But I had to have things in place before I opened up that can of worms.

"What about the fire, do they really believe it was me in the ashes?"

I thought I caught a glimpse of excitement in that question; her cheeks were flushed. I did a double glance at her to catch it again, but if it had been there, it had vanished. She appeared sincere.

"Yes, they believe it was you. All that is left is for you to be officially declared dead. People really do think you were charred in a house fire." She also could not know the cops were on to our plans. Who knew how she might react. "But if you don't follow protocol and stick to the plan, you are going to get caught . . . get me caught. Then what? You must be patient."

"I will . . ." She paced and bit her fingernails. I was getting agitated with each passing minute watching her. I thought I saw her lips move. Was she talking to herself? I was done with her shenanigans for the day. Without notice I turned and marched toward the door. "What about that bastard?" She raised her voice to get my attention. "Does he care that I'm dead?"

I was flabbergasted and insulted at the same time. This was the woman who had loved my husband as her own and did something for him that I had not been able to do—give him a child. Now here she was asking me if my husband was grieving over her. I twisted in her direction like a swivel. "Erika, I didn't come here to talk about my husband's emotions, or the tears he shed over you. Besides, as you made clear . . . he is a monster, remember." I gritted my teeth.

She stared at me. I assumed she was uncertain how to respond. "Hahaha," bellowed out of her piehole of a mouth. Only she knew the reason for her amusement. She then sucked her teeth and made that *tsk, tsk,* sound. Her head waved from left to right. "No need to get testy or jealous. A girl was only curious."

"Hahaha," I chuckled aloud this time. "Jealous, of what? You, sweetie . . ." I gave her a devilish grin. "Never, honey!" I ground my heels onto the floor and put my back to Ms. Erika Jones as I strutted toward the exit. "Watch TV, read a book, pray, or something. But be patient and do not leave this house until you hear from me," I threw over my shoulder as I exited.

As I made my way back to my car, I couldn't shake off the unsettling feeling that remained after my conversation with Erika. Her questions, her demeanor—it all hinted at a brewing storm of emotions and uncertainties. It also made me think about the fact I really didn't know much about her.

Driving back, the weight of the situation settled heavily on my shoulders. I had taken on a dangerous task, one that involved lies, deceit, and manipulation, all of which I disagreed with. And now, with Erika's impatience and curiosity bubbling to the surface, I realized the delicate balance of our plan was at risk.

When I arrived home, the quietness of the house felt suffocating. Andre was still absent, off in his own world of secrets and deceit. I couldn't help but wonder if he even cared about Erika's supposed death. Was he happy she was supposed to be dead?

I poured myself a glass of wine, trying to drown out the nagging doubts and fears that plagued my mind. The thought of Erika out there, restless and unpredictable, sent a shiver down my spine. What if she decided to take matters into her own hands? What if she jeopardized everything we had worked so hard to conceal? I really didn't know what she was capable of.

As the evening wore on, I found myself pacing the living room, my mind racing with scenarios and possibilities. I needed to stay vigilant to keep tabs on Erika and ensure she didn't make any reckless moves that could foil my operation. But how could I control someone who was already teetering on the edge of desperation?

Chapter 31

At the sound of my doorbell chiming I almost shouted that I would get it. I had to constantly remind myself I was home alone. There was no Melva and Sue. I twisted the doorknob, and my eyes widened with surprise at the sight of Detectives Kruz and Wize, unexpectedly standing at my front door. I paused momentarily, my mind racing as to why they were at my door without notice. I had updated them on my new living arrangement, but still had no idea they would come by without calling.

"Detectives, I wasn't expecting you." I gave them a polite yet cautious smile. "Please come in." I ushered them inside. While I didn't appreciate their pop-up visit, the last thing I wanted was their standing on my porch drawing unwanted attention. "Is everything alright?" I asked.

Detective Kruz quickly observed the surroundings but ignored my question. She shared a glance with Wize. My heart skipped a beat, a cold feeling settling in the pit of my stomach. What could they possibly want to discuss that couldn't wait for a scheduled meeting or a phone call?

"We are just following up." Detective Wize's tone was controlled and revealed no emotion.

"Have you spoken to Andre about Jessica?" Detective Kruz asked point-blank.

I knew this was coming. "Not yet, it's only been a few weeks. When I moved out, I told him the reason I was leaving was because I needed space. So, I've been doing just that."

"Listen, Mrs. Perry, we need to get this show on the road," Detective Kruz said with a sharp edge of impatience. She sighed. "Now I know you are sensitive to this situation, but we have an obligation here."

Kruz's words stabbed me like a knife. She seemed to consistently forget that Andre was not just a case to me, he was my husband. It also escaped her that I was his wife and a person too. Upset, my eyes narrowed, and my face tightened with anger. "You keep saying that, but what about me, Detective Kruz? Huh!" My voice boomed. "You want to solve this fantasy murder of my husband's deceased wife. A murder that I'm sure I'll never get him to admit to because I'm positive that he is innocent. Meanwhile, I'm losing my own life in the process. Do you know—or perhaps you don't give a damn!—I have been out on leave from Walter and Hanks, a job where I have worked my ass off since leaving college. And as a Black woman, only recently became partner at this prestigious financial firm by the age of thirty-three. But because of your department's obligations, showing up at my job giving the perception of arresting me for a murder that never even fucking happened, I'm losing everything." My heart was pounding so hard I could hear each beat. I was so distressed. A tear escaped my right eye and slid down my cheek.

"Mrs. Perry, first let me apologize to you, if I gave you

the misconception that I don't care," flowed from Kruz's lips to my shock. "I do care and I'm sure Detective Wize here does too, about your career. Our intention has never been anything else. But understand we do have a job to do, and unfortunately it is Mr. Perry and his double life that started this."

I couldn't believe my ears or the slight smirk that I could detect on her face. The woman was relentless in her narcissism and could not help herself. Her tone and body language held no sincerity, it was clear to me she was only interested in controlling the situation. She was full of it, building me up only to gut punch me back down. I burst into laughter . . . then stopped abruptly and glued my eyes onto Kruz's. "Listen to me, Detective, what my husband did . . . or did not do, is up in the air. At this point nobody knows. Not even you!" I smirked, hoping that would annoy her. "But you can bet I will get down to it."

Kruz gritted her teeth as she was becoming agitated with me. "You can—" Kruz started but Wize cut her off with his hand held in midair as a truce between us.

"Okay, okay," he interjected. "Mrs. Perry, we are going to get out of here. Thanks for allowing us into your home today. Call us soon with the plan." I nodded as he ushered Kruz out of the door. Her body language was stiff and combative, she was not ready to leave.

Kruz paused. "One more thing." I watched as her body slowly turned to face me. "We need to meet with Erika Jones in person."

"No . . . no." I shook my head, my eyes darted from her to Detective Wize. "You can't do that."

"Oh, but we must, we need proof that she is alive. So far, we only have your word." Kruz's statement was a checkmate move. I always felt as though she disliked me personally. Even now she wanted to spite me by considering I might be lying about Erika Jones being alive.

"But she is alive. Why would I lie about that? Don't be so *First 48*," I mocked them. "If Erika Jones found out that you all were aware of her being alive, she would be afraid Andre would find out and be in fear of what he might do. We have to be cautious."

I could see that Kruz was unyielding, her facial expression was matter-of-fact. "Listen, this is an active investigation. We must report to our chief that she is alive, to do that we need proof. You moving out of the home was the wrong move, we needed you there with Andre. It was the most important part of the plan."

"I could not have stayed with Andre. I was too upset to be around him my anger would have ruined it. But please," I begged. "Like I told you before, I promised Erika I would help her. She trusts that . . . just give me a few more weeks and you will have your proof if there is any and information that I can prove." I implored them to understand. My plea hung in the air as the room fell silent.

Kruz finally nodded, the skepticism that lingered in her eyes was undoubtedly thick. "Fine, but we can't keep this thing under wraps for too much longer." I had bought some time. Time I still needed to overcome my own uncertainty.

The pressure in the room slowly dissolved as Detectives Kruz and Wize made their way out of my front door. I stood by the door, feeling a mixture of relief and hesitation. Their unexpected visit had shaken me, but I was grateful for the opportunity to buy more time. As I shut the door behind them, I leaned against it, taking deep breaths to calm my racing heart. The weight of the situation pressed down on me, reminding me of the delicate balance I had to maintain.

After a few moments, I walked back into the living room, the encounter with the detectives still fresh in my mind. I knew I had to tread carefully, balancing my loyalty to Andre with the need to uncover the truth about Jessica's death and following through with Erika's baby being returned to her. Sitting down on the couch, I picked up my phone and dialed Reese's number. After a couple of rings, I got her voicemail and knew she was at the hospital on duty. I would have to wait to vent to her.

After hanging up I sat in silence, contemplating the whirlwind of events that had unfolded in my life. The promotion, being put on leave, the detectives' visit, the ongoing mystery surrounding Andre and Jessica—it was all a tangled web that I needed to unravel carefully.

But amidst the chaos, one thing remained clear—I was determined to uncover the truth, protect myself, my husband, and my career, and navigate the challenges ahead with resilience and determination. The road ahead was uncertain, but I was ready to face it head-on, armed with the support of my trusted friend Reese.

Chapter 32

"Ah, I needed this," Reese admitted. She closed her eyes briefly and savored the taste. I took her lead and sipped my drink. I, too, needed a good strong drink. The cool liquid slid down my throat. I also closed my eyes and allowed the taste of the rum to revive me. I sighed with relief on the inside.

"Yeah, that hit the spot." I slowly opened my eyes; I would have smiled but my lips that were usually curved into an easygoing smile just wouldn't cooperate.

Reese's wrinkled brow showed her concern as she leaned in to get closer. "Lay it on me, what's going on so far? Spit it out already, it's all over your face."

My fingers traced the rim of the margarita glass, my gut held a hint of uncertainty and anger as I took the time to clear my thoughts. The distant chatter of the other patrons in the restaurant seemed to fade out. "Time is running out . . . I've got to get this shit done. Those detectives are on my ass about Andre, and Erika wants her baby." I started to feel like I was underwater fighting for air. The overwhelmingness of the situation hung in the air like a thick fog. "I'm starting to feel like I'm trapped between two guns, with no way out. I simply can't successfully do one without the other," I declared.

"Well, you have to do it. You need to talk to Andre about his wife. Stop putting it off. Get that ball rolling."

"Reese, I don't even know how to bring that shit up. It's really complicated. " I gritted my teeth, then picked up my glass and sipped. The tang from the drink momentarily took me away from the pressing matter at hand. "Let's say, hypothetically, he did it, which he didn't," I said right away. "But let's just say he did. Why would he confess?"

A thoughtful expression spread across Reese's face. She leaned in with a supportive look on her face. "Shit, Brooke, I don't know . . . but I do think that if the detectives are so adamant that Jessica was murdered, maybe you should talk to Vivian. She seems capable of murder. I've said it before, that lady is evil."

A smile immediately spread across my face. Reese was forever calling Vivian evil. "Evilina," I joked. I believed Vivian was vindictive and bougie, but a killer? Never. "Oh, I must stop hanging out with you. You're starting to rub off on me," I teased Reese.

"Honestly, I think both mother and son are creepy." She smiled, then sighed. "But to satisfy these detectives you must try something."

"I know," I admitted reluctantly. "Listen, I heard something that I think is odd but I'm not quite sure."

"What?" Reese lifted her glass and sipped, then set it back on the table.

"Well, remember when I went to Vivian's place to finish up the packing of her heirlooms and such?"

"Yep, oh wait . . ." She held up a hand as to block my words. "Please don't say you found out that she cross-dresses as a male. Because she does sometimes have that male dominance air about her."

MY HUSBAND'S MISTRESS IS DEAD / 201

"Really, Reese, please focus."

"My bad. I'm sorry, go ahead."

I couldn't help but giggle. "Well, for one thing, while I was in the attic, I found a diary, but that's not it. When I was leaving, I saw this room that I've never seen before or maybe never paid attention to. So, I pointed it out to Vera, just prying as to if it was another guest room in the twenty-bedroom mansion," I added with sarcasm. The house was unusually huge for Vivian and her husband, and of course Andre when he was growing up. "Immediately Vera says no . . . she says that's the room Mr. Perry Senior stayed in while he was sick, up until he died." My eyes gave a slight dramatic bulge.

The wrinkle of Reese's forehead told me she too was surprised. "Oh, he was sick? I thought he had a heart attack out of the blue? Right?" she asked.

"That's what I thought as well. So, the next day I spoke with Vivian and I kind of hinted to her that I knew Mr. Perry had a sudden heart attack. I even mentioned it to her twice because I wanted to be clear about what I was pointing out. And Vivian never once corrected me."

"Hmmph, that is odd." Reese squinted her eyes into slits.

"I was told by both of them that Mr. Perry Sr. Had a heart attack. Why would they lie about that?"

"I don't know . . ." Reese seem to think it over. "I wonder if it's possible he'd been sick with an illness that had him bedridden but something else caused the sudden heart attack." She shrugged her shoulders.

I mulled over her assumption, allowed it to roam around my thoughts. As I did that, I saw the potential of this theory unfolding. It seemed very logical. I wondered why it had never crossed my mind. Talking to Kruz and Wize was causing me to take every thought to the extreme. "I guess you are right. Maybe I'm reaching straight into the suspicion pot for all my answers," I reasoned. "But I'm having dinner with him tomorrow night. We are supposed to talk about things. I'm hoping he'll admit to the baby once and for all."

"You still have hopes for that?"

I chewed on that question hard. I hunched my shoulders with uncertainty. "I know he cheated, and Detective Kruz will have me believe he is a murderer and Erika Jones swears he's a monster. But I still believe he's good . . . a cheater maybe, but those other things they say, I believe are untrue."

Reese looked at me, then gazed around the restaurant. A calm expression covered her face as she eyed me again. "What about that diary? What's in it?"

"Oh, that thing. I haven't opened it."

"You haven't opened it." She seemed surprised.

"No, I haven't . . . I'm afraid to find Vivian's sexual escapades floating all through it." My cheeks stretched into a huge grin.

Reese scrunched up her nose as if the odor of a rotten egg had filled the air. "Ewww." She chuckled.

"Welp, you asked." I finished off my margarita, while Reese continued to fake spit out her disgust. "I swear you are so dramatic. Come on, walk me to my car. You know I feel like someone has been following me." I gazed around at the patrons in the restaurant to see if any of them looked suspicious or to catch some unwanted stalker staring at me. But everyone was engaged with their own company. I was tripping.

"Who would follow you?" Reese asked.

"I don't know. I swear all this drama got me paranoid."

"I see. Welp, let's have one last shot before we go. This will help you sleep tight without the suspicion of the invisible man," she teased.

I rolled my eyes playfully. "You are not a comedian. So, stop." I smiled. "Anyway, I need you to catch me up on how your dates have been going with Dr. Anthony, so fine."

"That he is." Reese perked up. "Oh, but Brooke, for the first time I think I'm in love." A glow burst through Reese that I'd never seen before. A sparkle ignited in her eyes that pushed out through her cheeks.

My mouth still hung wide-open from the four-letter word that I thought would never leave my friend's mouth. "LOVE!" My right hand pressed to my chest in awe. "I've never heard you use that word in the same sentence concerning a man. I think I'm going to need a few more shots to celebrate this," I teased. We both burst into loud giggles that caused the other patrons to stare.

Chapter 33

Melva opened the front door and stood back. "Brooke, hi." She grinned so hard her cheeks were stretched all the way back; her right hand was on her hip. I stepped inside and she reached out and pulled me into a huge hug. "We've missed you around here," she admitted. I had arrived for dinner with Andre. I had been a ball of nerves all day long. It had been weeks since I'd spent time with Andre, and this was going to be the night I would ask the questions.

"I've missed you all too. Has Sue left for the evening?"

"Actually no, she didn't come in today. The youngest grandbaby was sick."

"Oh, poor baby. You must tell her I said hi and to let me know if she needs anything."

"Of course, of course. And next time use your key. I thought you were a real-life visitor." We both laughed, as Andre came around the corner.

"Brooke, sweetheart, I knew you would be on time." He smiled, leaned in, and kissed me on the lips. "Ummph, I've missed you." He licked his lips as if he could taste me on them. I grinned. "When will you move back in?"

On that note my smile faded. I hadn't come to discuss my return and he knew that. "Andre, don't do that." My tone was firm. "We've discussed this . . . I need space and time. Now you said—"

"I know . . . I know." He pulled me into his arms, and I almost swooned. He smelled so good, his cologne captivated me. I had to shake it off, I couldn't let him charm me. "I just miss you so much . . . I miss you in our bed." His soft lips kissed my neck and my legs nearly caved underneath me. My entire midsection thumped and came alive.

"Come on, are you going to behave?" I had to break free of his embrace.

"I'll try." His tone was full of the lust that I needed to run away from. "Did you come hungry, as I instructed? I had Chef Doug prepare some dishes."

"Yes, I'm hungry."

"Sounds good. Let's have a drink first until Chef Doug calls us in." We headed toward the bar. "Did you ring the doorbell?" he asked.

"Yes."

"Why not use your key? The locks are the same."

"No, I moved out. So, I figured I'll try the visitor protocol."

"Nonsense . . . use your key next time." He walked around the bar while I stood on the other side to be served. A bottle of champagne was lying in wait on ice. He filled my glass.

The bubbly tingled in my cheeks. I was enjoying the prickle as the doorbell chimed loudly. That got my attention. Who could come visiting at this late hour when we had dinner plans? My glass stalled midair; I looked at Andre. "Are you expecting someone?"

"Yes, we have a guest that insisted on coming." He smiled.

"Wh—" I was cut off.

"Mother!" Andre exclaimed as he exited the bar and into Vivian's arms. Like the dutiful son that he was, he kissed her on the cheek.

"Brooke, dear, it's so good to see you." Vivian turned around and greeted me so fast, I didn't have the time to shake off the stunned look I was sure had appeared on my face.

I opened my mouth, but nothing came out. So, I swallowed hard, then finally I forced out a "You too, Vivian."

"Dinner is served," Chef Doug announced. I must have walked to the table blind; I was so confused and unhappy. Why was Vivian at a dinner that Andre had invited me to? Why had he not told me beforehand? He had been adamant that he wanted to have an intimate dinner alone with me. Finally, I had worked up the nerve to speak with him, and here, bold as shit, was Vivian once again interjecting. The sound of silverware clicking against the plates filled the air as we forked food into our mouths.

Vivian's unexpected presence in Andre's home felt like a sudden gust of unruly wind on a calm day. I struggled to hide my displeasure and maintain a composed demeanor. She was dressed elegantly as always, her behavior calm and confident, opposing sharply with my inner turmoil.

"Andre, darling, I really hope you don't mind my being here," Vivian said with a warm smile, her eyes flickering between Andre and me. I felt as if she were taunting me with her fake game of nice mother-in-law.

"Of course not, Mother," Andre replied in a polite manner, but with a hint of reservation. "Please, don't worry."

I wanted to scream at him for being so insensitive to my feelings. He'd known why I was here. As we settled at the dinner table, the atmosphere screamed uneasy. I could sense the tension brewing beneath the surface, a silent battle of wills between Vivian and me. She seemed to exude an air of authority, as if she had every right to be there, while I felt like an intruder in my own space.

"So, Brooke, do you miss being at home?" Vivan finally took the lead. I was not surprised. There was no way she could sit and be quiet.

I swallowed the small bits of food that I had been chewing on, took my napkin and wiped my mouth. "I miss Andre, yes. However, I do own the house I'm in." I picked up my fork and stuck it in one of the glazed brussels sprouts on my plate.

"Oh yes, I remember the bungalow." She referred to my house as if it was a small piece of shit.

I smiled in spite of her shade. "I'm sorry, Vivian, but it's a four-bedroom, thirty-two hundred square foot house. It's a bit bigger than a bungalow." I picked up my wineglass and sipped. I was not in the mood for Vivian.

"Well, a wife's place is with her husband."

My eyes shot in the direction of Andre; I watched as he stuffed food into his mouth. It was now clear to me why Vivian was there. Andre thought his mother could convince me to come home to him. But as usual his dear mother Vivian had no tact or simple respect. But this was one night they had underestimated me. I was ready to play ball. I sucked my teeth and turned to Vivian wearing the sweetest innocent smile a daughter-in-law could muster.

"Vivian, how long were you and Andre's father married?"

Vivian stopped chewing, gazed at me, and then smirked. She then continued to chew and focused her attention back on her plate. "More years than I care to count." Her tone was full of sour sarcasm. Andre laughed out loud.

"Mother, that is no answer. Babe, they were married more than thirty years."

"Yes, we were, and in that time, I never left his side. No matter what." She looked upside my head like I had a bunion growing. "I carried that marriage contract to the very end."

"And you were lucky. I know it had to be devastating when he had that heart attack suddenly and died." I purposely locked eyes with Andre.

"Yes . . . yes, it was. But we had each other. Didn't we, Mom?" He stared squarely at Vivian.

"We sure did." Vivian kept her eyes on her plate.

A surge of sickening emotion went through me as I listened to Andre blatantly continue to lie to me. The weight of unspoken truth was stifling. I had to fight to keep a composed exterior. Maybe this was the truth. Maybe Vera was mistaken? It is possible that Vivan and Perry Sr. slept in separate rooms. And to keep gossip down amongst their staff said he was sick. There had to be another explanation. Andre just would not lie to me about something so serious. Would he? Reese had said that the heart attack could have been brought on by other illnesses.

"Brooke." I jumped at the sound of my name. I had been deep in thought. I found Andre and Vivian observing me. "Listen, I know being a foster child, being thought of as a bastard . . ." Vivian started to say.

A gasp escaped my lips and my eyes bulged at the nasty words that came out of Vivian's mouth. "Excuse me? Did you say *bastard*?" My voice boomed. Anger burned through my entire body. I could feel the blood boiling under my skin.

Andre sat forward in his seat. "Umm . . . babe, I think she meant—" I threw my right hand up in his direction to shush him.

"Vivian, with all due respect . . . Yes, I was a foster a child and I have no idea who my parents were or why I was given up for adoption. But I equally do not know that my parents were not married. Therefore, I don't believe you should automatically make the assumption that I'm a bastard child," I spat out. But I wasn't done, I was about to checkmate Mrs. Vivan. "By the way, was Andre an only child or did he have a sibling?" I stood up, politely excused myself, and left the table.

Inside the bathroom I was so upset. I counted to fifty. Vivian and her mouth was just out of control. Her rudeness was respected by no one. The woman had just told me I was a bastard child, like she was telling me I had just won the Miss America pageant. "Unbelievable," I mouthed to myself as I gazed into the bathroom mirror. That woman never ceased to amaze me. I just couldn't understand how such a beautiful, rich lady who appeared to have it all could be so nasty. Sometimes with no intention. I refused to believe she was naturally this nasty.

"Brooke." Andre tapped on the bathroom door. "I'm so sorry," he apologized as I stepped out. "Brooke, babe, I know Mother can be too much. But she really doesn't mean anything by it."

I smiled as I thought of Vivian. She never presented herself as anyone but who she was; I could expect her to be her. "I know it. And I don't know why I let her get me so upset. I'm just a bit stressed," I reasoned.

"Come on, let's have a drink."

This time I chose a tequila shot. It helped calm me.

"Forgive me if I over spoke, you are dear to me, Brooke." Vivian had snuck in beside me like a thief in the night. After two tequila shots I felt so good. For now, I was over her words.

Things had mellowed out and Andre had popped open another bottle of champagne

"Andre, we must discuss this Erika thing with the detectives. I have got to know everything is okay." I said.

210 / *Saundra*

"Andre, son, why are you letting this get out of hand? I've told you to send a team of lawyers down there to set them straight and prove your innocence."

"Mother, I would, but there is no need. It's about to be over. They were just trying to see if Brooke knows anything. So they turned up the heat. You know that thing they do. But soon, babe," he said to me, "you can return to work. And I promise you if that Detective Kruz, or Wize, starts hounding you again, I will have LA's finest dream team of lawyers all over them. And when we are done, they will be picking up trash on the side of the street."

"Okay, so let's say the Erika Jones situation is done. What about your wife? They asked if I was aware you were married before and that she died."

Vivian's hair seemed to stand up on her head. "Listen, that girl was sick, and she died!" she shouted, her forefinger pointed at me. "My son has suffered enough. Her parents badgered my son and accused him of not being a good husband. The truth is she was their only child, and they couldn't handle it. She was sick, she died, and we buried her. That's all. That's it." Bits of spit flew out of Vivian's mouth as her sharp, cold words seemed to land in the air and freeze. The hardness on her face mirrored the coldness of her words, and it sent a chill down my spine.

I couldn't believe the way the dinner at Andre's had turned out, but I was glad to be home. Even still there was an uneasiness upon my shoulders. *She was their only child.* Vivian's words had played over and over in my head on the drive home, and I simply could not shake it. But suddenly it made sense; I needed to speak with Jessica's parents. Maybe I could learn what type of person she was through them. Then maybe some of this could make sense to me. Maybe they could explain more about her dying.

MY HUSBAND'S MISTRESS IS DEAD / 211

But Vivian's behavior had been inexcusable. Was she really that cold? Was she not capable of grieving for her son, whom she loved so much? Who was Vivian Perry, really? Who was the woman behind the socialite? The diary—there, probably, lay the answers to my question. After a hot shower I would make reading it my entertainment before bed.

I brewed a pot of coffee then dished up a cup then I looked for Vivian's diary in the lucky spot I was sure I had left it. But the spot was empty. I sipped from my coffee mug and racked my brain trying to remember what I had done with it. Was I tripping? I spun around in circles, baffled that I couldn't find the diary. Where could it be?

Chapter 34

My bedroom that was normally an oasis of order was in chaos. Drawers were pulled out, papers scattered about, my moves had been swift and purposeful. But the diary was not anywhere, it was gone—vanished. Sleepy and perplexed, I climbed into bed. Maybe I was tired. However, the morning hours revealed the same results. So, throwing caution to the wind, I cleaned my room, took another shower, got dressed and hit the streets.

As usual, the line of cars at the Starbucks drive-thru was wrapped around the building. Finding an empty space, I parked and went inside. Right before entering Starbucks, an eerie feeling seemed to creep up from behind me. I stopped suddenly and looked over my shoulder, but nothing seemed to be out of the ordinary.

The Starbucks cashier, whose badge read Kylie, asked, "Hello, what can I get started for you?"

"Hi, let me get a grande caramel latte, hot."

I placed my order then stepped off to the side. Once again, that eerie feeling forced me to look over my shoulder, but nothing was there.

My Husband's Mistress is Dead / 213

"Brooke." I jumped at the calling of my name. But it was only the Starbucks employee letting me know my coffee was ready.

"Thank you," I said, reaching for my coffee. I had to get it together. I was really becoming a walking body of paranoia, and I didn't like it. Why would anybody be following me, of all people? Shaking it off, I prepared to do what I was about to do. I had made up my mind that I would go and speak with Jessica's parents. That's exactly where my next destination was going to be.

My stomach was tied in knots with nerves but that didn't stop me. There was no doorbell, so I balled up my right fist and knocked twice. I counted to fifteen and there was no answer. I balled up my fist for one last try, but then the door opened.

A tall, middle-aged White woman with golden blond hair answered. Her eyes held the look of weary, but pleasant. I was quiet, but she spoke up. "Can I help you?"

"Mrs. Lawrence ... are you Jessica Lawerence's mother?" I stuttered. For a brief moment I lost all courage.

"I'm Mrs. Lawrence, yes? May I help you with something?" Curiosity gripped her face.

"Mrs. Lawrence, I'm Brooke Perry ... I'm married to Andere Perry."

The pleasant expression on Mrs. Lawrence's face when she first opened the door seemed to fade into shock and anger. "Why are you here? You can't be looking for Jessica, as I'm sure you know ..." She paused and pain switched to anger. She looked away and grunted to clear her throat. She put her eyes back on me. "Jessica is no longer with us," seeped through her lips.

"Yes, I'm—"

She cut me off. "If you will excuse me." The wooden

door started to shift forward as she stepped aside so that it could shut.

"Mrs. Lawrence, please." I leaned forward quickly and held up my hand to stop the door from closing. The door made a light thud against the palm of my hand. I was desperate to speak with her. "Mrs. Lawrence, I really must speak with you," I begged.

With the doorknob still gripped in her hand, she paused. Her eyes, full of despair, met mine. I felt horrible for landing on her doorstep, bringing back memories that she clearly wanted to keep behind her. But I didn't know who else I could speak with to get information about her daughter. She gave a deep sigh. Still hesitant, she slowly pulled the door open.

Taking that as an invite and in fear that might be the only one I would get, I stepped inside quickly. As soon as I crossed that threshold, I was swallowed up by a wave of warmth, love, and the feeling of being home. The air was filled with the scent of homemade meals and a hint of vanilla. The furniture, though showing signs of age, equally showed timeless charm.

"Please have a seat," she offered. I sat on the comfy sofa that was closest to me.

"Mrs. Lawrence, please, let me first apologize to you. I did not come here with any intention to upset you. But—"

She held up her hand to cut me off again. "Let me guess, Andre Perry, the millionaire, is not the perfect man you thought you married. How long have you been married to him?"

I was caught a little off guard with her statement followed by her question, so my words failed me. "Umm . . . almost seven years now." I nodded as if that would add proof to my calculation.

Mrs. Lawrence sucked in her lips deep and shook her head side to side. "Hmph, Jessica's only been dead eight of those years. See, it didn't take him long to move on with the rest of his life."

Eight years bounced around in my thoughts like a dribbling basketball. That was a surprise number for me to hear, because from what I understood and by my calculations, she should have said ten years.

"So, how'd you two meet?" she asked before I could complete my wandering thoughts. "Let me guess, you were an ordinary female, not rich like him and with no prestige. Those are the ones he goes after, or should I say, hunt for, you know."

Stunned by her accusation, I struggled to comprehend her implications. I considered how to respond, though nothing came to mind. "Well, I did have a college degree. The first time I met him we were at the gym." My answer was short, and it seemed pointless.

"Yeah, Jessica, she was educated as well, but ordinary. He dated her and groomed her to be his trophy wife. She had to check off all his boxes. While I can admit he did treat her okay, he cheated on her and I mean more than once. When she would find out, he always somehow convinced her that it was something between the two of them that caused him to go and cheat." She stopped, looked away, and gave a light, sarcastic chuckle. Then she looked straight at me. "Let me guess, he's cheated on you?"

The room that only a few minutes ago felt like an escape of comfort now bore a tangible discomfort. The lids of my eyes fell, and I could not control it. I found a safe spot to dump those emotions because I was here for a reason. My eyes fluttered open. "Yes," I finally said. "See, I had a couple of miscarriages. I suffered from that pain immensely and because of that became distant. And . . ."

The light chuckle that she released stalled. I knew there was no humor in the words I had just shared from the depths of my being.

"As I said, his excuse was it's your fault . . ." The realization of the point she'd made, made my stomach flip. "I tried to get Jessica to leave him. But she witnessed her father and I being married for all those years, so marriage was serious to her. And she loved Andre. Sometimes, I actually thought he loved her"—she paused as if in deep thought—"but Andre Perry was an entitled whorish man. And that mother of his, she never liked my daughter. She always thought Jessica wasn't good enough . . . beneath her precious son, and their social class. She took every moment she had with Jessica to make sure knew it. Here my daughter was beautiful, smart, educated, and respectful, with a huge heart. And that woman single-handedly sought to emotionally destroy her. And Andre never stood up for Jessica. He only made excuses for that overbearing bitch he called *Mother*.

"Well, one day I'd had enough. We were at their house for the Christmas holiday, and she was going on and on chastising Jessica, insulting her in front of their family and friends. Basically, my daughter was a nobody. I threw my wine at Vivian. To my dismay, it missed her, but I went after her like the White trailer trash she thought I was. I ripped her dress, nearly tearing it from her body before they could get me off of her. Bullying my child like that . . . but after all that, things got even worse. Something was bothering Jess. I tried but I just couldn't get her to tell me." Mrs. Lawrence stopped abruptly, sniffed back all the tears that had soaked her face.

"What do you think could have been bothering her? You think it could have been Andre with another woman?"

"I don't know. I just don't." She shook her head. "But really, why are you here? Why the questions about Jessica?"

"Some of the things you've said about Vivian . . . I've witnessed firsthand." I swallowed back the contempt in the words I hated to say, but as of late, it was a part of all conversations. "The infidelity with Andre." With that Mrs. Lawrence's head dropped as she shook it from side to side. She lifted it back toward me. "I found myself wondering about Jessica, who I knew as his first wife. You know . . . I can't find one picture of her in Andre's things."

Mrs. Lawrence grunted and stood up. "Follow me." She led me through another room, which I assumed was the den, then up some stairs we went. We stopped at the door on the right of the split hallway. She pushed the door open. "This is our daughter's room." I stepped inside and it was like time stood still. I could tell they hadn't changed anything since Jessica had graduated high school. The walls were lined with posters, all kinds of academic awards. "She was smart, huh!" I commented, amazed at all the awards she received from grade school all the way through.

"Yes, she was. She graduated as valedictorian of her high school class. At college she was magna cum laude. We were proud parents, her father and I." A smile covered her face as she remembered Jessica's graduation. She walked over to a desk drawer that was over by the bedroom window and pulled out Polaroid pictures. She handed them to me. In the first one she pointed at Jessica, and she was beautiful. She had long black hair, thick eyelashes, tall, light-skinned, with a big smile.

"She was beautiful," I commented as I looked through the pictures. I nearly gasped as I came upon the next picture. I was too dumbfounded to speak, but I had to ask. "Who is this with Jessica, they seem close?" Mrs. Lawrence had turned her attention from fussing with Jessica's curtain. She stepped over next to me.

"Oh, that was her best friend at the time."

"Welp, you can tell they had lots of fun together." I tried to keep my voice normal as I handed the pictures back to Mrs. Lawrence. It was time for me to leave. We headed back toward the living room. "Thank you so much for sharing your memories with me," I said just as we landed back in the living room.

Mrs. Lawrence stopped and gazed at me with the initial unease that lined her face when I'd first announced who I was. It was a look of skepticism, but that pain as she spoke of her daughter had already returned. "I almost had my daughter back. Whatever was going on with her had to do with Andre; she was going to leave him."

"How can you be sure?"

"She told me right here at my kitchen table. The next time she came by, she brought some personal items with her like her birth certificate, a will, passport, you name it, she had it. Even a few clothes and some jewelry. And what's more . . . she had spoken with a divorce attorney. Like I said, she was leaving him. But then . . . then she suddenly became ill. I mean, so ill doctors didn't know what was exactly wrong. Then she drowned while bathing . . . when he was not home." She spat that part out calmly. Every piece of venom that seeped out with it said loud and clear she didn't believe it. "I will never accept that my young, healthy daughter, who suddenly became ill, just drowned because she was too weak to save herself. Now I don't know what happened, but I don't buy that story for a second." She was firm, yet her face fulfilled with tears of despair. She sniffed. "I'm not sure why you are really here. But heed this word of advice while you still can, get out of that marriage."

I felt horrible for not telling Mrs. Lawerence the police were looking into Jessica's death. But I didn't want to upset her without knowing all the facts. I left that house feeling like a thousand bricks were on my back, and there was uneasiness in the pit of my stomach. I sat behind the wheel of my car. I couldn't shake off the feeling of anxiety that had settled over me like a dark cloud. The revelations about Jessica and Andre's past, coupled with the suspicion surrounding Jessica's death painted a grim picture that I couldn't ignore.

When I arrived home, I couldn't find solace in the familiar surroundings; every corner of the room seemed to hold a hidden truth waiting to be uncovered. I paced back and forth, trying to make sense of everything. Andre's lies, the affair with Erika Jones, Jessica's mysterious illness and death—it was all too much to process. I still had way more questions than answers. I wondered if the diary that had gone missing could shed light on any of my unanswered questions.

With the things I had just learned I needed some reassurance they were not as they seemed. Because listening to Mrs. Lawrence had shaken my confidence in my marriage, and beliefs. Who was my husband, really? Was he capable of murder? Was I in danger as Mrs. Lawrence had all but suggested? Andre had lied to me with a straight face about more than just the affair. The affair with Erika Jones was not just about me being distant. He had known Erika Jones all along, since according to the picture I'd seen, and Mrs. Lawrence's confirmation, Erika was Jessica's best friend. And according to that picture, which was clearly taken when they were still in high school, Erika Jones was also a liar. She had been careful not to mention that small detail. How deep was my husband's betrayal? And why had I ever believed a mistress?

Chapter 35

The sharp crack underneath my feet and the thickness of something below caused me to look down. There was nothing but a tree branch, and several others scattered over the road. Then my eyes followed the outstretched hand that was connected to my elbow giving me a slight tug. I froze at the sight of her. Was she really there?

"Come on, Brooke, we still have to walk up the road a little way." Jessica's voice was calm and sweet. I wanted to move, but my feet were frozen to the spot I stood on. I held my head up as I gazed around at all the tall trees that surrounded us. I had no idea where we were, but it appeared to be a secluded road out in the middle of nowhere. I used my free hand to shade my eyes as the sun beamed down directly on me.

"Come on, slow poke." Her cheeks stretched into a smile.

The sun suddenly felt like a burden weighing me

down. *"We can't, it is so hot."* I continued to shade
my eyes from the sunlight.

"Oh, come on, it will cool off. I promise." This
time her slight tug put my feet in motion. I gazed
down at a few other stray tree branches as I
followed her lead. Gradually, the sun faded, and it
turned to slight fog that quickly became thick. There
was a loud crack like a tree branch falling. I paused
and looked around, but Jessica only tugged again so
that we could keep going.

The fog was starting to devour us. I couldn't see,
but then a tiny light revealed Erika Jones, with a
bloody apron wrapped around her waist and streaks
of blood in her hair. She reached out for her hand.
"GIVE ME BACK MY BABY." She released a
hurtling cry that came from deep within and clawed
at my skin.

"But there is no baby." I shook my head. *"He . . .
he smothered it."* I lifted my finger toward Andre,
who now appeared wielding a knife.

My entire body rattled from fear as I tried to pull
on Jessica so that we could run. Then to my horror,
she disappeared. *"Jessica!"* I screamed as I turned
around and around in circles. *"Please, Jessica! Don't
leave me . . . please!"* I begged.

"Brooke, Brooke, Brooke." I heard someone calling my name from a distance. I felt my body jerk
and my eyes popped open. I had been dreaming all
along. My entire body shuddered at the memory of
my dream. I was home in bed alone but certain I'd
felt the presence of someone standing over me. Then
there was the sound of someone calling my name
and it felt so real. I quickly sat up and gazed at the
entire room. It was semi-dark except for a little light

*creeping in from my bathroom. An eerie feeling
swept over my entire body; I could feel my heart
pounding in my chest. I made a dash for my closet
and retrieved my Ruger pistol. Shaking and afraid, I
checked every room in my house, and nothing
turned up. I had to get it together; I was losing a
grip on reality.*

"Shit!" Once again, I was jolted awake. This time it was
my ringing cell phone. I had dozed off on my living room
couch after having a little scare. Detective Kruz was on the
line requesting I come down to the station. I sighed and
agreed.

"Well, have you asked him? Gotten him to confess
yet?" Detective Kruz paced the room with her hands in her
pantsuit pocket.

"Of course not. I still have not spent much time with
him. We had dinner the other night, but his mother was invited without my knowledge. She was in our faces the
whole time. And trust me, Vivian Perry would not allow
him to even discuss his pension, let alone his deceased
wife." My tone was sarcastic on purpose.

Detective Wize tapped his knuckles on the table. "Look
we've been patient . . . now it's time we wrap this up, Mrs.
Perry. We need . . . no, we *must have* a confession or we
need to have proof that Erika is still alive. If not, we have
to charge you with the murder of Erika Jones."

I was somewhat surprised with Detective Wize's ultima-
tum and attempt to put his foot down. He always played
the good cop. But today he was matching the same energy
as his partner. I'd had a long night of nightmares and was
simply fed up with the threats from them both about arresting me for shit that had nothing to do with me. "Look,

you can stop with the threats, okay. Now I've told you both, Erika Jones is alive. And I will produce her . . ."

Suddenly, I thought the table might crumble as Detective Wize's huge hand balled into a fist and slammed into it. I reflexively jumped. *"No, Brooke!"* His voice boomed throughout the room. "It's time you stop protecting that murderous bastard of a husband of yours. He took Jessica Lawrence's life away without a second thought, then he moved on with you. And now look, he has a mistress and a baby while being married to you. The man is vicious and calculating. If you don't stop protecting him, it may even be you that he murders next."

My emotions swirled inside of me. His words had been overwhelming and clawed at my mind. I wanted so desperately to reject his accusations. Then Jessica's mother's words started to haunt me. The sadness she conveyed over the loss of her only child. The trust that her daughter had given so freely to the man she loved. And that exact same man was my husband, Andre. Yet, in the end, Jessica had reached whatever she deemed had been her breaking point and was ready to risk it all and walk away. Was there something else going on other than infidelity? Was Detective Wize right? Anger, resentment, and uncertainty simmered at the surface. But something stubborn in me simmered with the same intensity.

"Regardless of what you both may think"—I addressed Kruz and Wize, making sure to give them both equal eye contact—"I've been over what you've said in my head a thousand times. I've weighed the what ifs. But as I've said to you, Andre is my husband, the man I stood before God and made vows to. Even still, I went and knocked on Mrs. Lawrence's door, Jessica's mom."

Their jaws dropped in surprise.

"While I was at Mrs. Lawerence's home, I somehow

resurrected her pain. And trust me when I say, I took no joy in that. She is a truly kind, honest, and loving individual. But I had to know who Jessica was. Because I kept hearing *she was sick, and she died* from Andre. Then here you all come to tell me *she was murdered by him.* No one has told me who the real Jessica was, nothing about her. But Mrs. Lawrence did. I even saw a picture of Jessica when she was alive. See, the ones you showed me of her dead body looked nothing like the real person. I found out she was beautiful inside and out. I actually learned she was a lot like me, educated, ordinary, and most of all devoted to Andre. Oh, and another all-time favorite, she was ridiculed by and never good enough for Andre's mother, Vivian. Just like me, she was also cheated on by Andre. Even still, she didn't allow none of that to keep her down. She was happy in her marriage and wanted nothing more than to be with the man she wed."

I paused as I remembered Mrs. Lawrence's final revelation to me. Detectives Kruz and Wize hung on my every word; it was like a vampire waiting for a taste of blood. They were so thirsty to know what I would reveal next about Andre.

"In the end something troubled her. She was planning to leave him, even took steps to do so. I also learned that Jessica has been dead only about eight years. I had been under the impression it was closer to ten. In short, I found out my husband lies to me about things. Things that I wouldn't think he needs to lie about. What's more, I found out Mrs. Lawrence agrees with you. She doesn't believe that her daughter drowned. And that, I don't take lightly. If Andre is guilty of murdering his wife, you get him, and see Erika alive and well at the same time. So . . ." I sighed. "What I'm saying is, I'm ready to hear Andre's truth. Just tell me how we are going to get this done," I laid out. I left out the part of Erika being Jessica's best friend on purpose.

MY HUSBAND'S MISTRESS IS DEAD / 225

Detective Kruz slapped both her hands together and acted like she'd just won the lottery. "Now this is some good information. And now we have the motive that we never had. We never knew that she was planning on leaving him." She licked her lips like she was about to bite off a piece of juicy pound cake. But some of this I thought they might have been abreast of, but it was clear they were in the dark about some things. All they wanted to do was nail Andre. Yes, he was a habitual adulterer but that did not make him a murderer.

"But didn't you ever talk with Mrs. or Mr. Lawrence after their daughter's death?" I asked them.

"We did . . . or at least you can say we tried, but she was always distraught. They kept her sedated for nearly two weeks. Afterwards her doctor was afraid she was on the verge of a nervous breakdown and was adamant we should let her rest. And, well, Mr. Lawrence was mute. Grief left him silent; we were told."

Just listening to Detective Wize brought back the emotions I felt the day I visited Mrs. Lawrence, and again my face was wet with tears.

"Mrs. Perry—" Detective Kruz started to talk, but I cut in.

"Please continue to call me Brooke."

She nodded. "Brooke, we are going to need you to wear a wire."

"A wire?" My voice screeched and it seemed like the air had been sucked out of the room. The words *a wire* echoed in my mind and sent a shiver down my spine. "Will it be attached to my body?" The thought of being wired up carrying hidden equipment seemed surreal.

"Yes, this is a for-sure way for us to get a word for word account of the confession out of him," Kruz said.

My eyes widened in disbelief and my breath caught in my throat as I listened. "Look, I'm uneasy about this, what if he suspects something?"

"You have to continue to gain his trust. You're his wife, he has no reason not to trust you. Right now, he's just focused on getting back together with you." Detective Wize tried to sound convincing.

"And if nothing else, remember this. Andre is rich, and the rich always think they can get what they want. You can probably get him to confess by convincing him you are on his side and will stand by him no matter what. Narcissism is sometimes the trap for such people." Kruz smirked at the thought of her theory being a fact that could be proven. I only felt apprehension about the whole idea.

"Aggh!" I grunted. "I'm really nervous about all this," I shared. A million questions flooded my mind. Could I even pull this off? I sighed and threw up both of my hands in a dramatic motion. "Oh, what the heck. I've been nervous a lot these days. Feeling like someone is following me, or I'm being watched. Hell, I even woke up in the middle of the night thinking someone was in my home standing over me while I slept." I left out the part of Vivian's missing diary. I still wasn't sure what that meant. Maybe I had moved it and forgot. I did have alot on my mind.

Detectives Kruz and Wize turned to each other, both perplexed about my statement. "Do you think Andre could be watching you?" Kruz quizzed, her eyebrow raised in suspicion.

"No . . . no," I said. "Andre wouldn't engage in such tactless things. What possible reason would he have to do that?"

"Okay, I guess." Kruz nodded. "We can put an officer on the streets to follow you around a few days, see if they find anything."

"That's not necessary," I replied, shaking my head. "Really, no one has a need to follow me. I just think all this talk of murder and conspiracy has made me paranoid." I glanced around the room and allowed things to sink in. I would be glad when this was all over. "Tell you what, let's take a few more days . . . only a few. Clear your head and we'll put the finishing touches to this," Detective Wize suggested. I couldn't believe that Wize had decided without consulting Kruz first. She almost always made the decisions on what the next moves would be. For a moment it appeared as though she might open her mouth to speak, but for the first time she remained quiet, and nodded in agreement. I left the office with a nauseating feeling of unease that might spill from my gut at any moment. I wasn't sure I would ever be able to betray Andre by not sharing with him my full intentions.

The drive home was quiet. My mind was a whirlwind of conflicting emotions. I wanted to believe in Andre, to trust that he was innocent, but the evidence seemed to stack against him more and more with each passing day. The image of Erika Jones with blood on her apron and the haunting cry for her baby echoed in my mind, reminding me of the darkness that lurked beneath the surface.

As I entered my house, the familiar surroundings offered little comfort. I couldn't shake off the feeling of being watched, of someone lurking in the shadows. I checked every room again, but everything appeared normal. It was just me, alone with my thoughts and fears.

Chapter 36

Two days had passed since I'd met with Detectives Kruz and Wize, and I was still no closer to accepting my duties than when I'd left their office. The only thing I was certain of was the sense of uselessness I felt at not being able to work. I craved the love I had for finance and the art of crunching the numbers for a business and forging miracles. I even missed the simple things about going to work, like the familiar hum of the office atmosphere. The hustle and bustle of everyone. Something I was guilty of taking for granted. Never in a million years had I thought I'd be uprooted from the place that brought me a fulfillment and sense of purpose that I could not describe.

Determined to revisit my workspace, I jumped in my Porsche and shot off like a bullet, headed for the interstate, into the downtown area. It was past rush hour, so I didn't have to put up as much of a fight to reach my destination. I pulled into a parking space in the parking garage and an instant feeling of nostalgia came over me. I hadn't been back since I was put on leave, and it seemed like ages ago. I sighed before opening the car door and stepping out.

MY HUSBAND'S MISTRESS IS DEAD / 229

I smiled at the thought of being back on my old stomping grounds where my career had started. Even though it was way past five and nearing eight o'clock at night, the garage was still full of people who were overachievers, just like me. Suddenly, there was a prickling sensation at the back of my neck, a gut feeling that I wasn't alone. I shut my eyes for a moment; again I was paranoid. I sighed and tried to shake it off. But there it was again. Fear kept me from looking over my shoulder, so instead I picked up the pace. My smile faded and the prickling sensation on my neck intensified. Panic set in full throttle as I could hear the footsteps that tried to match mine. I was not alone. I broke into a full run and so did whoever was behind me, the footsteps filling the quiet.

I frantically pushed the button on the elevator, it opened, and I jumped on and repeated the frantic pushing of buttons. The door closed just in time, as the footsteps sounded close. I leaned up against the wall as my body trembled from fear. I could hear my heart beating so hard I thought it might burst through my chest. The elevator delivered me to the lobby, where my eyes scanned the open area. Nothing seemed suspicious, I could see two of our armed security guards. I jumped on the elevator that would take me to my floor. The only way for anyone to get up there would be with a security clearance, so I tried to calm down.

Inside my office my tired body fell into my work chair. What had just happened? Had someone really just followed me? I hadn't noticed anyone pull in behind me when I entered the garage. What was really going on? Was someone out to hurt me? Who?

Taking a few deep breaths, I pulled out my cell phone. My hands were trembling so hard I thought I might drop it. "Detective Kruz, it's me, Brooke Perry," I blurted out. "I'm sure now, someone is following me." I realized my voice was now also shaky.

"Someone is after you? Are you sure?" Her tone was urgent.

"Yes, I'm sure!!" I yelled out of fear.

"Calm down, tell me what happened."

"Well, I am down at my office in the city. I get out of the car, I'm making my way inside the building, next thing I know, I'm being chased. And I do mean chased. Thankfully, I was able to get away."

"Did you get a chance to see who it was?"

"Hell no, I was scared to look back. I only focused on getting away."

"Okay, that is fine. Do you remember if anyone was following you in traffic when you were on your way there?"

"Ummm, no. But then I wasn't paying attention. It's like I told you all the other day. I thought I was being paranoid; I didn't believe anyone was really following me. I mean who would do that? And for what reason?"

"I can't say."

"Detective, do you really think whoever was chasing me is out to hurt me? Do you think they would have if they'd caught up with me?"

"Brooke, I would like to tell you no. But I can't. I just don't know. We have no idea who is following you. I do believe it has something to do with this case. We must end this. But for now, I'm going to assign a cop to follow you for a few days. For one, to keep you safe. And two, maybe they will see something that might help us figure out who's following you. Since, you are in the office now. I'm going to send someone over; they will text you when they are outside in the garage. Do not leave until then," she instructed. As nerve-racking as the situation was, she didn't need to tell me twice.

"Thanks, Detective Kruz. But please, can you have them be discreet?"

"Of course. The car will be unmarked."

She was right though; it was time we ended this. Enough was enough and I simply could not take it anymore. Something had to be done. "I'm ready for this to be done. And I think I know what to do. Now here it is . . ."

After hanging up with Detective Kruz I did a bunch of breathing exercises to get my heart rate back on track. I relaxed in the moment and was glad to be back in a place I absolutely enjoyed being. The sudden knock on my office door came as a surprise. Still reeling from my recent scare, I felt sick with nervousness. But the face I recognized on the other side of that door eased my fear.

"Mr. Hanks, hi. I didn't expect you to be here," I greeted him. I had been sure that by now he and Mr. Walter would be gone for the evening. They usually left the office around five, no later than six.

"Brooke, how many times must I tell you? You are one of us now, Norman will do." He smiled.

"Sorry, sir, old habits die hard." I grinned.

"I understand. I won't have you penalized this time," he joked. "I was about to leave when I noticed your light on."

"I know . . . and I know I'm not supposed to be here." I grunted lightly to clear my throat. "But I just missed the place. I had—"

He held up his hand to stop me. "There's no need to explain. Trust me, I get it. Brooke, I've always said you are too young to be so serious and driven. But Jack and I respect it so much we can only admire you." I nearly swallowed my tongue. Did he say they admire me?

"Admire . . . come on. You two are my idols. You've taught me everything I know and inspired me to reach for the unreachable because it is achievable," I summarized from my heart. I truly respected them and their hustle.

"Thank you. But yes, we admire you. And we have missed you in this place. What you bring to the table can't be taken for granted. Putting you on leave was hard, and not because you wouldn't be here to bring in clients or to make this company shine. But because we know the love and passion you have for what you do. That is why we reached a unanimous decision today along with the board members, to bring you back."

Tears instantly welled in my eyes. The sense of the suffering I'd endured, and happiness, all filled me at the same time. This, I had not expected when I'd decided to invade my office space for a few minutes of comfort. "I wasn't expecting this." I covered my mouth and sucked back tears. I opened my drawer and pulled out Kleenex to dab the wetness. "Thank you all so much, Mr. . . . Norman," I corrected with a laugh. "This means so much to me."

He nodded with a smile. "Like I said, I was shocked to see your light on. Jack and I were going to call you tomorrow for a short impromptu meeting to let you know that you can return whenever you are ready. Just pick the day."

"Oh, trust me, I will. I might need a little more time. I'm wrapping some things up. But don't worry, I'll be back as soon as these feet can carry me."

"Good. I'll inform Jack tomorrow. He'll hate that he missed you. Tell you what, let's do dinner sometime next week. Let Leah know when you are available, and she can put it on our calendar."

"Sounds like a plan to me," I agreed as a text came through. It was that cop Detective Kruz had told me about. He told me he was in the parking garage close to my car, so to come out when I was ready, no rush. Inwardly, I breathed a sigh of relief.

"Welp . . ." Norman exhaled and looked at his Rolex resting easy on his wrist. "It's late and I'm getting ready to head out. Are you parked in the garage?"

"Yes, I am."

"Okay, if you are ready to go, we can walk down together," he suggested.

"Sure, I think I'm ready to head out." I stood and glanced over my office one last time before we left. I couldn't wait to return for good. Norman and I made small talk on our way down. Getting on the elevator that would lead us out to the lobby, my heart started to pound lightly. Even though I knew a cop would be waiting to protect me at all costs, I couldn't shake the uneasy feeling.

As the elevator doors opened to head to the downstairs lobby, I couldn't control the feeling of unease. Was my life truly in danger, or was it just a series of paranoid thoughts fueled by recent events?

Norman noticed my anxiety and placed a reassuring hand on my shoulder. "Are you alright, Brooke?" he asked, concern evident in his voice.

"I'm just a little on edge," I admitted, trying to keep my composure. "It's been stressful times."

He nodded in understanding. "I get it. But remember, you're not alone. We're all here for you, and we'll make sure you get through this."

I managed a weak smile, grateful for his words of reassurance. We made our way through the lobby toward the exit, where the unmarked cop car was waiting. As we stepped outside, the cool night air offered a brief respite from the tension inside. I felt a sense of relief knowing the cop was close by.

Norman and I parted ways as we walked to our cars. As I drove away from the parking garage, I couldn't help but glance back, feeling a sting of nerves mixed with uncertainty. Would I ever feel completely safe again, or was this just the beginning of a new chapter filled with danger and mystery?

Despite my efforts, my mind kept drifting back to the chase in the parking garage, the mysterious footsteps, the feeling of being followed. It was all too surreal, like something out of a suspense novel.

As I approached my neighborhood, I couldn't get rid of the feeling that something was off. Every shadow felt like it held a hidden threat.

Once inside my home, I made sure to rearm the alarm right away. Since the diary incident I'd had my alarm system replaced and updated. My old one had been inoperable since I last lived in the home, and I'd never bothered to get it repaired. But the missing diary encouraged me to get that fixed right away. I checked it to be sure it confirmed all doors, windows, and locks were secured. I was mentally exhausted and ready to be rid of all this madness. I had no idea what my future held. Would we uncover the truth behind the mysterious follower? I just couldn't grasp the fact that someone was intentionally following me. *Who?* was the biggest burning question. For what cause? What else in life did I not know? If we didn't end this, who would it be the end of?

Chapter 37

At the ringing of the doorbell, I approached the door, with a hint of nervousness causing my heart to skip a beat. I smoothed down my mini cocktail dress, took a deep breath, and made my way to the door. I wanted to encourage Andre as much as I could. The dress fit every curve on my body, and it had every intention of speaking for itself.

"Hey there." Andre greeted me with delight, his eyes ate me up from head to toe. I had invited him over for dinner so I could, as Detective Kruz advised, gain his trust and play nice. And of course, woo him with the personal agenda in mind. Judging from the intense hunger all over his face I was already on the right track. I waved him inside and he never removed his eyes from me. "You look absolutely incredible, Brooke."

With a smile I put on the charm. "You look damn good yourself." And that was no lie. Andre was always easy on the eyes, his masculinity undeniable. I gave him a seductive wink as he moved into my space and kissed me passionately. I had to step away as usual because I knew what was on his mind. I gave a light chuckle and a knowing smirk, then led the way to the dining room. I wanted to get dinner started immediately. It was crucial that I kept everything on cue; this way I kept up the courage to go through with what I had planned.

After a delicious meal we headed back to the den, where I poured us each a glass of champagne. We sat down in front of the television, relaxed, and enjoyed the calm atmosphere. "Dinner was wonderful. It's been a long time since you cooked," he said. I could hear the appreciation in his voice.

"I know. I thought about having it catered but decided to pull out my own recipes. I'm glad you enjoyed it," I replied warmly.

He nodded in agreement. "I did enjoy it." He sipped his champagne and so did I. He set his champagne glass down, his expression turned serious. "Listen, a while back you asked me for space . . . you made it clear to me that it was something important to you. As hard as that was for me, I relented and respected your wishes. Because at that time I believed I owed you that much. And don't get me wrong, I still believe that. But now I want you to come home . . . it's time. All these things . . . that were in the past have blown over." Before I could respond, he had gotten down on his knee. My heart raced, and so did my mind as I tried to understand why he was down there.

"Brooke Perry, I know we have been through a lot recently, our relationship tested, but being married to you is a gift. I simply can't imagine my life without you by my side. Will you marry me again?" With every word that came from his mouth there was a depth of his emotions present in his eyes.

My heart once again skipped a beat, and my pulse quickened, as a mixture of emotions took over me. Then the guilt hit me like a ton of bricks, as the questions flowed through my mind. What was I doing? This just couldn't be

MY HUSBAND'S MISTRESS IS DEAD / 237

the man who was being accused of murder. Tears welled up in my eyes as I cried "Yes," my voice trembling. I had a feeling of fear and hope vibrating through me.

A smile covered Andre's face. He stood up and pulled me into his arms. "We will renew our vows in front of our friends and family," he said. We then shared a passionate kiss. It was a moment of bliss I hoped I never forgot.

But suddenly Mrs. Lawrence's face flashed through my mind like a Polaroid. And her words followed: *He's not who you thought he was, is he?* The words seemed to echo as if I was in a tunnel. Then an uneasy feeling stabbed me in the chest as I remembered the picture of Erika Jones standing next to Jessica. And Mrs. Lawrence confirming they had been best friends. The grip I had around his neck loosened. I needed to get back to the agenda at hand. Marriage sounded good but there were some things I had to be sure of first. Questions that were gnawing at me had to be answered. Manipulation was in full play as I offered to refill his champagne glass. Before committing to anything I would unravel any truth that was hidden beneath the surface, surely vindicating my husband.

"Andre, this year we have been through a lot, and as you said we've been tested in ways I could have never thought we'd be. But we are weathering this storm, and look, we are stronger because of it." I gave a light smile. "And there is no doubt we will be together." This time I leaned forward and planted my lips on him for good measure.

"Yes, we are, and I promise I will never let no one or anything come in between us again. Because I love you more than life, Brooke Perry." He kissed me again. He had no idea what I had brewing. I had only warmed him up for the kill. But I wasn't out to get him, but I had to get Wize and Kruz off of us.

"In that case there can't be any lies between us. None

from you and none from me." The gloat that was on his face shifted to concern.

Andre's eyes widened, as they searched mine for unsaid answers. "What lie are you keeping from me, Brooke . . . is there another man?" His tone was filled with urgency and his face etched in fear of what I might reveal.

"What!" I screeched, caught off guard. The question pierced through me like a knife in my heart. Shock reverberated through me, sending a jolt of adrenaline rushing through my veins. How could he ask me something like that? "No . . . no, there is no other man."

His face seemed to regain the color that had drained from it.

I decided to continue. I was about to drop the bombshell. "There is this one thing Erika revealed to me that I kept from you. And believe me, I had my reasons. For one, I did not want it to be true. Two, it intentionally hurt more than the infidelity, so I thought out of sight, out of mind . . ." I paused. "Erika told me about the child. The one you two conceived together . . . the one you never mentioned to me."

To my own surprise Andre's expression remained unchanged. But I knew better. "The baby, Andre, I know about the baby you had with her."

He took a step backwards. "What baby?" He had the nerve to maintain his facade of ignorance but there was a shift in his features. His expression remained stoic and there was a flicker of unease that danced in his eyes. For a brief second, I was sure I could see the turmoil that was raging inside of him. His jaw clenched tight as he tried to keep his composure intact. "Listen, I don't know what that woman told you, but I didn't have a baby with her. She's lying to you." This time he chuckled and kept a straight face.

I felt the surge of nausea come over me like a tidal wave

My Husband's Mistress is Dead / 239

with the ease of Andre's lie. He didn't even blink as he told that lie and denied his child.

"Brooke, I'm so sorry for what that lunatic put you through . . . put us through. Her lies have destroyed—"

I held up my hand to cut him off, I couldn't stomach another word of his bald-faced lies. The bitter taste of his betrayal was starting to overwhelm me. How could he stand in my face and lie to me with so much conviction? "Andre, please stop with the deep-rooted lies, okay. I know about the baby, that it is real and alive. Erika is not lying. In fact, Erika even knows where you hid the child."

That hit the jackpot of where Andre lived in that fleeting moment. His facial expression shifted from shock to alarm, to a grimace. "Where I hid her?"

"Yes, she knows. See, Andre, Erika never believed her baby to be dead. She knew you had lied again. She said at first it was a feeling that she couldn't shake. Then she set out to prove it." I lied about that part. I would not tell him yet what my role was. "See, that is why she came to see me. She didn't come to see me because she wanted to tell me about the affair. She came because she wanted her child back. And she wanted my help."

"Okay . . . okay, there is a child," he finally admitted with a dumb look on his face that annoyed me. "What is it she thought you could do to help?"

"I don't know." I continued to lie with the same straight face he had used to lie to me.

"Brooke, listen, I couldn't tell you about the baby. I did it to protect us. You are everything to me."

"I know that. And I understand." It was time I played the understanding wife. "I wish you had told me though. What's more, I wish you had told me about the relationship you had with your sister. Sweetheart, I would have welcomed her even if Vivian won't."

"I'm so sorry, baby. Please try and forgive me," he begged with puppy eyes as he came closer.

"I do forgive you." He pulled me into his embrace, and I folded because I had more. "Andre, I would like for you to bring the baby here."

"Here?" he repeated.

"Yes, home with us. We will raise her together. I will love her as if she is my own."

Andre sighed and I could see the apprehension all over him. "I can't do that. I can't."

"Why not?" I instantly cried. "She is yours. I thought you loved me, Andre. Please, bring her home and we will raise her, so we can live as a family."

"I'm sorry, Brooke, baby, but I just can't do that. It's really not that simple. Look, Kara has had her since day one, she loves her too. And I promised her she could keep her. She will be hurt. She's been so hurt by my family already."

"Your sister will be hurt, what about me? Huh, Andre? I can't have any children, and you know that. Two miscarriages . . . two precious babies lost to us. I have hurt until I wanted to die. That pain is still buried deep inside of me. You of all people know what being a mother means to me." With no more words of compassion to push him to ruling in my favor, I dropped to my knees and cried. And as I expected, he dropped to his knees to catch me.

"Oh, Brooke, baby don't cry . . . I'll do it. I will bring our baby girl home."

I threw my arms around him and hugged him tight. Andre stood up and assisted me back to my feet. "Now will you please move back in the house?"

"Yes, I will move back in, but not just yet. Maybe you can move in here with me for now. For the past few months, I've enjoyed being here, living simple. Please bring our daughter home here. I can hardly wait to meet her.

Oh, I need to go shopping." I jumped excitedly and started pacing. "When can you bring her? Can you bring her tomorrow? I just can't wait." I clasped my hands together with excitement.

Andre grabbed me. "Brooke, calm down." He laughed. "I can't bring her tomorrow. I'm totally booked at the office. But in two days she will be home here with us. Tonight is all about us." He pulled me to him. And for the first time ever I almost cringed at the thought of being with Andre. I was no longer sure of anything when it came to my dear husband. But I had to seal the deal of the plan. Andre had to believe that we were a go.

Chapter 38

"I tell you—you go and fall in love and just forget all about your best friend." I was on the phone with Reese, pouting. As I glanced over my shoulder as I made my way inside Neiman Marcus, I didn't see anything suspicious. I felt comfortable knowing that one of the cops who had been assigned to protect me was close by, watching. A week had flown by since the incident in the garage and I was finally getting to the point where I wasn't so jumpy. I had decided not to tell Reese about the incident because I didn't want her to worry. So, I tried to keep up my usual jolly to keep her suspicion at bay.

"Brooke, don't say that I have forgotten about you, friend. I've been so busy at the hospital. I was on call again for the past week. I actually have good news. As you know, my residency is coming to a close . . . they offered me a position here." I could hear the tremble of excitement in her voice.

I covered my mouth with astonishment. "Oh my God, Reese, I've been so wrapped up in my own crap I forgot all about your residency coming to an end. Oh, best friend, I am so proud of you, congratulations." Tears welled up in my eyes, I was so elated. I had watched Reese work hard and sacrifice so often to finish medical school, internship, and then residency. In the beginning there had been so many times she wanted to quit. But I had encouraged her until she believed she could do it. And she had. "My best friend is a whole doctor out here. WHAT!" I sang with excitement.

I could hear Reese sniff on the other end. I could tell she was crying tears of joy. "I know, I can't believe it either."

"Well, Ms. MD, I have a surprise for you," I said, my tone mischievous. I was almost unable to control myself.

"What is it? Come on before I burst from curiosity." Reese was intrigued.

"Well, for one, we are going to party for like a month straight. We are going to turn up until we drop."

"Aye. And you know I'm down for that."

"You better be, because I'm taking you to Saint-Tropez for two weeks," I revealed, full of excitement.

"*Aggh!*" Reese screamed through the phone. "Are you serious? No fucking way, Brooke!" She was clearly unable to contain her excitement, and I was equally happy.

"Yes way! Complete with a yacht and all. So put the hospital on notice when you accept that position," I added.

"I sure will. Brooke, you are simply incredible. Two weeks in paradise, this has got to be the best gift ever. Can I invite Anothony?"

"Oh damn, this girl is too in love?" I teased as I laughed out loud. This was definitely a first and new Reese. And I for one was giddy for my friend. I loved seeing her in love. "Of course he can come. He can be our bodyguard in a strange land."

"Hmmm, that does sound like a good idea, he is strong.

Oh, I have an idea . . . how about I ask Anthony to invite Terrell? Did you know that every time we're all hanging out, he always asks about you? Every time." She giggled.

I stopped in my tracks. That was a cause for a pause. The mere mention of Terrell was a surprise. The fact Reese shared that he had asked about me on more than one occasion was flattering, but that was quickly replaced with concern. "Why would he do that? I told him I was married. I said exactly that."

"Welp, clearly he could see you were unhappy. A good man knows."

"Hmmph," I grunted. "Too bad I didn't. I thought I was the picture of happy." I used sarcasm to cheer myself up.

Reese sighed, then laughed. "You are something else, the things you say. But, on another note, you're out shopping for baby furniture. You know the baby is not going to stay permanently?"

"Yep, I know. I thought all that through but concluded, what the hell. Besides, it keeps Andre under the impression she is. He might wonder why I haven't prepared." I exhaled with a hunch of my shoulders as if Reese was in front of me. "Also, it's not like I have anything else pressing to do. I'm going into Neiman Marcus to grab the baby a gold bracelet with her birthstone. You see, I figured that with a rolling-stone father like Andre, and with a no-loyalty heathen like Erika for a mother, she'll need something that's really her own when she grows up. What better than something that represents her true identity."

"I guess now that you put it that way, I see your point. But I still can't believe that bitch was Jessica's best friend."

The thought of Erika being Jessica's best friend still turned my stomach too. "Please don't mention that tragic truth, I need to get through this ordeal without thinking about it. Every time I think about it, I want to confront

MY HUSBAND'S MISTRESS IS DEAD / 245

her about the betrayal she bestowed on her friend. I mean, how disloyal can a person be?"

"Do you think Jessica knew something was up with them and just kept quiet about it? Do you think it started before she died, or after?"

Those questions really burned in my mind. I had thought about them over and over. They were questions that truly deserved an honest answer. But how might I get them? Andre, I was sure, wouldn't be an open book about such an embarrassing truth. He'd denied his own child until he no longer could. I had to show him the picture from Mrs. Lawrence's house to prove I knew; Jessica and Erika had been best friends. Even then, he'd probably deny knowing it. But the one thing I was sure of was Mrs. Lawrence didn't know about Andre and Erika's affair, because had she known she'd have mentioned it. "I just don't know. For Jessica's sake I hope she never knew. I know she knew of his infidelity but hopefully not with whom. If, they had the decency . . . well, if you can find any decency in what they have done. Hopefully, they waited until she was deceased," I finally said. "But nevertheless, there are good things ahead. Saint-Tropez, here we come." I changed the subject.

"Awww! I can't wait!" Reese cheered from the other end.

"But listen, I got to go talk to the jeweler here." I ended the call as I admired some of the cutest baby chains ever. There were so many to choose from.

"Wooo?" I gasped. I abruptly took a step back to avoid the collision of nearly bumping into a familiar face. My eyes widened in surprise. "Sorry about that," I apologized.

"It's fine." He let out a gentle chuckle.

"Terrell, right?" I queried. I couldn't believe it had only been a few hours ago that Reese had been teasing me about him. And here he was in the flesh. After shopping at Neiman Marcus, I was in the mood for a drink and quick bite to eat so stopped at a nice bistro that was close by. My timing was good.

He grinned. "Yep, that would be me. How are you, Brooke?" My name sounded like silk coming out of his mouth. He wanted me to know that he remembered me. I fought back the flattery.

I kept my composure and replied with a casual tone, "Oh, I'm fine, kind of had a long day out shopping, thought I'd stop in for a nice margarita before going home. How about you?"

"Ah." He exhaled, and I could hear the exhaustion in his tone. "It's been a long stretch. I've been at the hospital since about two o'clock this morning, and it's now eight o'clock at night." I could hear the weariness in his voice but there was a stronger sense of commitment and responsibility, showing that he took his job seriously. "So, in light of that, I thought I'd have a drink, and some hot food not prepared in the hospital cafeteria. Care to join me?"

"Sounds like school lunch." We looked at each other and laughed. "Trust me, I understand."

I paused for a moment as I considered his unexpected offer. I felt a mixture of curiosity and caution moving through me and I was tempted to decline. But then there was this sense of intrigue to enjoy something I had not for a while: the possibility of pleasant conversation. I softened my resolve, as I said, "Yes."

We sat down and ordered drinks and food. "So how have things been at work? I know you had the promotion and all."

"Well"—I sipped the Long Island iced tea I had ordered before speaking on my cracked-up life at the moment—"I kind of have some personal things going in my life right now . . . and I've been off work for a while. But on a good note, I do plan to return soon. And I can't wait." I gave a light smile. Just thinking about my job at Walter & Hanks saddened me in ways I could not describe. My career was a huge part of my life; next to God and my marriage, nothing else was more important. "So, how is working going for you?"

"Oh, busy, busy. The last few weeks I've been on twenty-four-hour days, but I should be getting a break soon. But I can't lie. I love it." He was not lying, the truth was shining in his eyes.

I laughed. "You know the nature of the beast is to eat your passion. But twenty-four-hour days. Welp at least you're single . . ." I paused. I could have kicked myself. Why would I say that as if I knew how his life had changed. "Wait, please excuse me, my bad, here I am pretending to know your relationship status."

He held his head back and let out a deep chuckle. I wanted to duck, I felt so ashamed. He must have sensed it. "No . . . no, it's okay. You were right, yes, I'm single . . . and . . ." He shrugged, wearing a smile. "I guess it does ease things . . . But that is not why I'm single." He gazed at me with a sense of attraction and interest.

"Oh." I snatched my eyes away from his. They were so big and deep.

"Does marriage dictate one's career? I know you're married," he added.

"Hmm. Not really, or I guess it depends. When I was marri—" I paused. What was I saying? "I mean, marriage hasn't dictated mine," I corrected. "My husband and I are both career driven, so it worked out."

"Excuse me if I'm being too forward or overstepping. But twice you have referred to your marriage in the past tense. Are you still married?"

248 / *Saundra*

Again, he gave me a reason to pause. I could have easily said yes, of course I was still married. But I was in no mood to pretend. It was just not who I was. "I'm married, yes."

"Ah, I see." He nodded slowly.

"But . . . there's there's been a few unforeseen circumstances that have weighed heavily on my marriage." A sense of surprise washed over me as I realized I was opening up to him about personal aspects of my life. I couldn't explain it, but there was something about him that put me at ease. I had never considered discussing my marital situation with someone I barely knew.

"Listen, I apologize for asking, and I'm truly sorry for what you're going through, Brooke." His facial expression was covered with genuine concern.

"There is no need for either. Anyway, this Long Island iced tea is clearing up a lot. I really would like another." I giggled.

He smiled. "I think we can handle that." He gestured to the waitress at the nearby table.

Chapter 39

The day I had dreaded for more than a month had finally arrived. The sting was in place and there would be no turning back. Detectives Kruz and Wize and a few other detectives were close by, where they would be listening to the entire conversation I would have with Andre. I was so thankful they had come up with a new way to use a wiretap other than hiding it on my body. Instead, there were wiretaps throughout the entire front portion of my house, from the front door to my living room, den, kitchen, and hallway. I had even had them put one in the baby's room. Any room that we might possibly visit was wired, except for the other bedrooms and bathroom. So it was critical that I kept to those rooms throughout our conversation. But the plan was to keep him in the den exclusively, and the other areas were just a backup. I was so fidgety I could barely keep still as I paced, waiting for Andre to show up. I was racked with anxiety, but determined as well to get this over and done with.

This moment was crucial and the responsibility that weighed on my shoulders was relentless. I had rehearsed my lines on how I would try to carry the conversation carefully, with the hope everything went as planned. Erika was tucked away in one of my guest bedrooms. The plan was, once, and if, Andre confessed to the crime the detectives were so sure he committed, the cops would move in to arrest him, I'd hand the baby off to Erika and be rid of her for good.

My heart skipped a beat at the ring of the doorbell; adrenaline surged through my entire body. "We are here." Andre smiled at me as soon as I opened the door. He was holding the cutest little girl I thought I'd ever seen. With a head full of curly hair, big, deep, glossy eyes, and the most adorable cheeks, she was lovable. My heart melted.

"Oh, Andre, she is beautiful. Hi, London." I spoke to her gently from my heart. "Can I hold you, London?" My arms were outstretched and immediately she came. I gave her a gentle hug.

"Oh, wow," Andre said. "First, I can't believe she let you hold her. And second, a squeeze. She must like you."

"Of course she does," I cooed at her, heading toward the den, leaving Andre to shut the door behind him. "You are just the cutest baby ever, little London. I'm Brooke—can you say Brookie?" I sounded it out and she just gave a slight grin then yawned. "Wait, are you tired, sweetheart?"

"Yep, she is. It's actually time to put her down. She fought it all the way here, but she likes to watch the clouds and trees go by when she's riding in the car. So . . . she stuck it out." Before he could finish, London had laid her head on my shoulder and was out.

"Welp, I got her room all set up. Let's go put her down," I suggested. Andre followed me with the diaper bag he had on his shoulder. I laid her down in the crib I had set up. I walked up and picked up the wireless baby monitor we could use to listen while she slept. "Come on," I whispered to him. "See, it has the camera and all."

"I see you are fully prepared, Mrs. New Mom." He smiled as we headed back toward the den. I set the monitor down nearby. I turned around and Andre was on my heels. I beamed.

"I love to see that smile on your face. And I plan to keep it there," Andre said, as he pulled me into his arms and kissed me. I had to pretend to welcome this because I had to keep the flow steady.

"You better," I said. "How about we have a toast to you bringing London home. I have some wine chilling."

"Sounds good," he agreed. That was my way of breaking free of his embrace so I could start my quest. I returned with two glasses and the wine, and I poured.

"Now, to our baby girl, this marriage, and happiness." I held up my glass.

"Here, here," he added, and our glasses clicked together.

"Andre, I can't tell you how happy I am to have London here. You doing this means the entire world to me. Thank you for sharing her with me. I will be forever grateful, and I promise to love her as if she were my own."

"I know you will, Brooke. Everything about you is good."

"Thanks." I smiled, then sipped my wine. "You know, I've been thinking a lot about Jessica Lawrence . . . your first wife." He gazed at me but said nothing. "Since the cops brought her up, I don't know, I've just considered who she was, to you. I know you loved her."

"I did," he added.

"You know we talked about us being totally honest with each other. No matter what. I know you to be a good man. And I know that you would never do anything to intentionally, or for any reason, cause anyone harm. I know you said Jessica was sick. The cops think it's something else. But I was thinking she could have been sick and not in control of her balance? She could have slipped in the water if she was not feeling well? With little or no energy and no help? But also, when people are sick, according to Reese, they can be like dead weight and need more than one person to help lift them. One person could use all their own strength trying to lift someone, especially in slippery water. Or they could have entered the room just as Jessica was about to slip and didn't have time to catch her." I tried to present a few scenarios to help him see that he might have been guilty even though it had been an accident. Andre just listened, but he said nothing. He finished his wine then reached for the bottle and poured another glass.

I continued. "Those cops, they just want to twist things around so that we turn against each other. But you and I are a team. I hope I have proved that on my part. Your infidelity hurt me to the core, as I've said, and finding out about the baby initially hurt me double. But in the end, none of that mattered. I'm here and I've stuck by you. And I plan to never leave your side. But as I said before, there can't be any lies between us."

The silence was so loud I could hear it ringing in both my ears, and Andre still had not budged and uttered a single word. He was nearly done with his second glass of wine. I had to increase my manipulation or end this conversation before he got suspicious.

"Remember when I told you I had no lies except keeping from you that Erika had told me about the baby." I dropped my head for a second to appear ashamed of what I was about to confess. But I was desperate and felt I had no other card to play. "I murdered Erika Jones. I . . . I'm responsible for the fire that took her life." And there was

MY HUSBAND'S MISTRESS IS DEAD / 253

my reaction. Andre's curiosity seemed to stand at attention as I saw a thousand questions glisten through his eyes.

"You what?" he mouthed. For a moment I thought I saw a hint of fear in his eyes, of what I might reveal.

"Please, don't be angry with me. But I hated that bitch! I hated her arrogance. She gloated when she spoke about her plan to take you away from me!" I screamed and managed to produce spit balls that flew out of my mouth on cue to prove the intensity of my anger. "And that I refused to tolerate," I said through my clenched teeth.

There was a look of flattery that captured his face as he listened to my revelation of what I did to keep him. There was a sense of resignation and acceptance of a cold-blooded murder. He was proud as he placed his wineglass down. "Damn, baby, I never knew you had it in you . . . and you are right, listen, when it comes to Jes . . ."

Chapter 40

I had taken a deep breath as my insides quivered with curiosity and anxiety, when Andre opened his mouth to disclose what I was sure had happened to Jessica. I froze as an image emerged from the darkness like a ghost materializing from thin air in my very own home. My mouth fell slightly open, and my words got caught in my throat as I struggled to comprehend what was going on. I blinked to be sure I wasn't seeing things, but the flesh was clear.

"Vivian," fell from my tongue. I had so many questions, but I started with the obvious one. "How did you get into my house?"

With her tall posture, exuding confidence and bearing her usual arrogance, she smirked. "Dear, a key of course. I've always had one." Her tone was unapologetic, as if she dared me.

"Mother, please, be nice," Andre said. I looked at him like he was as crazy as his mom.

"Be nice. Is that all you have to say to her? Why is she here, Andre? In my home, the one I own. Who barges into someone else's home unannounced? I didn't invite you." I scowled at her. "Andre, did you?" I stared him down with malice.

"Who, me? No, I had no idea she was coming. I'm just as surprised as you. But after all, this is Mother."

Vivian made a sucking noise with her teeth. "Oh, you two." She taunted us with a smirk. "There is never much I don't know. And Brooke, dear, there is never anywhere I'm not invited. You'd do well to remember that." Her tone in that moment reflected the power she held. Her gaze pierced me. I was too appalled to respond.

"Now let's get to the situation at hand." Her tone took on a more sinister edge. This was different to what I'd heard from her before. "Brooke, my dear, all the questions about Jessica. You must know what happened to her, eh." My eyes widened in disbelief at this person standing in front of me; my heart pounded in my chest.

"She's dead and I, your dear mother-in-law, killed her. No one else, only me." Her words were blunt and voice free of guilt or remorse as she took all the blame. A wave of shock and horror washed over me as I struggled to process what she had just confessed and the boldness with which she had done it. A chilling shiver went up my spine as I watched the gleam and sense of satisfaction in Vivian's eyes.

"Mother, why do that? Huh? Why can't you just keep your mouth shut? Go on, get out. Can't you see my wife and I are trying to work on our marriage? Go on, leave, now." Andre uncharacteristically spoke to her in a harsh tone. I'd never heard him take that approach with his mother.

The smirk on Vivian's face turned icy as she glared at me, through me. "I knew it . . . I always knew this manip-ulative ward of the state was up to something," she spat out. "I told you from day one not to trust her. That she came from nothing, so she would not understand anything that has to do with family values!" she shouted. "I mean, boy . . . are you so blind, can't you see it?" She gazed at Andre for only a second before she turned back on me. "This bitch is just like the first one. Are you really stupid enough to believe she wants to raise another slut's child?" Her words were full of venom as she threw daggers and continued to bash me.

I could suddenly feel Andre's eyes on me. Unsure, I looked at him and to my surprise there was a look of confusion and apprehension on his face that rendered me momentarily speechless. His expression changed to one that I wasn't familiar with as his eyes darted between Vivian and me. I could see his mother's words were working, casting a shadow of doubt over my intentions. His eyes now glared at me with scrutiny and my nervousness intensified as the air in the room grew thick.

"Mother, should we get rid of her too . . . kill Brooke?" Andre then burst out into odd, gut-wrenching laughter. I stopped breathing as the room fell into a chilling silence. He turned to me, the emotions on his face conflicted, like a scared little boy.

"Brooke, I told Mother not to kill Jessica. If she'd given me time, I would have done it myself. But you know Mother, if she hasn't taught you anything else about her. She's shown you that she has no patience for that which she will not tolerate. And well . . . that bitch of a wife Jessica just wouldn't stop with the threats. See, she wasn't trusting like you. Nope, that one, she was always snooping around, and she found out that Dad had left my sister Kara seventy-five percent of the company."

I gasped as it hit me like a ton of bricks, and it was all suddenly clear. This was the motivation behind Jessica's death. She had known something that had cost her life.

"Can you believe that bastard only left me twenty-five

percent? Boasting some bullshit about what he owed her because he'd never done right by her. Even worse, he had the nerve to say I was incompetent. Me. Can you believe that shit? See, he never understood me. It wasn't my fault that I was born into wealth . . . into privilege. Yet he scrutinized me and then resented me for not being like some page boy." I could see the pain behind his eyes as he delved into deep-seated turmoil with the relationship with his dad.

"Yeah, he thought leaving me millions would suffice for cutting me out of what was my birthright. I was his one and only son, his heir. The same as he had been with his father. But no, he proceeded to write me off with the stroke of a pen. Because he felt it was his right to do so. But no, that never would have happened. It just couldn't be allowed. As you can see, it all turned out fine. What Kara never knew hasn't hurt her. I take great care of my sister. There isn't anything she wants that I wouldn't give her. But Elk Perry's Brokerage will always be mine. And that fake will Mother created says so."

In that moment of clarity, I found my voice. "And your father . . . the heart attack? That was a lie? Or is there truth to it?" My tone was hesitant, and a sense of dread hung in the air. My eyes searched Andre's face for a sense of denial.

He nodded his head yes. "Yeah, that heart attack part was a cover-up," he said it flatly. His voice carried no emotional attachment. "That was a project between Mother and I. We were his legal caretakers at the time. It was arsenic that did the trick. You know that stuff doctors refuse to look for in death." I was disgusted at his almost robotic type of demeanor. A wave of sickness and sadness washed over me as I realized the extent of deceit and greed that had torn this family—a father, son, and wife—apart.

"I just . . . I can't believe what I'm hearing." My voice

quivered as my eyes darted between Andre and Vivian. "The heinous acts you two committed are a story of horror . . ."

"See, Brooke, you should have listened to me. I told you that this man who you thought was dipped in honor and his beast of a mother were monsters." Erika's sudden presence sent a shockwave through the atmosphere, her tone was vindicative. If looks could kill, Andre and Vivian would have dropped dead on the spot. Their eyes grew wide as saucers, as they shot uneasy glances at one another.

"Did you see this shit!" Erika tossed something that I immediately recognized as familiar. Vivian's diary that was missing from my room.

Stunned, I mouthed, "How'd you get this? Have you also been in my house uninvited?" I caught the book as it almost tumbled from my unsteady hands.

Vivian's voice cut in. "And just why would that be in your house? It belongs to me. You've been taking things that are not yours. I believe the law calls it stealing."

"No . . . actually I found it while packing up the attic. A job you recruited me to do." I didn't really know what else to say so I winged it. "I had plans to return it."

"HAAA!" A chilling laugh rose from Erika and spread through the air like a snippet from *A Nightmare on Elm Street*. "Fuck all the explaining, did you read it? Or should I just share? You know—what you wrote about in secret— or will you?" Erika chuckled.

"This gutter rat is crazy. Andre, son, you sure know how to pick the loonies, I tell you." Vivian squinted her eyes at Erika as if she were a piece of shit that was not worthy of her time.

"No, actually, Vivian, I'm Saint Christopher compared to you. You, lady, belong at the top of the pile on *Cold Case Files*, with a pair of handcuffs on your wrists at the end of the show. Brooke, did you know that Andre had a dear old aunt? Your father's sister. Well, she was named in his will too. So, Mrs. Vivian here, along with her beloved son, murdered her and buried her—before they killed Mr. Perry Sr., of course. You know, follow the line of succession to be sure and snip out any threat."

Bile rose and tore through the pit of my stomach up through my esophagus and threatened to spill over. I gagged from the burning feeling as I covered my mouth and tried to breathe in deep to fight it back down. I couldn't take any more of Vivian's and Andre's *how to get away with murder* classes. My eyes landed on Andre, whose mouth was still wide-open, staring at Erika like he had seen a ghost. He was stunned by her presence. I doubted he'd heard anything she'd just revealed, nor did he care. Her mere presence was all that concerned him.

"What are you doing here? Do the dead really come alive? Because I thought you were six feet under in ash and bone. Didn't you die in the fire, you evil bitch?" His voice was sharp, almost accusatory. His hands were clenched into fists at his sides. "I thought I was finally rid of you." The room fell silent with only the echoes of Andre's angry words.

"Just consider me back from the dead, you arrogant asshole, and I'm not going anywhere without my child," Erika said.

Andre laughed out loud as he took a step forward, approaching Erika. "Bitch, you really are crazy. Just because you helped deliver my baby does not mean you can have her."

My right hand went straight to my forehead. I felt light-headed, I wasn't sure about what I had just heard. "Wait a minute . . . helped deliver the baby . . . Erika is the child's mother." I stuttered over my words, my voice full of uncertainty. I had no idea what was true or false at this point.

Andre laughed out loud again, which only heightened my sense of confusion. "This is not Erika Jones. Erika died in childbirth. This is Tammy." My head snapped around so hard on my shoulders I thought I heard it crack. What I really heard was a gun that was pointed at all of us—cocked, held in the hands of Erika or Tammy, whatever her name was.

"Give me my fucking baby. NOW!" she yelled. "Or I'm going to light your ass up with bullets. And for the record, I'm not crazy. Your mother alone fits that category." She chuckled. Vivian said nothing.

"What is really going on here?" I asked. "Andre, if Erika died in childbirth why didn't you say something to me when I first came to you with this whole Erika Jones thing? Why didn't you shut this down a long time ago? You could have done something. Yet you allowed me to believe this Jones impersonator was who she pretended to be."

Erika aka Tammy shook her head and sighed with frustration. "You are too smart to be this dumb, wifey. Why do you think he didn't tell you? See, Brooke, Andre always thinks he's so smart. And in this case, he might be. The same way he never told you about the child until you brought her to him. He thought it would be better than admit that he had a whole other mistress. That's how I knew that he wouldn't tell you who I was when I decided to be Erika Jones."

"Brooke, if you believe this, then you are crazy. You can trust my words when I say that this delusional bitch is crazy." Andre followed up.

"No . . . all of you are fucking crazy. Just plain monsters. Erika or Tammy or whoever the fuck she really is, was your first wife Jessica's best friend. Yeah . . . I know about that too. Y'all been fucking." I eyed them both with accusations. "I saw the picture at Jessica's parents' house. Yep, I met Mrs. Lawrence. Thankfully, she doesn't know about you two sickos' double lives." I shook my head in disgust. "Mrs. Lawrence shared with me that you were Jessica's best friend, but she never gave me a name."

"Listen, in the beginning my intentions were never to hurt Jessica. I wanted our marriage to work. But this psycho always wanted me," Andre claimed.

"Hah, don't flatter yourself. You wanted me too. Ever since Jessica introduced us at that dinner party, you couldn't keep your eyes off me. Shit, you damn well flirted with me in front of her. She was just too green to catch it. You wanted your marriage to work, ha, don't make me laugh." The imposter I now knew was Tammy waved the gun, and I flinched as I was close to her. "No matter this bull-shit, I'm just here for my baby. I thought I would have her before now. I even started following Brooke after a while because I thought she would lead me to where you were hiding her. But that was useless."

I gasped as I realized she had been the one following me. The one who'd chased me in the parking garage. It had been Erika, the one I was going out of my way to help this whole time. "So, you were the one following me. The one who chased me like a mad person out trying to mur-der me in the parking garage?"

"Murder you? Chase you in the parking garage?" Her eyebrows raised in a clueless manner. "Girl, that wasn't me. Yeah, I watched you sleep a few nights with the chance you might scream out where the baby was." I cringed, re-alizing it had been her standing over me when I thought I had been dreaming. That is how she'd gotten the diary. "But I have never chased anyone in a parking garage. Not the way I roll. That was probably Andre's crazy ass mother, she is unpredictable. Aren't you, Mrs. Perry?" She sucked her teeth.

Andre huffed as he took another step. "Brooke, this one is a mental case. Don't believe a word that comes out of her mouth, it can cost you dearly. I thought I was done with your crazy ass when you allegedly died in that fake-ass house fire. But I guess luck wasn't on my side. But, bitch, know this, you will never have my daughter. I think I told you this before. I should have had your ass killed then."

Tears instantly swelled up in Tammy's eyes, I could see the sorrow that engulfed her. Her body seemed to tense up as her grip on the gun became tighter, pointed directly at Andre. The hardened look on her face was torn between heartbreak and determination. "Andre"—her voice quivering, you could see the anguish and trauma that she was suffering—"you owe me this baby, remember . . . you beat mine out of me, you piece of shit." I saw a flash that turned out to be Andre as he dashed across me toward Tammy. The sound of a click followed by a pop cracked loudly. I watched as a bullet cut through Andre's chest. Andre stalled, then stumbled backwards, a look of shock and pain covered his face as he patted his chest.

"ARRGGHH!" Vivian screamed out and fell to Andre's side.

It all seemed like a dream as I heard the sudden entrance of the detectives. "Freeze, drop your weapon!" I could make out Kruz and Wize among the booming voices. So much had occurred, I'd long forgotten all about the cops and the sting. Tammy's gun was now aimed at Kruz. I heard another pop and watched this time as Tammy's body hit the floor.

Epilogue

Four Years Later

What can I say? Four years have passed since that chaotic and horrific night that my life and the lives of those I loved and thought loved me changed drastically. The images that are embedded deep in my memories still haunt me. The revelation of Vivian's involvement in Jessica's murder had been a shocking blow. The cold, calculated, premeditated incident had left me feeling numb, I couldn't understand how someone I had known for so long could harbor so much evil and that I could be so oblivious to it. After all of Vivian's cruelty toward me I still had never considered her to be capable of such madness.

Then there was my loving, caring, devoted husband, Andre, the man who I was certain adored me. Never in a million years could I fathom who he really was. If the secrets and lies weren't enough, to learn his true nature and role in all of it was a punch in my gut. The realization that I had for seven years closed my eyes at night and lay beside a man who was capable of such atrocities shook me to my core. His role in the entire ordeal had left me questioning everything I thought I knew about love and loyalty. The man I had once believed to be my rock had crumbled under the weight of his own lies and indiscretions.

Then there was Tammy, who had single-handedly christened herself as Erika Jones to manipulate me, while getting revenge on Andre, and in the end leading to another tragic event with the loss of her life. After Detectives Kruz and Wize had busted in, Vivian was taken away, kicking and screaming for her son, and placed under arrest for all of her monstrous acts. Put on trial, she attempted to finesse her way through the jury, thinking her uppity ways and riches would set her free. Once again, she'd overplayed her hand, her confession was on tape and heard live in court.

That insanity plea was the joke of the trial. In the end, Vivian was convicted of the murder of her late husband, and Jessica. But she got away with the murder of her sister-in-law because they didn't have a body. Either way, she was found guilty and sentenced to life in prison. However, the aftermath of Vivian's conviction had brought a sense of closure, albeit tinged with bitterness. Justice had been served, but the scars left behind were a constant reminder of the fragility of trust and the depths of human depravity. As it turns out though, prison was not something she could adjust to. She aged overnight and deteriorated mentally, and after six months she died of a heart attack. And the world was finally rid of her.

In the midst of it all, I had emerged stronger, wiser, and more cautious. Life had taught me harsh lessons, but I learned to navigate its complications with a newfound clarity. The chaos of the past had sculpted me into a woman unafraid to confront the truth, no matter how painful it may be.

As I looked toward the future, I vowed to never let my-

My Husband's Mistress is Dead / 265

self be blindsided by illusions again. The road ahead was uncertain, but I faced it with a steely resolve and a determination to carve out a life built of authenticity, trust, and genuine connection. And I had my reasons to do just that.

"Oh, Shelly, what can I say, you have once again outdone yourself." Shelly joined me in the kitchen. She was still my go-to, one-and-only party planner for any event. Today's event was beautiful inside and outside.

"You are welcome. Now I just have one more thing I need to add, for the balloon float," she said. The doorbell rang.

"I'll get that, Melva," I yelled. Melva and Sue now worked for me. I had sold Andre's house and purchased another one just as big. I still owned my own home, I never planned on selling it. But what can I say, I'd gotten used to living in that mansion Andre had insisted we live in and now I too craved the same space. "I'll meet you all out back," I told Shelly, then excused myself.

I smiled as I reached for the door, ready to greet whatever guest was now arriving. The outside heat rushed in; my mouth was wide-open prepared to greet him or her. But I found no one. Stepping closer to the edge, I looked out the door, but no one was in sight. My eyes reverted downward and there on the ground was a letter-size envelope. I stuck my head out the door and looked around; still nothing and no one. I could see the envelope was addressed to me, which was no surprise, it was my house. I looked out again but saw no one. Picking up the envelope, I shut the door.

I pulled out the contents from the envelope and my heart skipped a beat as I recognized the familiar pictures. Memories flooded back to that terrifying night in the parking garage. I could still hear the sound of the footsteps echoing, my heartbeat had matched my fear. My hands trembled as I looked over the photos that had seemingly caught every moment of that night. My stomach started to turn as I considered. Who took these pictures? Was it the person who chased me? I'd been so busy moving forward in life I had forgotten all about the fact that Erika, aka Tammy, and Andre both had denied chasing me. Oddly enough, after all the atrocious acts they had both committed I somehow believed them. But who else would do this? Why go through the trouble to deliver these to me now? A flash of nausea swept over me; I felt the need to lie down. The doorbell rang again. "Shit," I mouthed. "I'll get it," I yelled out again. I really wanted to greet all of my guests. I scrambled over to the kitchen counter as I slid the pictures back into the envelope and inside a drawer. Digging deep inside, I swallowed hard and forced a smile. I had to get through this party.

I pulled the door open to find Reese standing there alone, with both her hands cradling bags that I knew were gifts. "I'm here," she sang out. I pushed my concerns aside and gave my friend a warm greeting. The last thing I wanted to do was warn Reese of the photos and put her on alert. Reese knew me well, so I had to contain my composure in body language and tone. Besides, I too wanted to enjoy this day. I would figure out the contents of the envelope later.

"You had better be on time," I threatened playfully. "Where is your husband?" Yes, Reese and Anthony had actually tied the knot a year after my life had fallen apart. Even though my life was glazed in turmoil, I was so happy for my friend. Even now I loved teasing her by reminding her that Anthony was her husband.

"Don't you start." She smiled. "He's at work doing another twenty-four-hour shift. I pulled one yesterday, so you can say we haven't seen each other in two days. But what can we do?"

"The life of doctors who work in hospitals."

"Exactly, that is why we are really considering opening our own practice."

"Gosh, I'm so proud of you two." I smiled.

"Enough about me, where can I put these bags down? You know I bought up the store."

"I see. Let me lead you out back to Shelly's gift corner."

"I see, as usual, Shelly done did her thing. It's so beautiful." She set the bags down and sighed. "Now where is she, where is the birthday girl?"

"Mommy, Mommy!" London saw me and took off toward me. Today we were celebrating my daughter London River's fourth birthday. Yes, London was Andre's and Erika's daughter. After Andre's death and since Erika was deceased as far as anyone knew, me being Andre's legal wife and no one else to claim her, I was granted full custody. And I named her London River. She was the spitting image of Andre, but she had the prettiest deep green eyes I had ever seen. I could only assume they were from Erika, but with no pictures of her we would never know. I didn't dwell on that. I made sure that she knew she was loved, and she was my entire world. I had even cut back at the office. I was still full of ambition and gave Walter & Hanks one hundred percent. But I was a mom now and refused to miss out on any of her important moments. She would have the love that I never did.

"Hey, princess. Come here and give your aunt Reese a hug." Reese bent and London jumped in her arms.

"Happy birthday to the birthday girl." We turned toward the voice of Terrell. Yes, recently, we had been going on a date here and there. After Andre, I had a lot to put into perspective. But now my life was going great. It felt good to know there were no more tricks inside. Surely, I had enough of those to last me a lifetime.

"Come on, everybody, it's time to sing happy birthday

to the birthday girl," Shelly announced. London and all the other little kids who had been invited from her preschool cheered with excitement.

The ring of my cell phone interrupted my grin as I delighted in the whole scene. "Shelly, one second, I need to take this." I didn't recognize the number. "Hello," I said. My tone was cheerful as I stepped away from the noise.

"Hi, can I speak with Brooke . . . Brooke Perry?" the voice on the other end inquired.

"This is Brooke." The voice was just as unfamiliar as the number.

"Ummm . . . I . . ."

Whoever the person on the other end was seemed to be hesitating. I gazed over at everyone gathering around to sing "Happy Birthday" to London. "Excuse me, can I help you with something? This is not a good time," I said.

"Yes, I know . . . you're probably having a birthday party today." That grabbed my attention. I pulled my eyes away from the gathering as it hit me like a ton of bricks. Was it a coincidence that I'd just received photos at my door? Now this strange call on my phone. Was it all connected?

"Who's this? Did you just leave photos at my door? How do you know I'm having a party?" I threw questions at whoever was on the other end. My heart sped up, and I suddenly felt overwhelmed, as if I might pass out.

"Well, it's her birthday. And since I gave birth to her, I will never forget. Oh, and since you asked, this is Erika . . . Erika Jones."